THE BARON'S RETURN

The Rakes of Mayhem
Book 4

Anna St. Claire

ARE YOU SIGNED UP FOR DRAGONBLADE'S BLOG?

You'll get the latest news and information on exclusive giveaways, exclusive excerpts, coming releases, sales, free books, cover reveals and more.

Check out our complete list of authors, too!

No spam, no junk. That's a promise!

Sign Up Here

www.dragonbladepublishing.com

Dearest Reader;

Thank you for your support of a small press. At Dragonblade Publishing, we strive to bring you the highest quality Historical Romance from some of the best authors in the business. Without your support, there is no 'us', so we sincerely hope you adore these stories and find some new favorite authors along the way.

Happy Reading!

CEO, Dragonblade Publishing

Additional Dragonblade books by Author Anna St. Claire

The Rakes of Mayhem Series
The Earl of Excess (Book 1)
The Marquess of Mischief (Book 2)
The Duke of Disorder (Book 3)
The Baron's Return (Book 4)
A Gift for Agatha (Novella)

The Lyon's Den Series
Lyon's Prey
The Heart of a Lyon
Once Upon a Winter's Tale (Novella)
A Lyon of Her Own

Also from Anna St. Claire
Once upon a Haunted Heart (Novella)

PROLOGUE

The outskirts of Boston
United States of America
August 1815

S IN SAW THE yellow light through a thick, rolling fog, and
stumbled toward it. It must be a house this time. Thick fog
enveloped him, adding to his confusion as he staggered through
the trees and low-lying shrubs in his way. His body was on fire,
and his vision wavered—it was failing. The fever was making
everything impossible: seeing, speaking, thinking.

Sin couldn't stop staring at the light, even though he could no
longer trust his eyes with this beastly fever. So many times, there
had been a light in a window, only for him to find it was nothing
but the moon's reflection on wet ground.

Damned fever. Why had he stopped to speak with the soldiers
in the marsh? He'd known about the mosquitos and the deadly
disease and had avoided it—or thought he had. Many men had
dropped dead from it, and now, he would likely join them.

If I stop walking, I won't survive, he told himself over and over.
His feet tripped over a thick root on the path, but he wouldn't
stop as he stumbled toward the light. Did it belong to a house?

What was so heavy? He reached around and felt his rifle pull
forward. His favorite rifle and leaden feet pushed him into the

moist ground beneath him.

The light was closer. He prayed he could reach it. Rivulets of cold sweat trickled between his shoulder blades and made their way down his backside. The beacon was just ahead of him… If he could go just a little farther. Forcing his eyes upward, he saw the light grow into a ball of fire. "No! Not a fire. You're a candle," he said, reaching out and touching the cool wood of a thick door. His head thumped against the door…once, twice.

Edward Sinclair opened his eyes and watched the door open as if it were happening in front of someone else. In his feverish state, he would have sworn he was looking into the luminous green eyes of an angel. A soft halo of light surrounded a beautiful face framed by waves of golden hair.

"Can I help you?" the angel asked.

"P-please, I-I m-mean you no…harm." He wanted to say more, but when he opened his mouth to speak, black vomit spewed forth. An instant later, Sin pitched forward into dark oblivion.

CHAPTER ONE

25 Curzon Street, Mayfair
London, England
February 15, 1817

"WELCOME HOME, MY lady, and Mrs. Pritchett," Jenkins, the butler, said as Lizzie and Lady Beadle entered the foyer. "Your correspondence is in the large silver salver, with a missive from Lady Armstrong on top."

"What's that, Jenkins?" Lady Millicent Beadle held her ear trumpet to her ear.

"Your correspondence, my lady, is in the silver salver," he repeated in a loud voice. "Lady Armstrong's invitation is on top of the pile."

Lady Beadle nodded. "Take this blasted horn, dear Lizzie."

Lizzie hid a smile as the viscountess handed her the conical brass hearing device, while the butler assisted her employer with her hat and pelisse.

"Thank you, Jenkins. I'll attend to the post tomorrow. However, I'll read Lady Armstrong's now." Lady Beadle beamed as Jenkins handed her the invitation. "This is exactly what I've been waiting for, Lizzie!" she said, waving the vellum envelope in the air. "My niece and her husband always throw the most delightful parties. You will have a grand time, my dear." She turned back to the butler. "Jenkins, can you have Agnes make sure my sweet kittens are in the parlor?"

"Very good, my lady," the tall, gray-haired retainer said.

Lizzie swiftly returned the ear trumpet to Lady Beadle as Jenkins took her pelisse and hat and hung them in the vestibule next to the older woman's. She hoped Lady Beadle would allow her to stay home. She had no desire to go to a ball. Especially after the many social engagements they had attended in Bath. She wasn't used to being so much in Society. Certainly not after living in America for five years, more than half that time on her own.

"How was your visit with your cousin, my lady?" Jenkins asked.

"A thoroughly lively sojourn, Jenkins. Didn't we have a wonderful time, Lizzie?"

"Indeed, I thought it was most enjoyable and quite edifying," Lizzie replied. "Lady Massey seemed in good spirits throughout our stay."

Lady Beadle harrumphed. "She dragged us to every milliner, mantua maker, assembly room, and all the other sites Bath has to offer in the six weeks we were there. Not even the wet weather slowed her down." She rolled her eyes. "I love my dear cousin, but she's been claiming to be at death's door for nearly twenty years. Honestly, she missed her calling as a Drury Lane sensation."

Lizzie's lips twitched as she and the viscountess made their way upstairs to the parlor. "She seems to derive a great deal of joy from her grandchildren."

"Yes, yes. She adores them, and I'm happy for dear Althea." Lady Beadle waved the envelope at the butler. "Jenkins, have Rosalee bring a tea tray to the parlor. I'm positively parched."

"Very good, my lady," he said, with a slight bow and a wink at Lizzie before he turned and left them.

"It's nice to relax, finally." The older woman heaved a deep sigh as she settled back against the gold and white striped settee. "Yoo-hoo! Come here, my darlings," Lady Beadle called out.

As if on cue, three cats emerged from three separate corners of the parlor.

"Ah, there you are, my pretties," the dowager said, as a long-haired brown-and-white cat leaped up on the settee beside her. "Athena, my sweet. Have you been napping in here all day, or did you just sneak down from Lizzie's room?" she asked, petting the now-purring cat. "Have I mentioned, dear Lizzie, that I named my pets after my favorite mythological gods?"

"Yes, my lady. And they are perfectly named." Lizzie had lost count of the number of times Lady Beadle had told her about the cats' names, and she had replied in the same way each time. Lady Beadle was a sharp lady, and Lizzie often wondered if the old woman repeated herself on purpose just to see what she would say.

Lizzie suppressed a chuckle. In truth, she had never owned a pet and adored the trio of cats. Athena often slept at the foot of her bed. Lizzie usually left her chamber door open during the day, allowing the cat to come and go as she pleased. Athena's favored perch was the windowpane, where she watched the birds. The twitching motions she made with her nose and the low growling sounds left no doubt that, given the opportunity, Athena would succumb to her natural feline inclinations.

Lady Beadle patted the cushion on her other side. A big orange-and-white cat leaped onto it and plopped his head on her lap, next to Athena. "Zeus, dear, you seem to have put on some weight in the past six weeks," she said. Zeus lifted his head lazily and meowed as if in protest. "We shall have to curb your treats." She wiggled her fingers at the third cat, a lovely black-and-white tabby sitting alert on the carpet, patiently waiting her turn for her mistress's attention. "Venus, you look sated as well. Did you catch a mouse?" Turning to Lizzie, she said, "As far as I know, we have never seen a mouse in this house!"

Rosalee walked in with the tea tray and set it down on the side table next to the settee.

"Rosalee, tell Lizzie. We have never seen a mouse in this

house, have we?"

The maid began to pour as she responded, "No, my lady. The cats—they do keep us mouse-free. Cook loves 'em and feeds 'em leftover kippers."

"Ah! That's why our food bill is so high," Lady Beadle said with a chuckle. "But these skilled mousers are worth a few extra kippers..."

"And rashers of bacon, my lady," Rosalee added. "Zeus loves his bacon."

"Perhaps we should reduce Zeus's rations a wee bit," Lady Beadle said. "I'm concerned that he lacks the agility of his sisters."

"He's always enjoyed his treats," Rosalee said with a smile.

"Yes, and I know you're too polite to say it, but Zeus is on the lazy side, and it's his sisters who do most of the mousing. Isn't that true, Zeus?"

"Meow," Zeus replied, lying on his back so she could rub his belly.

Lizzie giggled. "They are sweet—and all with such unique characters." The cats were cheeky, but they were adorable and affectionate. Lizzie was touched that Lady Beadle treated them as part of the family.

She smiled as Athena leaped from the settee and settled at her feet. Reaching down, she petted the purring cat. Sitting back, Lizzie picked up her cup and sipped her tea. With a relaxed sigh, she gazed around the room, eyeing it appreciatively and noting that, despite the rich color scheme, the parlor exuded warmth and comfort. Gold and white dominated the space, beginning with an Aubusson rug in white, gold, and pale blue over gleaming, pale-oak-planked floors. The settee was covered in a subtly patterned pale-blue-and-white damask fabric, and behind the settee hung a large gilt mirror. The walls boasted a rich cream color, adorned with tastefully painted scenes of Cornwall's cliffs and canvases depicting English meadows full of poppies, Queen Anne's lace, cornflowers, and other wildflowers. A tall walnut escritoire with a matching chair dominated the wall next to the doorway.

Lizzie had come to know her employer well these past six months as her companion. The widow was kind and warm-hearted despite her occasional ill humor. But from what Lizzie could tell, that was mostly because she was irritated at using an ear trumpet. As a child, the viscountess had survived a severe fever and sore throat, but it left her with hearing loss—an affliction that had grown worse over the years. By her forties, Lady Beadle had become reliant on the hearing device.

"Those beautiful grandchildren are no doubt keeping Althea going. They are all she talked about," Lady Beadle murmured, changing the subject, as she was apt to do. "Dearest Arthur and I weren't fortunate enough to have children of our own, and while I simply adore my niece and nephew, do you see me carrying on and gushing about them? Of course not!"

"Lady Althea was most enthusiastic, my lady," Lizzie said in a discreet manner, knowing how mercurial Lady Beadle could be. She reminded herself of what her mother always said—*blood is thicker than water.* "She was probably trying to make us comfortable, my lady."

"Nonsense! She was showing off," Lady Beadle countered.

"Hmm," Lizzie said noncommittally as she lifted the delicate cup to her lips. "Such fragrant tea, my lady, wouldn't you agree?"

"Fragrant, indeed." The older woman gave Lizzie a shrewd look as she opened the invitation. "By the by, I took the liberty of ordering you a new gown for the ball this evening."

Lizzie raised her brows in surprise. "You did, my lady?" *Oh dear*—she had hoped Lady Beadle would forget about the ball.

"Indeed," Lady Beadle said again, her lips twitching as though she suppressed a grin. "I'm pleased that I thought to ask Madame Soyeuse to make an additional ball gown for each of us before we left for Bath."

Lizzie set down her cup as she tried to maintain a placid demeanor. "Another new dress is too generous, my lady. My pale lavender will do just fine for a more formal affair." The older woman had already infused Lizzie's wardrobe with several brightly colored gowns, day dresses, and even nightgowns that she could never have afforded to buy on her own. Although Lizzie thought the gowns were beautiful, the shades and fabrics were far more vibrant than was acceptable for her station. After all, she was not a naïve debutante preparing for her come-out. She was a penniless widow who had accepted her lot in life and felt extremely fortunate to have secured a position as Lady Beadle's companion.

"I'll not hear another word on the matter, my dear. The soiree is tomorrow, and you shall have a new dress. In the morning, the modiste will deliver our gowns."

A knock sounded at the door, and Jenkins stepped into the parlor. "My lady…"

"Jenkins, you will take my ear trumpet and hold it until Mrs. Pritchett here consents to wear a decent dress to my niece's party, as I have requested." Lady Beadle turned to Lizzie. "You've been here for months, my dear, and it's time to spruce up your wardrobe. Since you are attending events at my behest, the expense is mine, and the matter is closed."

"Er…yes, my lady," the retainer said, eyes wide, as he accepted the ear trumpet. "What should I do with it, madam?"

"What do you usually do with it when I don't wish to hear fustian nonsense?" Lady Beadle thumped her cane in annoyance. "When Mrs. Pritchett comes to her senses, I'll have it back."

"Lady Beadle—" Lizzie began.

"Tut, tut," the older woman interrupted with a flick of her wrist, then added in a gentler tone, "Lizzie, you are a lovely young woman. You should dress in a manner befitting your station as a lady when you attend events at my behest. As I said, the expense is mine, and the matter is closed."

"My lady," Jenkins said, "I forgot to mention that Lady Armstrong favors a reply as soon as possible."

Lady Beadle pointed to her right ear and shook her head.

The butler handed the trumpet back. Once she positioned it in her ear, Jenkins leaned down and repeated in a louder voice,

"Lady Armstrong favors a reply to her invitation as soon as possible."

Lady Beadle gave a satisfied smile. "Thank you, Jenkins. I can count on at least one person in this household to do my bidding." She handed the trumpet back to the servant. "Send a footman to tell them we'll be there on time."

"Yes, my lady. Do you wish me to keep the ear trumpet?"

"Why would I want you to do that? Of course not. If you take it away, I won't be able to hear Lizzie."

Jenkins nodded, smiled at Lizzie, and handed the hearing device back to his employer.

As petulant as Lady Beadle could sometimes be, Lizzie had grown to care deeply for her and couldn't help but be tickled by the humorous antics of the household.

After living alone for several years in America on the outskirts of Boston during a war, Lizzie was thankful for her position and appreciated being back home in England in a lovely home with a kind, if somewhat stubborn, employer and her equally kind staff. But letting go of the pain of her past was proving to be more challenging than Lizzie had anticipated. And despite how much she liked Lady Beadle's niece and nephew-in-law, Lizzie felt uncomfortable attending Society soirees. "Lady Beadle—"

"Tsk, tsk! Dear, please call me Millie! It sounds like you're speaking to my mother when you call me Lady Beadle. It makes me feel old."

Lizzie swallowed. "My la—Millie. It's not that I don't appreciate your many kindnesses—but I am out of place in London Society. I am happy serving your needs as a companion, but I feel more comfortable remaining here." As an Englishwoman in the Americas, she'd gotten used to being ignored. The American-born women spurned her for being English, and the wives of the English officers snubbed her for being the daughter of a country vicar. The men, on the other hand, whether American or English, seemed politely solicitous when standing next to their wives and all-too-eagerly lascivious when those wives were on the other side of the room. Lizzie would rather spend a quiet evening reading by a cheery fire than be subjected to leering looks from men who believed widows were fair game, and cool glances from women who believed all widows were on the prowl. The wounds of the past five years had not fully healed.

"My lady, I appreciate your kindness, but I am not ready—"

"Claptrap! You are the daughter of a vicar and the widow of Lord Peter Pritchett, the son of the Earl of Newnes. You have every right to take your place in Society, something you've refused to acknowledge, despite my encouragement. I'm not suggesting you go on the hunt for a husband—but why not have a bit of enjoyment? There is nothing wrong with attending a dinner party or a soiree. You are no longer in mourning—you are a vibrant, intelligent, and charming young woman and should experience what life has to offer."

"My lady—" Lizzie tried again.

Lady Beadle interrupted once more. "I have received reliable information that the old earl…um…Lord Newnes and his wife are not in town and will not be returning for a while. But you cannot go on avoiding them forever, child."

Lizzie had no wish to see Peter's parents. They had never accepted her marriage to their son and had treated the union with disdain. Her husband, a British officer, had been certain they would come around to accepting her by the time they returned to England. But the War of 1812 lasted into 1816—longer than anyone had imagined. When her husband lost his life in Major General Robert Ross's attack on the American capital on August 24, 1814, Lizzie's world had come crashing down. Because he had been an officer of the British Navy, Peter's body was returned to his family in England. All she had received was a letter informing her of his death and that his body had been shipped home. The vessel had been a warship, and given the danger of a possible attack, they had deemed it safer if Lizzie stayed behind, according to the letter. But in truth, she had been given no option.

She had remained on the outskirts of Boston in the home she

and Peter had made together. But losing her husband had left her alone and nearly destitute, with little of value she could sell for necessities, on the verge of becoming dependent on the charity of a community that had never fully welcomed her into their midst. Despondent and in mourning, she'd missed the opportunity to leave with the last of the British troops and other officers' families.

Looking back, her only brush with happiness after Peter's death had been when she had nursed back to health Edward Sinclair—a man with ties to the Crown who seemed completely comfortable in the American wilderness. He had been in pursuit of a friend's son, who had disappeared after the Battle of New Orleans. It had been a shock to see the tall, bearded man with startling blue eyes on her doorstep. Even more shocking, he was barely able to stand, his knees almost buckling. She'd helped him inside and determined he had contracted yellow fever as he asked her for help in a raspy, reedy voice. Lizzie's heart had gone out to the poor man, and she vowed to do what she could to save him.

The contagion, unknown in the British Isles, had brought him near death. As if by Providence, Lizzie had not succumbed to the fever herself. Moreover, returning Mr. Sinclair to health had given her a renewed sense of purpose. She was barely nineteen years of age when she married Peter and had never traveled beyond the village where she grew up. Then, within a matter of months, she'd married, crossed an ocean, set up house on the fringe of an American colony, and watched her new husband march into battle—and then grieved his death after less than two years of marriage.

Determined to shake off her feelings of loneliness and despair, Lizzie had regained her spirit, the same spirit that had served her well as a vicar's daughter. But that was not the only transformation she had undergone. Caring for Edward had given her renewed hope. As he began to heal from his illness, Lizzie had also begun to heal from her grief.

Edward had had more than enough coin to provide for his

stay, and Lizzie had acquired the necessary supplies to feed and nurse him back to health. During those weeks, which seemed like months, she had experienced a sense of happiness she had not felt since those early days of her marriage before everything changed. Even though she'd known Edward would have to leave eventually, her heart ached when he departed to resume his search for his friend's son.

She remembered so clearly that last day. Barely healed and still gaunt and haggard, with that long, shaggy hair and beard, he had held her hands and thanked her for everything she'd done for him. Telling her he had to continue his search for his friend, he placed a purse full of coins in her hand, enough money to see her through several months. At first, Lizzie refused, but Edward had insisted, telling her he owed her far more for saving his life. He said he would do his best to send word to her. She'd gazed into those striking blue eyes and hoped and prayed with all her heart that he would keep his promise and come back to her.

Weeks turned into months, and Lizzie despaired that she would never hear from Edward again. She knew all too well how harsh life could be in America, especially when one ventured into the wilderness. Lizzie had no way of reaching Edward and did not know where he could be. Despite her blossoming feelings for the British agent, she could wait no longer. She'd shed too many tears for her husband, and then she wept for what might have been with Edward. She had no one and nothing to keep her in America.

Michael was the only family she had left, and she didn't know where he was. It had been five years since she had seen her brother, but she thought she would feel it if he had died, and she sensed he had somehow survived the war.

The funds Edward had left her eventually ran out, so she'd sold the last thing she had of value—the gold band that Peter had given her when they married—and booked passage on a ship bound for England. She'd start there to find her brother.

Upon her arriving in England, Lizzie's first stop was the Admiralty and Marine Affairs Office, to inquire about Michael. She'd learned he had joined Wellington's transition team in Paris. But they would tell her nothing more. Except for a brief letter from Michael, which they had doubtless read—a letter she had read so many times, it was committed to memory.

Dearest Lizzie,

Thank you for alerting me of your return—something that warms my heart immensely. I have missed seeing you these many years, dearest sister, and was not surprised you knew to send your missive to the admiralty's office.

I had hoped to be here to greet you but have been called away on orders. I will do my best to write and send letters to you here.

Some very dear friends—Viscount Armstrong and his wife—have asked that you stay with them. You will be safe, and I promise to find you as soon as I return.

The address is Grantham Place, Mayfair. Lady Celia Armstrong and her husband are looking forward to having you as their guest. However, if you are insistent on finding a position, she may know of one.

I look forward to seeing you as soon as possible.

Your loving brother,
Michael

I will be here when Michael returns.
"Well, my dear Lizzie, what say you?"
Lizzie shook off her melancholy memories and breathed a deep sigh. She had been lucky indeed that the very day she'd visited Lord and Lady Armstrong, they informed her of a position as a companion. "Lady Beadle, I don't wish to sound ungrateful…"
"Then I suggest you do not, Mrs. Pritchett. In the end, I will have my way," Lady Beadle said teasingly before clearing her

throat. "Madame Soyeuse will deliver a new dress tomorrow. We must look our best."

Wily woman! Lizzie noticed Lady Beadle had not used the ear trumpet to listen to her last comment, and yet she had answered. Lizzie had begun to wonder if Lady Beadle could read lips, considering the older woman recently related that she had volunteered at London's Braden School for the Deaf as a young bride. She and her husband had been silent patrons and helped fund the construction of the school and had been actively involved in the institution for many years.

Biting back a smirk, Lizzie held up her hands in mock surrender. "Fine. I will accept the new dress. But you must allow me to make future decisions on any more gowns."

The viscountess beamed and clapped her hands. "Excellent. We have a glorious event to attend, and my niece is expecting our attendance. I've been hoping my nephew would come, but I have gotten no updates from him. He hasn't been to see me in an age—not since near the end of that unfortunate dustup with the colonies. I do adore him, though." Mumbling to herself about the last time she saw him, she munched a sandwich.

Summoning up her courage, Lizzie cleared her throat. "I realize the timing of your niece's ball did not give us adequate time for me to provide my input on the gown, but in the future, I would prefer some choice in the colors and fabric for my clothing." She held her breath, unsure of her employer's reaction. But Lizzie was determined that she would have some say over what she wore and not be treated like a child. Her preference would be for a more sedate wardrobe, befitting her position in the household.

The older woman sniffed. "Of course, my dear, as long as they are not too dreary. It would be a shame, given your beautiful coloring."

I knew it. Lady Beadle would have her way. Lizzie bit down on her lip to contain a retort. *There's no use. She means well and is the first person to care about me in years.* She sighed. "Millie, if you don't mind, I will return shortly. I'd like to freshen up."

"Of course! Take your time, dear. We have a very busy day tomorrow."

LIZZIE CLOSED THE door and leaned against it, staring wordlessly at her apartment. The room was the same size as the small, rented cottage where she and Peter had lived in America.

What am I doing fretting about gowns? It's a complete waste of time. Walking to her bed, she kicked off her shoes and lay down, staring at the blue-and-white lace canopy that matched perfectly with the walls, painted in a soft blue. There was little doubt that Lady Beadle's insistence on suitable gowns would result in nothing Lizzie wanted. *So what?* Lady Beadle had been the soul of kindness, and Lizzie had much to be grateful for. What was one dress in the grand scheme of life? If she were honest with herself, it was Michael that troubled her. Not knowing where he was or when he was coming home. He was the only family she had left.

But her brother wasn't the only person she missed.

When she closed her eyes, her mind went where it often had since the day she said goodbye to him—*Edward Sinclair.* Those incredible blue eyes still haunted her dreams. And yet she had no way of knowing if he were alive or dead.

Rolling over, she groaned into her pillow. After those many weeks of nursing him back to health, she'd found herself smiling again. When he announced he was leaving, she had asked him to stay a few more days and even offered to cut his beard. He was barely out of danger, and she worried about him relapsing. He said he would be fine. But she had no way of knowing that.

"No, it's better to keep the beard where I am going," he had said.

She'd touched his cheek and said, "I will miss you."

Lizzie opened her eyes. A tear rolled down her cheek and she wiped it away. It all felt strange. She had grieved the loss of Peter, her husband. So why did she keep thinking about Edward? She couldn't understand why the man occupied her thoughts so much—they had shared no declarations about a future together, and yet her vivid dreams had conjured up his handsome face and broad shoulders too many nights to count, and she'd wake up almost feeling his very presence. She had felt the flutter of something between them, something rare and wonderful, but she had held back, afraid to give words to her blossoming feelings, afraid to encourage someone who might break her heart.

Since she had been back in England, she realized that seeing couples flirting and strolling arm in arm or on carriage rides only reminded her of what she'd lost. That, with the tragic loss of Peter, left her afraid to relive that kind of all-consuming grief. She would not—*could not*—risk her heart again.

Despite those haunting yearnings of her heart, when six months went by with no word from Edward, Lizzie had decided she needed to pursue her life as if he had never been a part of it. Besides, wherever he was, he had most likely forgotten about her.

CHAPTER TWO

S TARING AT HIS bearded reflection in the mirror, Edward Sinclair considered the dispiriting task ahead, unable to escape the memories connected to the unruly growth. Raising the blade, he could almost hear her cajoling words envelop him, taking him back to that last day. The last time he had held her in his arms. The sound of Lizzie's voice was as clear as if she were speaking to him now. A wave of longing swept over him. Lizzie's teasing tone and the mischievous glint in her eyes had lightened his mood like no other.

"Come on, Edward, it's so ratty. I'll bet you have a handsome chin under those scruffy whiskers. At least allow me to shave you and rid you of the beard. You'll feel more comfortable," she had said. Her words echoed in his mind.

He'd shaken his head. *"No, it's better to keep the beard where I am going,"* he recalled saying, a choice that now gave him a heavy heart. The beard would have grown back by the time he'd reached New Orleans.

Wordlessly, she'd stood on her tiptoes and kissed his cheek tenderly. He felt the wetness of a tear as her lips touched his skin.

Never had he met anyone like her, and the desire to see her again had grown into a palpable ache. By the time he'd returned and located anyone who knew anything about her, it had been too late. She had sold everything of note and booked passage to

England—but what ship and when? The man who told him the news had been unsure of any details.

Sin was desperate to find her. She'd probably left to find her brother, as he was her only remaining family. The man's name danced in the periphery of his thoughts. He thought it began with a D, but he wasn't certain, and his head throbbed from memories clouded by the persistent fever that had gripped him. He recalled Lizzie saying she had not heard from her brother in years and did not know where to look for him.

He didn't know her brother's name or anything else about him, but Lizzie was unforgettable. If her missing brother was the only clue to her whereabouts, he would visit every military office in London. If she had visited one of them looking for her brother, someone would remember her.

"God's oath, I miss you," he murmured, staring at his reflection, absorbing the look of regret and resolve in his eyes. Inhaling deeply, he gripped his blade, determined to cut away the growth and shed the weight of lingering regret of a time he longed to reclaim. "I will find you, Lizzie. I promise."

TWO HOURS LATER, Baron Edward "Sin" Sinclair leaned back in the brown-leather-upholstered armchair in front of an enormous hearth in his favorite room at White's. He'd only just returned to London, and it had felt good to shed himself of that shaggy beard and don clean, dry clothes. He primed his cigar, leaned forward, lighting it from the dancing flames, and returned to his relaxed position, warming himself by the fire while he waited for his friends, Viscount Hugh Wright and Lord Matthew Romney, the Earl of Romney.

As he stared into the crackling fire, he thought of *her*—the only woman who filled him with longing and regret. *Lizzie. God, how I miss you, Lizzie.* Once he'd completed his mission, he returned to her as soon as he could, but the cottage where she had been living was locked and empty. He'd searched everywhere for her, making inquiries throughout the surrounding area and the town of Boston. But her widow's status and beauty had most likely made her a threat to the women in the small community, and no one seemed to know her whereabouts. Finally, he found the owner of the cottage where she'd lived, who said she had sold everything and left. *But to where?* Sin recalled Lizzie saying she had an older brother named Michael who was in the British military service. Although the man's last name continued to escape him. He knew it wasn't Pritchett, but... *Damn and blast!* He couldn't recall the man's name or the military branch he served.

Frustratingly, he'd forgotten much of their conversations because of the fever and its lingering remnants he had experienced with the yellow jack. Miraculously, he had survived when many didn't, thanks to Lizzie's ministrations.

He was a tracker, by God, though he had been unsuccessful in finding a slip of a woman. But in no way was he ready to give up on locating her. If she had returned to England, he would find her.

Heaving a deep sigh, he flagged a footman to refill his brandy. "Lords Wright and Romney will be here soon. If you see them, point them my way."

"I'll see it done, my lord," the footman said.

"Thank you," Sin said, accepting the glass of brandy and taking a sip. The warm liquid coated his throat as it went down. "I don't recognize this one. Is it new?"

"They've just promoted it to our house brand, although we've had it for a while. It's St. Remy, my lord," the footman replied.

"Excellent. I have some space in my wine cellar to restock, and this is a perfect blend."

"I'm pleased to check, my lord."

"And if you would be so kind as to bring a bottle of this fine brandy and two more glasses for my friends, who should arrive shortly."

"Very good, my lord." The footman nodded.

Sin leaned back in his chair and sighed as he took another sip of the amber liquid. Its heat chased the chill away from yet another bleak day. The gloomy weather appeared to be a continuation of last year's unusually cold and damp climate. Most days had been sunless, wet, and cold. With the famine, disease, and uprisings throughout the kingdom, he was rarely in London. But when he was, he enjoyed relaxing at White's.

Thoughtfully, he slowly swirled his brandy in the glass and watched the familiar dark-red legs of alcohol ease down the sides.

"Sin! I see you're in your favorite chair with your favorite drink," Romney teased, taking the matching chair next to his.

Sin sipped his brandy and smiled. "I am, and this brand may become my new favorite."

"You've got influence here, my friend. Or does no one else wish to claim this warm seat for themselves?" Viscount Asher Wright said, moving to the other seat across from Sin and Romney.

Laughing, Sin said, "If you refer to how I managed to find this seat waiting for me when I arrived, I thought of it as my good luck. That there were two empty chairs was good luck for you."

The footman returned with the brandy and glasses and closed the door to the room as he left, leaving the three men alone.

"Speaking of special treatment, I ran into the Widow Louisa Parker. She asked that I give you her regards," Wright said with a puckish laugh.

"Code for 'come see me,'" teased Romney, using the fireplace to light a cigar. "I thought you dashed her hopes years ago?"

"Correction, Romney. I never gave her hope in the first place." Sin snorted. "Are you sure she extended regards to *me*, Wright? When you saunter into a room looking every bit the rogue pirate, every woman practically contorts herself trying to catch a glimpse of your pretty face—including Lady Parker."

Wright shrugged and grinned. "I've heard she has a sword fetish," he said in a matter-of-fact tone.

Sin and Romney hooted.

"I had heard that as well," drawled Sin. "But I'm not sure I'm interested in *swordplay* with her ladyship."

"And she's also a fan of a fat purse," Romney added. "Bethany has complained about her flagrantly feline prowling of every ballroom she steps into. She vowed to give her a piece of her mind—*American style*."

"I'm sure it took something outrageous to get your sweet wife peeved. Tell us what happened," cajoled Wright.

"You're right. At a recent event, the widow approached me and, placing her hand on my arm, asked me to dance with her. As an enticement, she rubbed her leg against mine—and refused to accept *no*. Unfortunately for her, Bethany, who was standing nearby, noticed as well, and smoothly removed the widow's hand from my arm and inserted herself between us. With a no-nonsense smile, she said, 'My husband has an aversion to stray cats.'"

Sin nearly spat out his brandy. "Your little lady has gumption."

"Oh, she has that and more," Romney said with a sly grin.

"She held me off for weeks in the bayou," Sin added, "and from the look in her eyes when I first met her, I knew she wasn't afraid to employ that trusty shotgun she was holding."

The three men roared with laughter.

It had been a long time since Sin had shared a hearty laugh with his friends. Romney's praise of his American wife reminded Sin of another strong-willed beauty—Lizzie. If it hadn't been for her, he would have certainly perished from yellow fever. He'd never been jealous of his married friends in the past, but ever since meeting Lizzie, he could not help but feel a heightened sense of what was missing in his life—love, a wife, children, a warm hearth to come home to.

"That reminds me," Romney said. "As I was leaving, my wife reminded me of the party at Lord and Lady Armstrong's tomorrow evening. Please tell me you plan to attend."

Sin nodded. "Of course. My sister would never forgive me if I failed to attend a ball she hosted. I'm certain she has meticulously planned the guest list and counted me among the eligible men."

"And I'm assuming my invitation was for the same," Wright added, quirking a brow.

"Knowing my sister, she's probably already chosen your future bride," Sin said with a chuckle. "She's the consummate matchmaker. She's learned from the best—dear Aunt Millie."

"Your aunt will never forgive you if she finds out you're in town and don't show," Romney said. "My mother adores her and mentioned your aunt has spoken of your homecoming several times to her set. She'll be thrilled when she finds out you're back in London."

Sin groaned, imagining his aunt rubbing her hands together in glee. She was forever trying to marry him off. "I stopped by to visit earlier in the week, and she was away visiting a sister in Bath. At this late date, I've decided to surprise her at the party."

Romney blew out a breath. "It's nice to be married and not have to worry about marriage-minded mothers."

"Speaking of which, I'm surprised Lady Romney will be attending," Wright said. "Most women would be resting at home during their final months of pregnancy."

"Ah, well, there's the rub. My beautiful wife is American and unused to the mores and manners of the *ton*. Despite her station, she refuses to surrender her Creole ways."

Sin knew Bethany well enough to agree.

"You may recall my telling you she was gathering herbs with her dog on the plantation just before the Battle of New Orleans began. Confinement seems out of the question. I doubt I'll be able to get her to sit, much less lie in until the birth," Romney said.

The men laughed.

"Speaking of that courageous canine, how is Dandie?" Sin asked. "She is a perfect blend of brave, loving, and fierce."

"Agreed. She has been extremely protective of Bethany throughout the pregnancy. I've given up on coaxing Bethany to slow down before giving birth. My wife believes in adhering to the same schedule until her due date arrives, which, as you can imagine, drives the biddies of the *ton* crazy."

"Ha! One can imagine," Sin said. "She's been well trained in healing and herbs, and no doubt that helps frame her thinking on the subject."

"You are correct." Romney nodded. "While she respects doctors, she disapproves of bleeding a patient or using leeches and is forever peppering the doctor with questions. Luckily, our family physician is young, well trained, and patient. Having served on the battlefield, he respects her knowledge, and the two get along famously. He's even asked her opinion on certain matters."

"Most impressive," Wright said, swirling the brandy in his glass.

"How long will you be in town?" Sin asked.

"A few more weeks, most likely," Romney replied. "Bethany is due in late April or early May, so we won't tarry long in London. She wants to give us time to catch up with family and close friends and attend a few Society functions before we return home to Graceview Manor. Mother adores Bethany and plans to accompany us to Kent. She cannot wait to meet her grandchild. But while we are in town, we'd love to have you both drop by Romney House."

Sin nodded, looking forward to visiting his friends at their townhouse in Mayfair. "Bethany will be a wonderful mother," Sin said. "I remember her as extremely protective as she cared for you—before she had even gotten to know you. All she knew was you were a wounded British soldier who needed help. Had she been discovered housing you, she likely would have been arrested for treason."

"Yes, I am a most fortunate man. She is those things and more. After our shared experiences in America, you know her better than most," Romney murmured as he raised his glass of brandy to his lips.

Sin smiled. "She's a force of nature. Will Bethany's Great-Aunt Theodosia and Grandmere be coming for a visit?"

"The short answer is yes. The long answer is that I'm working on getting them here. Since travel is slowly resuming between America and England, the voyage won't be as adventurous as it was for Bethany and me."

"Few would want that adventure," Wright said. "You spent a year getting here."

"Yes," Romney agreed. "The storm that forced our ship onto an uncharted island left us with little hope of repairing it. I am forever in your debt, Sin. Thank God you had the navy send a search party. It was our good fortune you had people watching out for us."

"I promised your father before he died that I would find you," Sin said in a somber tone, "but I failed to get you there in time."

"My father went to his grave knowing he could count on you." Romney cleared his throat. "He was taken too soon. I miss him."

The men raised their glasses and shared a silent toast in memory of the late Earl of Romney.

"My apologies. I didn't mean to spread melancholy. What did you wish to discuss?" Romney asked, leaning back in the leather seat and lighting another cheroot.

"Your observation skills only sharpened when you spent those first few months blinded, after the battle. I've never failed to be impressed with your resourcefulness. There aren't many people who could have accomplished what you did without sight." Sin leaned forward and patted his friend's shoulder. "Few people could have survived, Romney."

"I had help," Romney said. "Bethany was my eyes."

Sin noted out of the corner of his eye a man walking in. Tall with long black hair and beady black eyes, the stranger took a seat at the far end of the long room. "Do either of you know him?" Sin asked his friends in a low voice, his instincts on high alert.

"Baron Percival Blackwood," Wright whispered. "Slick bastard, that one. He was recently accused of attempting to ravish a young woman from Sussex who had come to London for the Season with family friends."

"Bethany heard of the sad tale and reached out to offer assistance to the girl," Romney added. "Her family holds little influence in the *ton*. And while there were witnesses, including a footman and a maid, their testimony was largely discounted in Blackwood's favor."

Sin clenched his jaw at the story. Men like Blackwood used their power to hurt and demean those weaker than them, especially naïve and innocent girls. He'd crossed paths with many such men over the years.

"Despite this fine brandy, I'm sure you didn't just bring us here to polish off this bottle," Wright said as he refilled their glasses.

"Too true." Sin gave his friends a rueful smile. "I'm here on a favor from Wellington," he added in a low voice. "He requires sharp individuals to work for intelligence on this side of the channel, and he asked me about the two of you. Unfortunately, Napoleon was not our only threat. Given this cold and rainy weather, the effects have been dire on crops, as you both know. People are starving in many areas throughout the realm."

His friends nodded in understanding. "Unfortunately, this year bodes the same," Romney added.

"Indeed," Sin continued. "The Crown is anxious to prevent revolutionary ideas from taking hold in England. If either or both of you are amenable, Wellington would like to speak to you."

"I am honored," Romney said. "While I can offer some assistance from the sidelines, unfortunately, I cannot be part of the team. With a child on the way and after everything Bethany and I went through to get here, I'm not sure I want to sign on for any more adventures other than the kind that my darling wife provides every day."

Sin chuckled. "I understand, my friend. I thought that would be your answer, but I promised the duke I would ask."

"I, on the other hand, have nothing to hold me back," Wright said. "Father is in good health, but should he take a bad turn, I'd have to assume the earldom. Not something I'm looking forward to, as I much prefer travel and adventure."

"And winning the hearts of all the ladies you meet, I wager," Romney said with a wink.

Wright grinned. "Well, I have always held a soft spot for a damsel in distress."

"I don't know how if that is one of the direct duties of this assignment," Sin quipped.

"However, I don't want this to be my life's work, as you've done," Wright teased him. "But my life has become rather humdrum of late, and I would welcome a change of pace."

"Good. We expect much of the time you would be in London, but I cannot promise there won't be danger or travel," Sin said.

"As you know, I have one of my ships and crew in port. After a few weeks in London, the crew may get eager for a bit of adventure," Wright added good humoredly.

"Sinclair, Wright, and Romney! Three of my favorite people," a deep voice said from behind them.

Sin and his friends turned to see Evan Prescott, the Earl of Clarendon, approaching.

"Good to see you, Clarendon." Sin indicated an empty chair next to Wright. He'd noticed Blackwood had gotten up to leave. "Join us for a brandy."

"Was that Blackwood that left after I walked in? I wonder if I offended the poor chap?" Clarendon said sarcastically. "What was he doing here? He doesn't usually frequent White's."

"Couldn't say—but from what I've heard, he seems to prefer darker pursuits," Sin said grimly.

"Unfortunately, the man seems to have more lives than a cat," Clarendon said.

"Or a snake?" Wright added.

"Do snakes have many lives?" Romney asked.

"I'm not sure, but aren't they good at shedding their skin when they want to escape somewhere?" Wright said.

A footman approached, carrying a tray. "Would you care for a drink, my lord?"

"Lord Sinclair recommends the brandy," Clarendon said.

"Very good, my lord," the footman said, offering him a glass.

"I thought I'd find one or more of you here and came to ask if you'd like to help me pick out some horseflesh at Tattersalls," Clarendon said.

"Aren't you and your lovely bride attending the Armstrongs' ball tomorrow evening?" Wright asked.

"Oh, yes. Apologies. I meant the day after Lady Armstrong's soiree. I've heard Tattersalls has several new Arabians." Clarendon gave a sly laugh in Sin's direction. "Does your aunt know you're back in town?"

Sin laughed. "You're not the first to ask. She doesn't know yet. My sister and brother-in-law know. We thought to surprise my aunt at the party."

"Splendid idea. I cannot wait to see her reaction. You came back from America and went straight to Paris. My wife told me your aunt was crestfallen. She's quite the life of a tea, according to Charlotte. She thinks of you and your sister as more than a niece and nephew and seems intent on arranging a match for you."

He recalled his sister's letters to him while he was in France saying the same. As much as he loved his aunt, he could do without her meddling. "And similarly, no opportunity will be afforded this visit," Sin said. He raised his glass and toasted his friends. *There's only one woman for me, and Aunt Millie cannot help me with that.*

CHAPTER THREE

The next day

BRIGHT SUNSHINE STREAMED through the curtains and a throaty meow coaxed Lizzie awake. Opening her eyes one at a time, she found Athena sitting regally on the covers facing her, apparently studying her while casually licking her lips.

"I must thank you for waking me, Athena. It's going to be an exhausting day, but I'm glad it will start on your clock instead of Lady Beadle's, because I will need the extra time to inquire about Michael's whereabouts before our mistress awakens."

Lizzie followed Athena's gaze and saw a nest of baby bluebirds nestled on a sturdy branch of the oak tree outside her window. "Even though I'd like to reward you for waking me early, I'm afraid I cannot give you what you want." She rubbed the feline behind her ears. "Those baby birdies aren't bothering you, and you must leave them alone."

As if she understood Lizzie, the cat gave a fierce meow before standing and arching her back.

"I hope that's just a stretch and not some sort of show of force," Lizzie said, giggling. "You know you have food in the kitchen, and if I'm not mistaken, one of the kitchen maids probably added bacon to it. Let the birds enjoy their breakfast while you go to the kitchen and enjoy yours."

The long-haired, brown-and-white cat raised her paw and affectionately touched Lizzie's chin. Turning, she gave another loud meow before jumping off the pillow and taking up her usual post on the windowsill.

"Watch all you like. But the window will remain closed. I'd love to lie here for a few more minutes and watch them with you, but today will be challenging, and I must get started." Smiling to herself, Lizzie took a last look at Athena, whose paw touched the window, as though she were determined that should the glass magically disappear, she would be ready.

Lizzie couldn't help but admire the cat's persistence, as it matched that of her mistress. Lady Beadle exhibited an astonishing amount of energy, and little seemed to unsettle her. Lizzie admired the older woman's infectious spirit and hoped she could draw on it for the evening ahead.

After completing her morning ablutions, Lizzie donned one of her day dresses, a cornflower creation that complemented her blonde hair. She slipped into the dress, grateful for its simple cut and design that allowed her to do so without the assistance of a maid. As a country vicar's daughter, Lizzie had never had a maid growing up. And she certainly hadn't had one in America. The talented modiste Madame Soyeuse seemed to understand Lizzie's practical nature instinctively and had suggested the style. Lizzie had been secretly thrilled, also appreciating a similar design with her stays.

Once dressed, she fashioned her hair into a long braid, coiling it loosely around her head before securing a matching hat. "You've got the room to yourself, Athena," she said, dropping a light kiss on the cat's head and receiving a soft meow in response. Walking to the door, Lizzie glanced back over her shoulder and noted that Athena was still caught up in the birds' activities on the branches outside. Smiling, she left the door ajar for the cat to leave when she wished.

Making her way downstairs to the front entry hall, Lizzie wished the butler good morning as she saw him organizing the morning's post on the silver salver.

I wish there was a letter from Michael, she thought with a heavy sigh. However, she knew that was not likely.

"It looks like another cold and rainy day ahead," she said, accepting her warm pelisse.

"I expect you're right, Mrs. Pritchett." He smiled, handing her an umbrella and holding open the front door.

"Thank you, Jenkins."

"The carriage has been brought around and is awaiting you, as you requested, Mrs. Pritchett. When shall I tell her ladyship to expect you?"

"I shan't be long. No longer than two hours. I'm hoping to be back before she even misses me."

The butler gave a knowing smile and nodded before closing the door behind her.

A half-hour later, Lizzie arrived at the Admiralty and Marine Affairs Office, just as fat droplets of rain began to fall. She recalled that first visit just over six months ago as she knocked on the opaque-windowed office door. In a way, it had been a stroke of good luck that Michael had connected her with his friends Lord and Lady Armstrong.

"Enter," an almost high-pitched male voice said from behind the door.

Lizzie opened the door and stepped inside.

"Mrs. Pritchett. It's a pleasure to see you again," the young man said.

"You... Mr. Chester, you remember me?" The words escaped Lizzie's lips before she could retrieve them. But it had surprised her. She'd been away six weeks and only met the young man once before she and Lady Beadle left for Bath.

"Of course. We don't have many lovely ladies visit this office, so it's easy to recall them."

"Th—thank you." She wasn't sure what to say to his rather bold compliment. Swallowing, she addressed the thin, bespectacled man. "Mr. Chester, I've come to see if there's been any word from my brother, Michael—Captain Michael Robinson."

"I see. Let me look through my records." He stepped from behind his desk and walked to a standing cubby where communications were stored. Sifting through the meticulously shelved papers, he grunted. Then he thumbed through them again and turned back to her. "I thought I had heard something—" He paused, his face flushing red. "Please excuse me, Mrs. Pritchett. I shall return in a few minutes."

The young man stepped out a side door, and a few seconds later, Lizzie heard Mr. Chester and a deeper male voice from the office somewhere behind the door. A few moments later, the door opened, and a tall, auburn-haired man stepped over the threshold. "Mrs. Pritchett, I am Corporal Addis. I understand you are asking about Captain Michael Robinson."

"Yes, he is my brother. I was told he had been sent to Paris. I received one missive that I retrieved upon my arrival in London six months ago. Since then, I've visited this office several times, and I was told to come back in a few weeks each time. I was away for six weeks and only just returned to London yesterday. I was hoping to have finally received another letter or note from Captain Robinson. He is my only family..."

The two men exchanged a look that heightened Lizzie's worries.

"Mrs. Pritchett," Corporal Addis said, "I should not reveal this, but your brother is on an assignment from Wellington."

"When will he return?" she asked.

"I'm very sorry, but given regulations, I cannot share any further information," he replied. "I am certain that once he is able, Captain Robinson will send word to you."

His words revealed little, but his shuttered eyes said otherwise. Was Michael missing? Or was he wounded? She wanted to ask, but knew he would tell her nothing. *This is ridiculous.* She needed information.

Drawing herself up, she stated in a firm voice, "As Captain Robinson's only living relation, I expect to be informed of his circumstances as soon as possible. Can you please give me some indication of when that might be?" Michael would surely write as soon as he was able.

"I wish I could say, Mrs. Pritchett, but these things can take time." His face seemed to tense in frustration. "Perhaps you might check back again in a few weeks."

"Corporal Addis, you said *these things*. What do you mean?"

Addis's face flushed crimson. "My apologies, Mrs. Pritchett. I misspoke. I have no information on Captain Robinson's status at this time."

He knows something. She was certain of it. Both men knew more than they were telling her, and it infuriated Lizzie. Michael might be in trouble, and there was nothing she could do to help him. Her lips stretched into a thin line. "Thank you, Corporal Addis," she managed before turning on her heel and leaving the military office.

Deflated and defeated, Lizzie made her way back to the waiting carriage. What could she do? What recourse did she have? In truth, she knew no one who could help her find out. Even if she were able to learn of Michael's whereabouts, or what kind of trouble he might be in, how would she be able to help him? The dismal news weighed heavily on her shoulders.

As SOON AS she entered the townhouse, Jenkins took her hat and pelisse. "Lady Beadle wishes you join her in her suite of rooms. Madame Soyeuse arrived a few minutes ago," he said in a gentle voice.

"Thank you, Jenkins." She would have to set aside her worries about her brother's whereabouts for now. Lady Beadle never slowed. Perhaps that was a good thing, as Lizzie would likely be unable to think clearly until the shock and anger had settled. She knew with certainty the evening would be a late one. The last thing she wanted was to attend a ball. Unfortunately, she had no choice in the matter.

As she walked into Lady Beadle's suite, Lizzie recognized the familiar, lilting French accent of Madame Soyeuse.

"My lady, you look marvelous in that color," the modiste said.

"Yes! It simply cries out for red hair," Lady Beadle enthused.

Lizzie hurried into the dressing area, where she found Zeus, Athena, and Venus all perched on the back of a settee, eyeing a box of ribbons that the modiste was using. "I'm back, my lady," she said.

"Thank goodness! I had begun to fret. You've been gone so long. Is everything all right?" The older woman held up her ear trumpet, expecting an answer.

"I apologize, Millie. I stopped by the Office of the Admiralty to see if they had any word from my brother."

"And did they?" the older woman asked, adjusting her ear trumpet and holding her hand up for the modiste to wait.

"No," Lizzie said, unable to hide the despair in her voice. "It was more what they didn't say than what they did say."

"What do you mean, my dear? Let us examine this rationally. The war is over. Therefore, most of the danger has passed. Is that not so?"

"That is what I thought, but I'm no longer certain." Lizzie knew Lady Beadle was trying to help calm her fears. She did not want to worry the older woman, especially not on the day of her niece's ball. She knew how important the function was to Lady Beadle. "I was told by the office he was on an assignment with Wellington. But that was all they would tell me."

"What does that mean—*on assignment*?"

"I asked, but my question seemed to irritate the corporal in charge of the office," Lizzie said.

"My dear, we should not borrow trouble. It is conceivable that the young man simply has had no updates on the situation. Besides, Paris is now under English control. I am certain there is nothing to worry about. And all will be well."

"You're right, my lady," Lizzie said, mustering a reassuring smile for the older woman. She drew herself up. "How may I be of assistance?"

"Ah. That's much better, my girl." Lady Beadle smiled. "Now then, tell me what you think of this gown. Since we have no time for another, I do hope you love it," she said cheerfully as she modeled a sapphire-blue satin dress that sparkled as she made a slow turn in front of the floor-to-ceiling looking glass.

"I think it's wonderful," Lizzie said. The gown was indeed flattering both in style and color. She admired Lady Beadle's enthusiasm for life. The dear woman had had her share of sadness and tragedy, and yet she marched onward, deriving pleasure from each day. *I need to keep that in mind in my own life.* No matter what life brought her, Lizzie would do her best to face life head-on in the same way Millie did. "What type of turban will you wear?"

"I have ze most beautiful turban, my lady," Madame Soyeuse said, holding up a dark blue covering with a feather and light blue jewel embedded in the front. "It will show off ze blue silk."

"Perfect. And I know exactly what would match perfectly." Lady Beadle reached into a large hatbox beside the looking glass and whipped out a curly wig. "I've been saving this for a special occasion."

The modiste's eyes widened. "My lady, that is certainly...special."

"Isn't it, though?" Lady Beadle beamed. "It's called regal titian."

Lizzie hid a smile. The wig was not regal, nor titian. It *was*, in fact, a very bright orange.

The modiste turned to Lizzie, her eyes flashing a look of horror.

Oh dear, how best to sort this one out? It was not unusual for Lady Beadle to wear a turban or an outlandish hat. Occasionally, she added a wig of colored hair from her extensive collection—although many of them resembled the ancient hairpieces of the Georgian era.

"But my lady, you have perfectly beautiful gray hair," the modiste managed in a slightly strangled voice.

"Gray! That is exactly the problem." Lady Beadle adjusted her ear trumpet around the knotted orange hair. "It's bad enough that I must use this damned thing to hear, but I am also saddled with faded gray hair. At least I can hide the gray with my glorious wigs. Otherwise, everyone will think I am old, which I refuse to be. The red hair will tell them otherwise," she declared.

Madame Soyeuse opened her mouth and closed it, perhaps thinking twice about what she had planned to say. Instead, she dug into a bag and produced a large, blue-stoned brooch. With the utmost care, she removed the feather and pinned the jewel to the front of the turban, covering the smaller stone. She then pushed the turban down on the orange wig and allowed only a curl or two to show. "My lady, this will look perfect," she said. "You can trust that this addition will add an elegant touch."

Lady Beadle stepped back and eyed her image in the looking glass. "I love it. What do you think, Lizzie?"

"It brings out the blue in your eyes, my lady," Lizzie said.

"Your turn, Lizzie," Lady Beadle announced. "No further alterations are necessary, Madame Soyeuse. We should prepare Lizzie for the party."

Two hours later, the fittings were finally completed. Lizzie was pleased with the deep-pink gown Lady Beadle had chosen—although the lavender dress would have been equally nice. Lady Beadle looked splendid in the blue—orange hair and all.

CHAPTER FOUR

The Armstrong ball
Later that evening

S IN STOOD ON the upper landing of the ballroom stairs, his gaze sweeping the lively crowd below. *Celia didn't leave a soul in London off her guest list*—something that both intrigued and perturbed him.

At that moment, a familiar shrill voice sent a chill down his spine and filled him with a sense of dread. He riveted his attention to the back of the room and saw her…

The Widow Louisa Parker approaching his Aunt Millie.

"Woohoo, Lady Beadle! Woohoo!" she called, waving her gloved hand.

The exuberant greeting was met with a slow, stiff response from his aunt, who was engaged in a conversation with Lady Romney. She turned to face the interloper with a wan smile on her face, clad in a sapphire-blue satin dress with a matching turban. Sin was momentarily distracted by the unexpected sight of orange curls peeking from beneath the fabric of the turban. His aunt had always maintained gray hair, although now that he thought about it, his mother had mentioned, on more than one occasion, his aunt's collection of colorful Georgian wigs.

Beside her, a vision in rose-pink satin and shimmering muslin caught Sin's eye. The blonde woman stood with her back to him, elegantly sipping lemonade, her identity momentarily concealed. His breath caught at the lovely silhouette, but before he could ascertain her identity, his attention was diverted by a dark figure who suddenly appeared, blocking his view of the slender young woman, appearing to engage her in conversation. He stiffened as he realized the man was none other than the Earl of Blackwood. Why the hell did his sister and brother-in-law invite a man who was rumored to have attacked an innocent girl?

"Sin, it's good to see you," a voice said from behind.

Sin turned and greeted his friend and brother-in-law. "I had planned to say hello to Aunt Millie but heard the warning whistle of the widow," he said. He gave a brief nod in the direction of his aunt at the other end of the room. Thankfully, Celia knew he never stayed for the entirety of a function and often showed up late. His preference was always to come for a short while and then leave.

"I noticed her as well and had hoped we could take refuge on the balcony, if need be," Wright said. "Sorry to disparage a guest of yours, Armstrong."

"No need to apologize," Armstrong said. "I asked my wife the same thing. The widow is an irritation and makes herself an interfering nuisance wherever she goes. Celia never gave me a good answer—something about it being easier to avoid her here than all over London, should she not be invited."

Sin decided not to comment about Blackwood.

"Ah, I detect my friends may be avoiding the irksome widow," Romney said, approaching. "Indeed! This could be an interesting experiment! We could finally settle who the widow is more taken with—Sin or, as he so eloquently put it, the rogue pirate," he teased, a mischievous glint in his eyes.

The four men erupted into laughter at Romney's jest.

"Why don't we burn an hour and take in a game of billiards?" Wright asked.

Armstrong chuckled but declined. "As much as I'd enjoy a

good game of snooker, my wife would have my head—and more," he said. "I must remain among the guests."

"There you are, baron," Lady Parker said, strolling up to them.

"Good evening, Lady Parker. It's nice to see you again," Wright said, his lips twitching.

"Lady Parker," Sin said flatly, hoping she'd keep walking.

"They are getting ready to strike up the band. I'm sure you promised me a dance," she cooed, lightly tapping Sin's chest with her fan.

"I did?" he asked in a placid tone. This woman was a manipulative menace and up to her usual tricks. Her blatant lying made him want to dig in.

She playfully slapped his arm. "Oh, Sin, surely you recall our recent little chat."

"Er…perhaps there is some mistake," Wright supplied. "Sinclair and I have been out of the country…and we've only *just* arrived back in England."

Sin noticed Romney stood quietly by, smiling.

Normally, Sin would never contradict a lady—but he had a hard time considering the widow a lady. At least by the standards he had been taught. "Lady Parker, I am sorry, but I don't recall. However, if—"

"I'm afraid you are mistaken, Lady Parker," said his aunt, gliding up behind the widow and tucking her ear trumpet in the folds of her dress. "My nephew promised *me* the first dance—although, if you don't mind, I feel a turn around the room might be more to my taste. It's been a year since I've seen him, and we have much to discuss. And besides, your…er…companion Lord Blackwood awaits you."

"B-but we… He…" the widow sputtered as the older woman accepted Sin's arm and nodded toward Blackwood.

"I'm sorry." Aunt Millie pointed to her ear. "Perhaps another time, my dear," she said, taking Sin's arm. "I'm sure Lord Blackwood is eagerly awaiting you to dazzle him with your charms."

"How dare…" the widow started but turned on her heel and left in a huff.

"Armstrong, do be a dear. Hold my ear trumpet for me until my companion makes her way over," Aunt Millie said. "I won't be requiring it for a while. My adorable nephew will be doing more listening than I will."

"I'm happy to, my lady," Armstrong said, barely hiding a smirk while he accepted the conical hearing aid.

"Thank you, dear." She turned to Sin. "Nephew, we have much to discuss," she murmured behind her smile. "It might take us two turns around."

Sin chuckled. His aunt was one of the cleverest women he knew. And only she could get away with interrupting the widow and making the remarks she had.

He studied her as they began their stroll. For her age, she was a very spry woman. He had never known her to let anything keep her from something she truly wanted—not even the loss of her hearing or her much-loved husband. She stayed active. And he had noticed she didn't always need the hearing horn. It seemed a tool of convenience to him. But he would never admit his thoughts to her.

As they made the first turn in the room, Sin noticed Blackwood stride across the floor. It appeared the incomparable blonde he had noticed earlier was making her way toward the balcony and Lord Blackwood was still attempting to overtake her and speak with her. But it was her physical reaction that concerned him. Her head was down as she shook her head to something Blackwood had said. It appeared she would walk faster, but still, Blackwood seemed to persist. Was she trying to evade him?

"How long have you been in town?" his aunt asked, looking up at him and distracting him from his thoughts.

"Not long. I stopped by your townhouse in Mayfair, but Jenkins said you were not in London."

"Ah. I had been visiting my cousin," she said, still watching him. "She implored I visit her."

"I see. Were you there long?"

"Six weeks. But now I'm entirely versed on the layout of Bath and all it offers."

He chuckled. His aunt and her cousin were always at odds, but secretly, they depended on each other. "I had planned to surprise you, Aunt Millie."

"Well, I'd say you've done it. Will you be in town long?" she asked.

"I am not sure. As you know, I'm rather involved with some security matters—" He stopped. "How is it you are hearing me?"

She cackled. "I assure you. I cannot *hear* you. But I can read your lips. It's my secret power. Don't tell anyone."

He laughed and lightly squeezed her hand that was holding his arm. "You never cease to surprise—"

"But...you must look at me when you talk," she interrupted.

"I'm sorry." He turned and looked down at her, smiling. "I will keep your secret, Aunt Millie. But I must ask—where and when did you learn to read lips?"

She chuckled. "You know, of course, that my dear Arthur helped me establish a school for the deaf. And I volunteered—a lot! Over time, I realized that I was learning alongside many of the children who lived there. It's a remarkable way of communicating. You cannot hear voices, but sometimes when you read lips, you see more than you might hear."

Sin could relate to what she was saying. "In my work, I have to pay attention to similar nuances of the face and form."

"Exactly! Speaking of your work, there is something I would ask you to assist me with, my dearest."

"Are you missing one of your cats?" he teased.

"No," she said, swatting him. "I assure you, my cats are fine. However, I am rather concerned about Zeus. He is somewhat lazy and is getting quite..." She held her fan up and covered her mouth. "He is getting *fat*," she said in a hushed tone.

Sin started to suggest she feed him less, but that would have been impolite. Instead, he asked, "What do you plan to do about it?"

"I'll feed him less, of course!" she said. "He's dratted lazy, but I adore him. And the extra weight might cause him difficulty with his health later in his life."

Sin bit back a smile.

"I have a favor to ask of you, my sweet boy."

"Go on. I will do it if I can," Sin said. *As long as it doesn't involve your matchmaking.*

"I wonder if you might help my companion find a member of her family. Her brother is missing. She has no other family to speak of. You must do it in secret—she would be upset with me if she thought I was meddling. At the very least, it would make her uncomfortable, and I can't have that."

"Aunt Millie, you would *never* meddle," he said, holding back a smile.

"Of course not," she said, pulling her shoulders back in mock surprise.

"I will try to locate his whereabouts, Aunt Millie. But I should prepare you. I won't be in London long."

"Pish! I'm sure the duke would not mind you helping an old woman."

How did she know Wellington was involved with his travels? Surely his aunt didn't know he was working for the newly formed diplomatic corp. She was making a stab in the dark. And he had learned not to address those, or risk being ensnared. Instead, he answered, "I will do my best. You, my dearest aunt, may have years behind you, but you are anything but old."

"I knew it! The orange curls are working!" She clapped her hands together gleefully. "I told my modiste my red wig would be just the ticket," she pronounced and then narrowed her eyes as if taking his measure. "I'll let you in on a secret. After all my years of being happily married, it's lonely living without a man. So I've decided to find myself a man—just to share my time with," she added hastily.

"But what of your companion? Celia mentioned you've found one whom you adore."

"Your sister is right." His aunt's eyes sparkled with affection as she spoke of her companion. "I have no plans to let her go. She's young and absolutely lovely, and her family is even connected to the peerage. She has every right to be a part of this crowd—if she would just allow herself," she said, gesturing casually toward the bustling room. "She's bound to find her perfect match one day, and I don't want to be too far behind her in that regard."

Sin chuckled at his aunt's frankness. "You are one in a million, Aunt Millie."

She was swift in her response. "You couldn't handle me," she quipped, smiling. "Ah. We've come full circle. And reached the end of our journey."

Sin noted Armstrong was still patiently holding Aunt Millie's ear trumpet, but his other friends had scattered, no doubt taking part in the lively reel. He was relieved to see that Lady Parker had taken Aunt Millie's advice and was now dancing with her escort, Blackwood.

"It was a lovely stroll, Aunt Millie," Sin said, bowing over his aunt's hand.

"Yes, it was, dear. Now…where is she?" she said, turning and gazing about. "Oh, there she is!" Aunt Millie suddenly began waving excitedly at someone in the throng of guests. "Yoohoo! Yoohoo!"

Sin glanced in the same direction and saw a vision emerging from the crowd. A beautiful young woman with golden hair, wearing a rose-pink gown.

His aunt's voice was clearly filled with pride as she said, "Come here, my dear. Allow me to introduce you."

"Yes, my lady," the woman replied softly.

And then everything froze. Everything went still.

His breath caught in his throat and his heart thundered in his chest. And Sin felt as though he were being pulled back in time to that first moment he beheld her beauty—that golden halo of hair, that angelically lovely face, that mellifluous voice. And those eyes, those incredible emerald-green eyes that had haunted him from the moment he left her standing on the small porch of her cottage on the outskirts of Boston a year ago.

"Sin, allow me to introduce my companion…"

CHAPTER FIVE

LIZZIE STARED INTO the indigo eyes of the man she had dreamed about—the man whose memories had robbed her of a peaceful sleep night after night for the past year. He had been handsome even in his raggedy beard and gaunt state from the ravages of his illness…but now, he resembled a handsome knight from legends of yore. His heavy beard was gone, and his dark hair was neatly trimmed, albeit a trifle longer than was the current fashion for men, something she rather liked. But he was no longer frail or thin from the illness. He was healthy, strong, broad-shouldered…

She opened her mouth to speak, but at that moment, her voice failed her and her legs felt like they would collapse beneath her. When she faltered and feared she would fall to the floor, he reached for her hand and kissed it. His strength steadied her.

With a mixture of astonishment and disbelief, she whispered, "Edw—Mr. Sinclair, you are here? You…you are Lady Beadle's nephew?" She glanced at the dowager viscountess and noticed the older woman was watching their exchange with keen interest—as if solving an elaborate riddle.

After a long moment, Lady Beadle spoke. "Are you two already acquainted?"

Lizzie glanced at her and back at Edward. And then it dawned on her. *Of course! Sin is short for Sinclair—how did I not know that? I never even gave it a thought.*

Lady Beadle had mentioned her nephew Sin many times, but Lizzie had never made the connection. And now she recalled that Lady Armstrong had also referred to her brother by the name of Sin. Trying to find her equilibrium, Lizzie replied to Lady Beadle's question. "Yes… we are," she began slowly. "He… We…" She couldn't finish the sentence. She couldn't divulge how she knew Edward Sinclair. To admit she had taken him into her home and nursed him back to health—a woman living alone—could have disastrous consequences within Society for both her and Lady Beadle.

"Mrs. Pritchett." Edward took a step closer as if sensing her uncertainty. "It's a pleasure to see you again." He smiled and then turned to his aunt. "I met Mrs. Pritchett in Boston while searching for Lord Romney."

"I'll have my ear trumpet," Lady Beadle said, breaking the tension. She extended her hand and accepted the hearing aid from Armstrong. "I can't hear a darn thing. But Lizzie, *how* did you meet my nephew, and how am I just learning of this now?"

Lizzie exhaled a breath she hadn't realized she was holding. "We met in Boston," she said, realizing Edward had already stated that fact.

Lady Beadle arched a brow. Lizzie could read the impatience flickering in her eyes.

"Er…yes. Mrs. Pritchett volunteered at a hospital where I was a patient," Edward explained, saving her once again. "At the time, I had fallen ill, you see, and the prognosis was grim."

"Oh dear! I had no idea," his aunt said on a gasp.

"What happened to you, man?" Lord Armstrong asked.

Lizzie had forgotten Sin's brother-in-law had been standing there as well.

"I had *yellow jack*," Sin replied. "A wretched illness, although I try not to dwell on it. Despite that, Mrs. Pritchett's persistence in my care likely saved my life. She knew me as Edward Sinclair, not the nickname I go by."

"That is correct," Lizzie said. "I had no idea that Edward Sinclair and Sin were the same." She still couldn't quite fathom it.

Lady Beadle paled visibly and reached for Lizzie's hand. "I owe you a debt of gratitude, my dear, for saving my nephew's life."

"You do not owe me anything, my lady," Lizzie said to the older woman, who was clearly distraught. "I just did what I could to render assistance."

"This is a remarkable coincidence," Lord Armstrong remarked. "I'm afraid we would never have put this together either."

"Indeed," Lady Beadle agreed.

Feeling Edward's eyes on her, Lizzie turned and beheld him once more.

"Forgive me for staring, Mrs. Pritchett," he said in that deep, rich voice that had been imprinted in her mind. "I must say that seeing you again has me at sixes and sevens. Would you agree to a turn around the room? I'd like to hear more about your voyage across the Atlantic." He turned to his aunt. "But only if you are amenable, Aunt Millie."

Across the room, the orchestra had begun playing a few notes.

"Hmm... I see the orchestra is returning from their short break." Lady Beadle glanced at Lizzie, her eyes gleaming with that shrewdness Lizzie had come to know so well. "Lizzie has refused to dance thus far this evening, despite my badgering. Perhaps she will agree to dance with you, nephew."

Lizzie felt her face heat. "Lady Beadle, I haven't danced in an age. I'm afraid I couldn't—"

"Pish! You are selling yourself short, my dear. Dancing is a skill that one never loses. Besides, you have but to follow the man's lead. And I know for a fact that Sin is a very fine dancer." Lady Beadle waved her hand and smiled broadly. "Besides, it would do my heart good to see that lovely pink ball gown swishing its way around the room."

Edward held out his arm to Lizzie as the orchestra began to play the first strains of a waltz. "May I have this dance, Mrs. Pritchett?" he asked.

There was so much Lizzie wanted to say. She hadn't danced since her wedding, and she feared making a fool of herself. Everyone was already looking in their direction. But she wanted to be near him, hear his voice—that melodic baritone. Perhaps that was what was so difficult. She'd always feared that she would never be so fortunate as to meet another good man, like her late husband Peter. And then Edward had quite literally stumbled into her life. Just when she had begun to believe in the possibility of happiness again, he had left almost as suddenly as he'd arrived. And now, a year later, just as she had begun to put her life back together, here he was again. But oh, how tempting it was to just give in and let this strange twist of fate take its course.

"Yes…Lord Sinclair," she replied.

The warmth of his touch tingled up Lizzie's arm, and she felt a swirl of emotions. As they took their places on the dance floor, Edward placed his hand on the small of her back. "Follow my lead," he whispered in her ear. "You will do splendidly, I promise."

"I hope you're right," Lizzie whispered back.

And then she was surprised once again. Or rather, Edward surprised her once again. They fairly glided across the dance floor. With each turn, he pulled her closer. And she couldn't help but inhale the clean, masculine scent of leather, sandalwood, and citrus—a scent she recalled so vividly. "You dance well," she said.

"I thank you for the compliment," he replied, leaning down and speaking close enough that his breath tickled her ears. "But it is your gracefulness that is shining through."

"Thank you." She felt her face heat at his words and fought an impulse to lean into Edward—still unable to believe he was here with her. Despite the pleasure of dancing with him, she had so many questions and so much to say, she scarcely knew where to begin. "I waited for you," she suddenly blurted. "I waited as long as I could, but eventually, I'd exhausted my funds. When I had little more than enough left for a ship's passage—"

"Please, no explanation is needed," he said. "I know how difficult it must have been for you." His low voice sounded raspy to her ears. "But I want you to know, I did return for you, and finally found someone willing to tell me that you had set sail for England. Although I was saddened—and, I must admit, frustrated with myself—for not getting there sooner, I was also relieved to hear that you had returned home. America is a dangerous place for a woman alone. You were very brave, Liz—Mrs. Pritchett."

"Th-thank you," she said, stumbling over her words. "And please call me Lizzie."

"Lizzie," he said, his voice sounding like a caress to her ears. "My friends and family call me Sin, as you are welcome to."

"Thank you, Sin." She gave him a tentative smile. "I am humbled and yet gladdened that you thought so highly of me that you returned to Boston." Her heart soared that he had gone back for her. If only she had been able to stay… Would their lives have been on a different path today?

"Not even the devil himself would have kept me from returning."

She glanced up into his striking blue eyes and immediately felt the heat of another blush suffuse her cheeks. She dared not close her eyes or risk his disappearing the same way he had seemed to appear. And yet her gaze slid away, as a sudden shyness overcame her at the intensity in his regard. Those blue eyes—how unforgettable they were—made a heady awareness course through her veins.

Seeing him now, it was as though that feverish man, so ill, so near to death, had been someone else. Lizzie dared to look up at him once more and was struck anew by how different his appearance was, how broad his shoulders were, how muscular his arms beneath her fingers…and yet how warm and familiar his voice was.

They continued their dance in companionable silence, enveloped by the splendor of the elegant and glittering ballroom. Moonlight cascaded through the floor-to-ceiling windows, casting delicate shadows that danced upon the gleaming wooden floor. The air fairly vibrated with lilting notes from the orchestra, blending with the buzz of countless conversations, punctuated by the occasional burst of laughter. Candlelight flickered from massive chandeliers, casting them in a warm, golden glow as Edward guided her across the room with effortless grace, adding to the enchantment of the evening.

In the gentle sway of their movements, a silent conversation unfolded between them, speaking volumes in a shared language of lingering glances and light touches. With each step, each turn, their connection deepened, drawing them closer together amidst the whirl of the other dancing couples. It was as if the world around them faded away, leaving only the two of them suspended in this timeless moment of rediscovery.

"There have been so many times when I thought I saw you through a shop window or alighting from a carriage," he said, breaking the silence. "Once I thought I even spotted you in Paris… I, uh, rushed up to a woman who resembled you from the back only to discover it wasn't you." His lips curved up in a crooked smile. "It happened more times than I can count."

"I must confess that I thought I glimpsed you many times as well," Lizzie said, unable to keep her voice from trembling. "Even so, I never expected to cross paths with you again."

Edward looked at her, his expression softening. "Nor did I, Lizzie. At least not by chance. But it seems fate had other ideas."

She gave a shaky smile. "I would agree."

"Unfortunately, a ballroom is no place for a private conversation. Would you allow me to take you for a drive tomorrow afternoon?"

Lizzie nodded, her heart pounding in her chest. There was so much she wanted to ask him, but Edward was right—his sister's ball was not the place. "I'd like that very much." The tingling warmth continued to spread through her from knowing that he had journeyed back to Boston to find her. Oh, how she wished once again that she'd had the fortitude and the funds to be able to wait for him, but there had been so much uncertainty in her life back then. So much fear. And yes, she had also worried that fate may have had a hand in keeping him from coming back as he had promised. Traveling in the American wilderness, one never knew what dangers lurked about. Despite having so many questions and uncertainties fluttering through her mind, Lizzie felt a familiar sense of comfort in his presence.

As the final strains of the waltz played, Edward escorted her back to where his aunt awaited them. Lizzie stole another glance at his blue eyes and found them upon her, looking at her with that same intensity as before.

"I will call on you at two o'clock," he said, his voice low.

She smiled, feeling a lightness of spirit she had not felt in a very long time. "I'm looking forward to it." To spend time alone with Edward would be an unexpected gift she had only dared dream of. Not only did she want to know about his experiences in his search for his friend, but she was also anxious to ask Edward if he had crossed paths with her brother and where he might be stationed.

As he returned her to his aunt's side, Lizzie released her hold on his arm. She saw Edward's sister, Lady Celia Armstrong, approaching them. "Sweet brother! It's good to see you out and about. I noticed you dancing with Mrs. Pritchett and thought I was seeing things!" She looked at Lizzie. "It is well known that my brother rarely promenades around the room or dances—but tonight he's done both!" she teased. "I wasn't the only person to notice—you have set the marriage-minded mamas' tongues to wagging. So many have asked if I would introduce my brother to them, and they have been very generous in their donations. Please don't misunderstand my motives, Mrs. Pritchett—I am merely teasing my brother."

"Harassing me, is more like it," Edward muttered, but his eyes held a smile for his sister.

"You are trading introductions for donations?" Wright asked, stepping closer. "May I be of assistance?"

"I suppose it appears that way—because I haven't turned anyone down. But I assure you, Sin, I would never use you," Lady Armstrong said smugly.

"Bravo, my dear!" Lady Beadle said enthusiastically. "I thoroughly approve."

"Mrs. Pritchett, please allow me to introduce one of my best friends, Viscount Asher Wright," Edward said. "We have been friends for more years than I can count. Wright, this is Mrs. Lizzie Pritchett, a friend from my travels in America."

"Mrs. Pritchett, it is an honor to meet you," Wright said, lightly kissing the back of her hand. He turned to Edward. "Well done, my friend. I see why you dusted off your dancing shoes."

Lizzie found herself laughing along with everyone else. Wright was unabashed in his efforts to meet eligible young ladies.

"Mrs. Pritchett, I must apologize to you. I'm afraid I've been thoughtless. An unmarried man's movements are carefully observed by the *ton*," Edward said, turning to her. "Mrs. Pritchett, I'm afraid my actions may cause you some minor notoriety in the gossip rags."

"Please, do not think of it," Lizzie murmured, although her stomach was in knots. "I'm sure it will be forgotten by tomorrow." Noticing the keen look on Lady Beadle's face, she knew there would be more questions about her time in Boston. She would have to prepare herself.

"My goodness! I just realized that the two of you are behaving as if you have known each other before. Did I miss something?" Lady Armstrong looked from Edward to Lizzie before glancing at her husband for an explanation.

Lady Beadle piped up, "It seems my companion and your brother met across the pond. And now they have reconnected— seeing each other for the first time a year later—at your party."

"How remarkable! I've heard of such stories but have never witnessed such a fortuitous reunion. I observed you two dancing and was struck by how intently you were gazing at each other," Lady Armstrong said sweetly.

Lizzie wanted to wish herself anywhere but there, except then, she might never have crossed paths with Edward. She glanced at Lady Beadle, catching the impish glint in her eyes. If there were ever a time she needed her gumption, it was now. Straightening her shoulders, Lizzie explained, "It is most fortuitous, Lady Armstrong. I met your brother when he was delirious with fever, and under the circumstances, I had no idea that the Mr. Sinclair I helped through an illness was your brother. I was only aware that you and Lord Armstrong were friends of my brother Michael."

"It is indeed a small world. My God, we owe you a debt of gratitude." Lady Armstrong wrapped her arms around Lizzie and hugged her closely.

Lizzie felt her face heat. She was unused to such attention, particularly in the middle of a ballroom.

"Sin never sent word," Lady Armstrong said, her eyes swimming with tears. "So, until he returned, we had no idea how close we had come to losing him." She turned to her brother and embraced him as well. "Promise you will never put us through that again."

"I promise," Edward said, his eyes meeting Lizzie's over his sister's head.

"There is so much more to this that I want to know," she said. Her voice sounded wobbly, and her eyes brimmed with tears again. Her husband stepped forward and wrapped his arm around her shoulders.

"Come, darling—let us step away for a few moments of privacy." He nodded at Edward. "If you'll excuse us, we won't be long."

"Yes, of course, I must look a blubbering mess," Lady Armstrong said. "I do want to hear everything about Sin and Mrs. Pritchett, but I should get back to the guests as well. I still have more funds to raise."

"She'll be right as rain soon enough," Lady Beadle told Edward. "Your sister has always been emotional from childhood. But she married a good man who adores her. As it should be."

Lizzie watched as Lord Armstrong escorted his wife from the ballroom. It was true—the young couple was deeply in love, something to be cherished for its rarity. She felt a pang of guilt that she had inadvertently been the cause of the young woman's distress.

"Do not fret, Mrs. Pritchett," Edward said softly, stepping closer to her. "My sister has a soft heart, but a strong spirit. Much like you do."

"I thank you, my lord," Lizzie whispered, still quite flustered by his nearness. She chanced another peek at his deep blue eyes and felt his warm regard like a soothing balm. She felt almost mesmerized, as she did when he was twirling her around the dance floor, and forgot what she'd wanted to say.

"My dear, I just had the oddest conversation with Lady Pemberly," Lady Beadle said, her voice nudging Lizzie from the magical glow she felt when she looked into Edward's eyes. "I am quite concerned, Lizzie," she continued. "Lady Pemberly told me that Baron Percival Blackwood practically accosted you earlier."

Lizzie frowned in confusion, trying to recall Lord Blackwood.

"You do not know his name, I warrant," Lady Beadle said, jutting her head in the direction of a man who was speaking to a voluptuous, red-headed older woman in a scandalous crimson gown. Lizzie had been introduced to the woman, a widow by the name of Lady Parker. "Lord Blackwood is that tall man dressed in black with long, unkempt black hair and odious, beady, little black eyes."

"Oh, yes, I did encounter him at the refreshment table," Lizzie said, recognizing the man. He'd stood so close to her that she had to take several steps back, feeling most uncomfortable in his presence. "I was thirsty for another glass of lemonade, and he attempted to engage me in conversation."

"I would not describe it as such," Lady Beadle said. "Gladys said he was practically ogling you. Oh, what a loathsome man!"

"Yes, that is Blackwood," Edward said, an edge to his voice. "I am sorry that you had to go through that, Mrs. Pritchett. Allow me to have a few words with him."

"No, please, Edward," Lizzie said, laying her hand on his arm. "I mean, Lord Sinclair, forgive me." She quickly withdrew her hand. "I—It was of no consequence, really. I do not want to make a scene."

"Fiddle-faddle," the dowager viscountess declared with a shake of her head. "From what I understand, the blackguard practically stepped on the hem of your gown, to make you trip so that he could paw at you. That man is a bad one, my dear."

"May I ask what happened?" Edward asked.

"When I stepped away from the table with my lemonade, he seemed to appear out of nowhere and bumped into me, and some of it splashed on his coat," Lizzie replied. "I apologized, and he immediately began to pepper me with questions—asking me my name, when I had arrived in town, and who I knew. I found his questions most intrusive, and I attempted to evade answering him directly. When I tried to excuse myself, he laid his hand on my arm and quite bluntly stated that he wished to call on me tomorrow."

She could feel her face flush as she described the encounter. She could not help but notice the muscle working in Edward's jaw, nor the flash of anger in his eyes. The last thing Lizzie wanted was for Edward to call out the horrid man and risk his reputation.

"Please, it was nothing," she said, hoping she sounded convincing. "I told him I did not think his questions were the least bit appropriate, then I sidestepped him and quickly walked away."

"I will instruct Jenkins to turn the blackguard away should he dare darken our doorstep!" Lady Beadle proclaimed.

"I promise, I did not wait for his response," Lizzie said. "I pushed past him and made my way back to Lady Beadle. Besides, I am here as her companion, not as her guest."

"I rather think my aunt would beg to differ with you," Edward said, his lips curving up into a crooked smile.

"I certainly do!" Lady Beadle bristled. "You are here as a guest of mine, and you are a lady. And should consider yourself accordingly for any future events we attend. The man's lack of manners alarms me greatly."

"I am in full agreement there," Edward said. "Lizzie, if he bothers you again, promise you will tell me. The man has an unsavory reputation, and, I confess, it's a surprise to see him here." He sighed. "My sister has evidently invited any and all possible donors to this fundraising event for the children's hospital and orphanage."

"Judging from what Lady Armstrong said earlier, I believe she has been successful in her efforts," Lizzie said.

"That well may be, but I still don't like to see men like Blackwood accosting young women, no matter what his donation is."

"Hear, hear!" Lady Beadle said. "I might have a word with Celia about this."

"Good idea," Edward said, bestowing a smile on his aunt. Then he turned to Lizzie, his voice soft and husky as he added, "I still plan to call on you tomorrow—unless you've changed your mind."

"Of course, I haven't. I'm looking forward to it." And she was.

"Excellent. I will be there at two o'clock."

She gave a slight nod. "I will see you then."

CHAPTER SIX

Sinclair House
Berkeley Square, Mayfair
The next day

SIN AWOKE AS the first rays of dawn were filtering through the curtains in his chamber, his mind still tangled in the remnants of restless dreams. Despite the night's fitful sleep, anticipation coursed through him like a wild river. Today, he and Wright had planned an early morning ride at Hampstead Heath, a haven amidst the hustle and bustle of London. It was a chance for Eclipse, his faithful steed, to stretch his powerful legs, a respite from the confinement of cramped city streets.

And it was a chance for him to think. Lord, he needed to think. Lizzie was in London, but it still felt as if he were dreaming.

As Sin got up, the world outside his window was still cloaked in shadows, the air charged with the promise of a new day. He could already feel the pulsing vitality of the city reverberating in his bones. With a sense of urgency, he dressed quickly, his movements fluid and purposeful.

Outside, Wright awaited him, the faint glow of dawn painting his features in shades of gray. A knowing smile played at the corners of his lips, a silent acknowledgment of their shared eagerness.

"I thought we might delay our departure until after breaking our fast," he remarked, his voice betraying a hint of weariness. "After all the merriment of last night, I find myself in need of sustenance before embarking on such an adventure."

Sin's gaze flickered to his mount. The magnificent beast pawed at the ground in restless anticipation. "Eclipse is raring to go. And I feel the need for the cold air on my face. But if you wish to eat, you are welcome to. I shan't be long."

Wright chuckled. "I am always raring to go, my friend. But I'm also always hungry. Let us ride first, and then our appetites will welcome a hearty breakfast even more."

Twenty minutes later they approached Hampstead Heath. Without traffic to dodge, the journey was quick and easy. "I'll race you to the end," Sin said, already nudging Eclipse forward. He heard Wright close on his heels. The smell of clean, calming rain from the night before permeated Sin's senses as their horses churned the damp earth beneath their hooves in their quest to reach the finish line.

For Sin, the heath held the promise of mental clarity—and he needed that today. He felt one with nature as he and Eclipse raced, the familiar course he and his friend had followed since their youth. Today, he needed to sort out his feelings and what it meant to see Lizzie again after so many months.

Their first meeting had been etched in his mind and heart. He had been close to death—the closest he had ever been. Not even in battle had he felt that close to the end. From the moment she opened the door to him, everything had changed.

The first part of his stay with her was too vague to recall, except for snatches of memory retained in between the fierce spikes of fever and what seemed like a sickness that had taken hold of his very soul. He would have died had it not been for Lizzie's care. They had begun a strange journey together as strangers, and yet in a short time had become as intimate as a long-married couple, considering what she had to do to care for him. Even though Dr. Hastings had visited daily, there were many times that she tended to his private needs as a wife would her husband. At first, he was too sick to feel ashamed of his vulnerability, but as he began to heal, he realized how remarkable Lizzie truly was. She never made him feel awkward, and she always had a ready smile. She would sit at his bedside for hours, reading to him, telling him humorous stories from her childhood, about her brother, and loving stories about her late parents.

He felt as though he'd come to know every part of her soul.

And in that short time, he fell in love with her.

And when I was well enough, I abandoned her.

How often had the memory of that last day gripped his heart? Seeing the pain in her eyes, the sadness that she had tried to hide behind a bright smile as she packed food for his journey in her small cottage kitchen. The guilt had almost been his undoing then. But how could he have done otherwise? He had traveled to America on a mission, one that he could not have abandoned.

How many times had he thought about taking her with him? An impossibility under the circumstances. Too dangerous.

How many times had he thought about turning back? Too many to count.

Sin shook his head as he heard the thundering hooves of Wright's horse gaining on him. As they approached the familiar bend in the road where a mighty oak tree stood, serving as their finish line, Wright pulled up alongside him and signaled for him to slow down. "My God, man. Were you trying to race against the devil?"

The two horses slowed to a trot. "More like an angel," Sin said.

"Ah, the beautiful Mrs. Pritchett," Wright said with a rueful grin.

His friend knew him so well. Theirs had always been the most remarkable of friendships—almost without speaking, they always knew what weighed heavily on each other's mind.

"I've been thinking about her for a year, seeing her image

wherever I go, approaching strangers from behind, only to find they are not her," Sin said. "She's all I've thought about since returning from America. I had planned to search for her, beginning today, and...*poof!* There she was at the ball last night."

"You still haven't said much about her. But I know there's much more to this story than meets the eye. I can tell that your heart is engaged," Wright said, nudging his steed closer.

Sin nodded. "It is. I was there for two months, but during the first, I was barely coherent from the fever."

"Two months in the company of such a woman can form a strong bond."

"We were close—closer than I've ever been to any woman in my life. I should have taken her with me."

"Were there any words spoken between you?" Wright asked.

Sin shook his head. "No specific words. But I felt we had an understanding. Ah, but I hurt her when I left. I should have told her that I loved her."

"Love. That's quite an admission. But it's a year later. Do you still feel the same way?" Wright asked.

"I do," Sin said. "I should never have left her. It was the stupidest thing I've ever done."

"But you went back for her."

Sin nodded and continued with his story. He explained that he'd promised Lizzie he would do everything in his power to return to Boston. "But when I finally did go back, it was too late." He wasn't entirely sure about the details, but Lizzie had told him she had run out of money and her only other recourse had been to accept charity from the community. "Unfortunately, she had been accepted by only a few people, and many were less than charitable to her. Eventually, she used the last of her funds to book passage to England, hoping to find her brother, whom she had not seen in years." But when she arrived, she found out that he had been given some sort of secret assignment, and the navy wouldn't provide her with any information.

"Does her husband have any family in England?" Wright

asked.

"I'm not sure of their family surname—I only recall her brother's first name, Michael. I could ask Lizzie, but I must tread carefully. This is still so raw and new. I would not want her to feel that I was imposing on her life. I can certainly ask Armstrong and Celia, who I found out last night are good friends with him. My aunt also asked me to find Mrs. Pritchett's brother—before she became aware that we knew each other. I suppose that was a tremendous surprise for her. It certainly was a shock to me."

"I can't imagine finding out that the woman who had held your thoughts for more than a year was practically right under your nose as your aunt's companion." Wright shook his head. "Does Mrs. Pritchett know how you feel?"

"No. I've never told her."

"Come on, my friend. Let's head back. You need a strong cup of coffee and a big breakfast," Wright said.

"I do. Thank you for lending me your ear." Sin looked at his friend. "Your townhouse is still under renovation, isn't it?"

"Yes. And I tried to stay there, but it's blasted uncomfortable, so I'm staying in a hotel."

"Nonsense! Bring your things from the hotel. You'll stay at my home until your townhouse is finished."

Wright chuckled. "I thank you, my friend. I find I have a voracious appetite this morning. Let us hope your cook has stocked ample provisions."

Sin laughed. This had been exactly what he needed. And with a clear head, he could focus on Lizzie. He didn't know how she felt or whether she still held the same regard for him as he did for her. While he'd sensed her pleasure in seeing him again, was it *just* that, or was there more? Now that he'd seen her again, spoken to her, he would not let his good fortune pass him by. But he would have to proceed with care. Lizzie deserved to be courted.

25 Curzon Street, Mayfair
London
Later that morning

"LAST NIGHT WAS certainly a surprise. I never imagined you knew my nephew," Lady Beadle said between bites of toast. She lowered her copy of the *Ton Tattler*.

Lizzie prepared herself to be peppered with questions. Looking across the table, she noticed Lady Beadle's ear trumpet resting beside her teacup and smiled fondly. The wily woman! Her hearing couldn't be as bad as she pretended. But it was impossible to know whether she could read lips, or whether the hearing loss was minor—not that it mattered. She found Lady Beadle endearing. Sneaky, but endearing.

"I was curious to see what was said about last night's ball. Here it is. Listen to this," Lady Beadle said, straightening the paper.

> "The *Ton Tattler* is pleased to share that LLP attended the extremely successful Armstrong fundraiser last evening and was seen on the arm of LES. The children's charities sponsored by L/L Armstrong will flourish thanks to the generous donations by members of the ton, specifically LLP's..."

She tsked as she set the newspaper down on the table. "Typical," she said. "Many notable people attended, and almost everyone gave generously, but the Widow Louisa Parker's insatiable need to bask in the attention of others once again propelled her to take center stage. Of course, she would find an opportunity to connect her initials with those of my nephew—the only time her claws were on Sin's arm was when she was pawing at him to dance with her."

"Goodness. The woman sounds quite ruthless," Lizzie said.

"And she never danced with him, did she? As usual, there is nothing of note—which happens every time the empty-headed publisher of the *Tattler* chooses to use one of the Widow Parker's tiring cat-and-mouse *dramatics*," Lady Beadle drawled, pursing her lips. "My nephew knows her, although I don't know if there is—or was—a *relationship*. Based on his efforts to avoid her, I will ignore her baseless intrigues. But I shall make sure he knows about it." She snorted. "Little do they know that they missed the biggest story. I planned to introduce you to my nephew at Celia's party, but it seems that took place without my help." She gave Lizzie a knowing look.

Lizzie gave her a nervous smile. She hoped to escape Lady Beadle's relentless thirst for details—specifically her meeting with Edward. "I confess I cannot imagine why the widow felt a need to attach herself to Lord Sinclair's initials, my lady."

She had not seen Edward in well over a year. Goodness, she'd arrived in London in July, having cried for what was lost the entire journey. So many hopes and dreams. First as a naïve bride barely nineteen, and then a widow less than two years later.

Despite losing Peter, she had tried to make a home for herself in Boston. She'd spent most of her time volunteering at the hospital, for it was the only place where she'd felt useful, spending her days assisting wherever a helping hand was needed. It helped her cope with her grief. But when she returned to her little cottage at the end of the day, she would give in to her tears.

Edward's arrival on her doorstep had changed everything. But when he left, after his illness passed, she was alone once again.

It was only after she arrived back home in England that she decided she needed to reclaim her life. She would look for a position for herself somewhere, somehow, and finally let go of the grief and pain from her time in America.

She had been fortunate indeed that she had met such kind people as Lord and Lady Armstrong and Lady Beadle. She would always be grateful to her brother Michael for his sage advice. But now, her life was once again upended. And she no longer felt herself on firm ground. In the span of a few days, she had returned from a six-week trip to Bath with Lady Beadle and then been whisked off to the Armstrong ball, where she suddenly came face to face with Edward again.

To see him last night and find out that he was in London—and moreover, that he was the beloved nephew named Sin that Lady Beadle had often spoken of—was almost beyond Lizzie's imaginings. She had assumed Sin was his actual name, not a diminutive for Sinclair.

"What time did Sin say he would call today?" Lady Beadle asked, tugging Lizzie from her reverie.

Her face heated. She felt a little strange and a tad awkward about the upcoming outing. She was no debutante, nor was she a member of Lady Beadle's family. She did not want to overstep her employer's kindness. It seemed strange to allow Edward to call on her at her employer's home. Yet she had no other option, since it was her home as well.

"He said two o'clock." Lizzie took a sip of her tea to brace herself. "Lady Beadle, I hope my outing with Lord Sinclair does not interfere with anything you have planned."

"Poppycock!" Lady Beadle waved her hand in a dismissive gesture. "I had nothing scheduled. And I will not have you fretting over this. I am tickled pink about it. And as I have said before, please call me Millie. It is my name, after all."

"Thank you, Millie." Lady Beadle was a dear heart, but Lizzie could not help but worry. People did talk. What if she and Edward were spotted on their outing by a *ton* gossip? She wished she could stop herself from worrying. She wished she could give a flying fig about what Society thought. But the past several years had taught her too many harsh lessons. She sighed as she refilled her teacup.

"Tell me about your volunteer service at that hospital in Boston," the dowager said, spreading blackberry preserves on a slice of toasted bread. "Did you encounter yellow fever a great deal?"

"Occasionally. People working in the ports were particularly susceptible, making it common, along with a few other illnesses."

"I've heard of it, of course. But the only thing I've ever known about it—besides it being a ghastly illness—is that it's very contagious. How did you avoid it?"

"I didn't, my lady—er, Millie. Shortly after Peter and I arrived, I fell ill. Initially, we were unsure of the cause, as I exhibited symptoms like fever and chills, which could have indicated various illnesses. However, Dr. Hastings, whom I assisted with my volunteer work at the hospital, speculated that not all patients react the same to the fever. He'd seen milder cases in some people, including myself. He said the case that I contracted perhaps served to protect me from falling ill again."

"So, you cared for Sin at the hospital," the dowager said with a shrewd look. "And you chanced to get the illness yourself. I am relieved that you had that protection for your own health, and I am grateful that you were able to help my nephew and many others no doubt."

"I too am thankful for that, Millie. I was fortunate indeed."

"My dear Lizzie, I am certain that you went through a great deal during your five years in America, and I can surmise your experiences were beyond challenging. The fact that I see a strong, intelligent woman of spirit and kindness sitting across from me makes me think that what you endured had nothing to do with fortune, but with fortitude."

Lizzie blinked back sudden tears. How she wished she could stop being such a watering pot. But when she'd looked into Edward's feverish face so many months ago, she knew would do everything she could to help him, consequences be damned.

"You possess a remarkably generous spirit, my dear. But I must say, not many women would have taken such a risk," the dowager said as though reading Lizzie's mind.

A knock sounded on the door as Jenkins entered. "My lady.

Lady Armstrong is here to see you," he announced.

"Really?" She arched a brow. "It's not like Celia to visit this early. I assumed she would still be resting after last night's exertions. Please see her in."

"Hello, Lizzie. Aunt Millie, thank you for receiving me," Lady Armstrong said, pulling off her gloves and tucking them in her reticule as she entered. She glanced at the sideboard laden with steaming platters. "Oh! I know it's presumptuous of me, but I barely broke my fast with a cup of chocolate and a lemon biscuit—I was in such a hurry to get here. Oh, and you have bacon! My favorite."

"Child, please, take a plate, sit down, and eat whatever you like," her aunt said. "If you want chocolate, we can arrange that as well."

"I'd love more chocolate," Lady Armstrong enthused. "I usually have two cups."

"Say no more. I can't imagine you leaving your home without a proper breakfast, but we can't have you chocolate deprived. I make it a point never to neglect the needs of anyone under my roof." Lady Beadle chuckled good-naturedly and turned to a footman. "Reggie, be a dear and bring Lady Armstrong more chocolate. Bring a pot—I might have a cup myself. Mrs. Pritchett, would you care for some chocolate?"

"That would be lovely." Lizzie smiled. She'd missed making herself a cup, having overslept a tad that morning.

"Thank you, Aunt. You are most accommodating," Lady Armstrong said as she picked up a plate and helped herself to bacon, scrambled eggs, and two slices of toast from the sideboard. Then, smiling, she seated herself across from Lizzie.

Lizzie noted the speculative gleam in the Lady Beadle's eyes, a smile crinkling her lips as she silently regarded her niece tucking into the generous helpings heaped upon her plate.

Lady Beadle cleared her throat. "It was a lovely party last evening, my dear. Were you able to raise enough money for the *children*?" With an arched brow, she watched her niece.

Lizzie suppressed a smile as understanding dawned on her.

"Oh, Auntie! We exceeded our goal," Lady Armstrong declared, popping a piece of bacon into her mouth. She chewed enthusiastically and then continued, "There were a couple of surprise donations from people I had not expected to be so generous. It would be gauche of me to comment further about that. But I was delighted with the outcome. The evening was a resounding success."

Reggie returned with the chocolate and filled a cup for each of them.

"There may be more than one success for you," Lady Beadle murmured, her lips beginning to twitch.

Lizzie coughed, hiding her chuckle, and picked up her cup to sip the creamy, delectable chocolate. She had missed the treat while she was in America. She'd had to make do with a tea she learned to brew from natural herbs and flowers that grew in the small garden behind her cottage.

"Well, I should hope we shall continue to have future fund-raisers," Lady Armstrong said, scooping up a bite of fluffy eggs. "Simply delicious," she murmured. She didn't seem to have heard her aunt's comment, but her slender form indicated she was probably not usually the type to eat breakfast twice.

Lizzie wondered if the married woman was pretending to be unaware because she was not ready to divulge her good news, or if she'd simply missed the hidden meaning of her aunt's comments. Lady Beadle had sometimes lamented that her niece was so involved in so many charitable causes that she sometimes forgot to eat. And there was the possibility that she was just famished because she had not been able to relax and eat last night. Lady Armstrong had spent most of the night tending to the guests and donations. It had to have been nerve-racking. Now that Lizzie had established a routine with Lady Beadle, she would endeavor to speak with her about aiding Lady Armstrong with her causes.

"Now, what did you wish to discuss, Celia?" Lady Beadle

prodded.

"Oh, goodness!" Lady Armstrong said, dabbing her mouth with her napkin. "These eggs are delicious. It tastes like they have cheese—we have never had cheese cooked into our scrambled eggs! Simply delicious. I will speak to our cook about that."

Her aunt eyed the plate with bacon and eggs, a smile flickering at the edge of her mouth as she sipped her chocolate. "You do that, dear. However, I know you didn't come here to discuss bacon and eggs—although you are correct, there is cheese in the eggs." A look of melancholy crossed her features. "My mother used to prepare them like that for me and Cook knows it's my favorite."

"Now that you say that, I recall always enjoying a hearty breakfast at your house, but I never realized the eggs had cheese. William is always telling me that my palate is a little sluggish." Lady Armstrong laughed. Taking a sip of her chocolate, she turned to Lizzie. "I came to apologize to you, Lizzie," she said. "I realized that I might have come across as too exuberant in my comments to Sin about his marital state, and I hope I was not presumptuous. I simply had to apologize.

"Sin and I tease each other. We always have. We were thrilled that Sin showed up last night, as he rarely does. He hates these types of events. But to promenade and waltz—well! The ladies were quite enthused—several hoped they could gain his attention. And then to find out that you and Sin had met in America, well, that was a tremendous turn of events. A most remarkable and welcome surprise. And I was so pleased to learn of it. But I was so excited about the donations that I ran to tell Sin—and I fear I drew attention to both of you and embarrassed you. And then I started blubbering on top of it. I don't know why, but lately, I've been so quick to tears." She shook her head. "I apologize if I made you unconformable. I promise I did not do it on purpose."

"I thank you for your apology, Lady Armstrong, but please allow me to allay your discomfiture," Lizzie said. "It was indeed a surprise to see Lord Sinclair again after so long, and under such different circumstances. Given our parting in America, I had resolved never to see him again. And I must admit, I was quite overcome." She had revealed a tad more than she normally would have, but she trusted both Lady Armstrong and Lady Beadle and was certain they were not the sort of women to spread gossip, as other ladies in the *ton* enjoyed doing. "But I was not upset with you, my lady," she continued. Lizzie couldn't be upset with Lady Armstrong for her exuberance. She was naturally an effervescent woman whose warmth embraced everyone around her. And if not for she and her husband, Lizzie would not have found a home and a position with Lady Beadle.

"Please, we are past formalities. Do call me Celia," Lady Armstrong insisted. "Your brother is very close to us. We are quite fond of Michael, and you feel like a long-lost sister to me. I hope I am not forward in saying that."

"Thank you, Celia." Lizzie smiled. "And yes, I also feel a closeness with you."

Lady Beadle interjected, clearing her throat. "Well, now that we have discussed how tasty eggs are with melted cheese, and have indulged our love of chocolate and exchanged heartfelt endearments, pray tell, my dear Celia, when are you due?"

CHAPTER SEVEN

25 Curzon Street, Mayfair
London
That afternoon

"LORD SINCLAIR, IT'S a pleasure to see you again," Jenkins said, opening the door.

"Thank you, Jenkins," Sin said, handing the butler his hat and coat. "I'm here to see Mrs. Pritchett."

"They are expecting you, my lord. If you'll follow me," Jenkins said, escorting him to the parlor. "My lady and Mrs. Pritchett, Lord Sinclair has arrived."

Aunt Millie gave a brief nod. The retainer bowed and closed the door behind him.

Sin noticed his aunt's three cats had taken their chaperone positions on the opposite end of the settee from Lizzie and Aunt Millie. He greeted his aunt with a kiss on her cheek. Then he turned to greet Lizzie, taking her hand in his hand and kissing it lightly. She looked beautiful in her emerald-colored dress and simple pearl earrings. He had to stop himself from staring at her. He would happily spend the entire day doing so, but then she would likely think him daft.

"Sin, join us. I know you wanted to leave for your ride in the park. But humor an old woman. Cook brought us some refreshing lemonade and sandwiches, and I'd love to take a minute and enjoy them. Do you enjoy cucumber sandwiches?" his aunt asked both him and Lizzie.

"Certainly, sandwiches and lemonade would be most welcome," Sin replied with a smile.

His aunt, ever the curious one, prodded further. "Where are you two young people off to?"

He chuckled. "Nowhere too adventurous, I'm afraid. I thought we'd keep to tradition and enjoy a carriage ride through Hyde Park, but early, before the fashionable hour."

Lizzie's smile widened. "That sounds wonderfully relaxing, Lord Sinclair."

"In Boston, I was known as Edward Sinclair. Please call me Edward or Sin, whichever you prefer." He'd encouraged her to call him by his nickname at the ball, but realizing how Lizzie must feel in such different circumstances, he wanted her to feel comfortable using his first name and would continue to remind her.

"In that case, Edward it is," she affirmed.

Sin noticed a subtle rise in his aunt's eyebrows. But his heart warmed to the sound of his name on Lizzie's lips. She was the only one who called him Edward, as she did in Boston, and it felt like a special and intimate connection between the two of them.

"Tell me, how well acquainted are you two?" Aunt Millie asked. "And while I don't doubt your hospital work, dear Lizzie, something tells me that is not how you actually met."

Lizzie's lovely face reddened, and she looked down. "I'm afraid the truth might have caused trouble for you, Lady Beadle."

"We are friends, and I've asked you to call me Millie, my dear." Aunt Millie patted Lizzie on the hand before looking at Sin. She picked up her hearing trumpet and placed it on her ear. "I must know everything, and I don't want to miss a word. It is the only way I can help you—if need be."

Lizzie turned her gaze toward Sin, who responded with a subtle nod and a smile of reassurance. "We can trust my aunt," he said softly.

Taking a deep breath, Lizzie related the events to Aunt Millie. "Edward arrived unexpectedly at my doorstep in the middle of the night, his condition dire and urgent. There was hardly a moment for him to plead for aid, for he was in a delirium and a feverish state. Instinctively, I welcomed him into my home. Dr. Hastings, in his kindness, visited to attend to Lord Sin—Edward's needs."

The pretty blush in her cheeks deepened, and Sin couldn't help his heart rate accelerating. She was lovely, demure, and a true lady, and yet she had shown such courage and strength in America.

"With his expertise and the resources Dr. Hastings provided, I did everything in my power to help Edward through the illness," Lizzie continued, her voice quivering with emotion. "The fever raged on for many days. Its intensity would ebb for a day or two, only to surge once more. Dr. Hastings said it was one of the most challenging cases he'd seen, but I was determined to do everything I could to s-save Edward."

Sin yearned to recall what had transpired those few weeks, but for the past year, every attempt to recall their first month together had ended in frustration. Even now, he hung on every word that came from her beautiful, bow-shaped mouth.

"I begin to understand why you offered up the story about the hospital," Aunt Millie said softly. "You are a widow, but even a widow would not be forgiven such an impropriety. The narrow-minded *ton* would see things differently. But I think you showed tremendous courage, my dear. And I thank you for saving our Edward," she added, her voice cracking. She dabbed at her eyes with the fine linen napkin on her lap.

Sin stood and walked over to his aunt. Sitting on her other side, on the edge of the settee, he took her hand and kissed it, trying to suppress a smile as she grumbled about his fussing. He'd known his aunt would understand and agree that Lizzie was an exceptional woman. Sin had sensed Lizzie's anxiety and wanted to reassure her. But it had been impossible to do so at the ball. Now, in the privacy of his aunt's home, Lizzie had revealed the truth, and everything was much easier. As he looked into her green eyes, his heart thudded in his chest.

"Now then," his aunt said. "Lizzie, I want you and Sin to spend the afternoon together. I insist on it. My needs are small, and I can see to them this afternoon. If not, Jenkins is in charge. What I cannot do is allow the two of you to miss a most fortuitous opportunity to reacquaint yourselves. The circumstances of your first meeting were remarkable, only to be topped by your second meeting at the ball last night. Quite remarkable indeed." Her eyes sparkled. "And in the meantime, I'm going to bask in all the clucking and speculation—seeing you two together will disappoint the matchmaking mamas of the *ton*." She tapped her cane on the floor. "Go on. Get on with your afternoon. Enjoy yourselves."

A few minutes later, Sin helped Lizzie into his carriage. He positioned himself beside her. "Are you comfortable?" he asked her. "If you are chilly, I have blankets under the bench seat."

"I am well, thank you." She smiled.

He lightly tapped the ceiling of the coach, signaling the driver to set their journey in motion.

Lizzie's voice trembled slightly as she asked the question that must have been weighing on her mind. "Are...are we courting?" she asked, her words barely audible above the gentle rumble of the carriage's wheels along the cobblestone streets.

Sin noticed her clasped hands trembled slightly on her lap.

He reached over and delicately cradled her face in his palms, his gaze locked with hers, drowning in the depths of her shimmering emerald eyes. "Lizzie," he whispered. He could hear the mixture of longing and determination in his own voice. "I've traveled continents in search of you. Every silhouette that bore even a faint resemblance to your graceful form, every hint of your possible presence, prompted my heart to race, and I would call out your name, hoping against hope that *she* was you. Yet each time, it was a cruel twist of fate denying me. And now, here you are before me, a beautiful mirage turned into reality."

His words hung in the air, charged with the weight of unspoken emotions.

"There exists an undeniable connection between us, one that transcends time and distance," he continued. "Had we remained in Boston, I would have courted you and forged an everlasting bond. I regret that circumstances prevented that. That *I* prevented that. So, my dear Lizzie, unless your heart does not echo my sentiments, I implore you to allow me to court you."

Lizzie swiped at her eyes. "I have never heard more beautiful words from you, not even in my dreams."

"Am I in your dreams, sweet Lizzie?" he asked.

She hesitated before nodding. "Yes, you are in my dreams," she said in a husky voice. "But despite my feelings, I fear this will not work for us. Society will not accept me. Peter's parents refused to accept me as his wife."

"You base this conviction on your marriage to Lord Peter Pritchett?"

A tear spilled down her cheek as she tipped her head in silent acknowledgment.

"Then Society be damned. I care not a whit for what the *ton* thinks. Your late husband's parents were fools to ignore their son's heart and his good sense in marrying such an incredible young woman. Now that he's gone without a chance to repair their foolish perceptions, it is up to them to make peace with their actions. I care about you, Lizzie—the person you are, *not* your pedigree." His voice softened and he gave a brief chuckle. "Besides, have you met my sister and my aunt? They accept you completely, and their influence is no small thing."

She gave a shaky smile. "Yes, your aunt has said as much. She refused to listen to reason and has outfitted me in the finest of fabrics and lace, despite my objections."

Sin grinned. "The modiste did a marvelous job, but she had a perfect model to clothe. And you realize by now, Aunt Millie won't accept 'no' unless it's from the Almighty or the king himself."

Lizzie giggled. "Your aunt is a force of nature."

"Indeed," Sin remarked. "I hadn't anticipated Aunt Millie's thorough interrogation over refreshments. I love her, and I know she means well, but she can be quite formidable at times. Now, I had hoped we could stop by Gunter's."

Lizzie's smile brightened as she spoke. "Gunter's sounds delightful. I was too nervous to partake of the refreshments, though I do adore those sandwiches."

"Perfect. I see no reason for a change of plans. We can enjoy a ride through Hyde Park and stop at Gunter's."

"Thank you for suggesting a carriage ride before the crush of the *ton*," she said. "While I was in Boston after you left...I thought..." She sighed. "Well, never mind. It no longer matters what I thought."

"Please share your thoughts with me," he said, holding her hand. "I respect what you have to say, and your opinion means a great deal to me."

She closed her eyes, and her lips trembled as she spoke. "After you left, word got out about your presence in my home. I don't know how it happened, for neither I nor Dr. Hastings breathed a word. But gossip that I had kept a man in my home for many weeks began to fly. It did not matter that you were ill and that I was tending your fever, or that Dr. Hastings visited every day. It only mattered that I, as a widow, had allowed a man to live in my home without the benefit of marriage." She swallowed and then continued, "I waited as long as I could for your return, but after the gossip began, I could no longer remain there with no funds of my own, and with no means to make a living. There was no longer any goodwill for me there, and I could not cope with the lascivious stares from men when I went into town, nor the hateful looks from women."

"I am sorry you had to go through that," he said. "I wish I could have been there to protect you from those vile people."

That Lizzie had to go through it on her own and without any support, except from Dr. Hastings, tore at his heart, while at the same time left him in awe at her fortitude. She had been brutalized by town gossip over his stay. How could he not have realized what would have happened to her, had Society realized their living arrangements? It was no different than if she had been here in England. An ocean between two continents wouldn't change human nature. It had been so thoughtless of him. He would make it up to her somehow.

"It was a difficult time, but it is in the past and I must move beyond those memories."

"You are not alone anymore, Lizzie. I promise you that."

"Thank you, Edward. Please let us speak of other things that are more pleasing." Her lips curved up in a smile. "There is a question I've been wanting to ask."

"And that is?" he said. Her smile was infectious, and he could not help smiling back.

"Is there more to the name Sin than just a short form of Sinclair? Anything I should know?" she asked.

He chuckled at the arch of her delicate brows and the teasing glint in her eyes. "Almost everyone calls me Sin—since childhood. But I must confess that hearing my first name on your lips is something I cherish."

Her eyes widened. "You do?"

"I do." He leaned in and brushed his lips over hers. They had only kissed once. The day he'd left. But the feel of her lips had been branded in his memory for more than a year.

She breathed out a sigh as she caressed the side of his face. "I never thought I'd see you again. But I am so thankful I did."

They enjoyed the lush green trees and colorful flowers as they passed through the park. Several couples had stopped along the way to enjoy a picnic in the warmth of the summer sunshine. They held hands and kissed several more times, each kiss becoming more fervent, and Sin had to call on every ounce of discipline he had to hold his passion in check.

When they arrived at Gunter's an hour later, the bustling atmosphere made it difficult to find a place to stop. The carriage jostled past the narrow alley next to the establishment. Sin spotted a young boy behind a low wall made of stacked wooden crates. The boy looked no more than ten years old, and so undernourished that he looked small for his age. He sat huddled with a small brown puppy, whose ribs were also showing. They shared a roll obviously scavenged from the crates of refuse.

The sight twisted through Sin's heart. He'd seen other children, sometimes with a dog or a cat, scavenging during his travels and his work. What he'd witnessed was heartrending. There were times when he had been able to intervene and other times when he could not.

The back door of the establishment swung open, and a woman brandishing a spatula appeared, yelling at the boy to leave. Startled, the tiny, emaciated dog barked in protest as the boy hastily secured a worn rope around its neck and prepared to depart. "Come on, Josie. We can't stay here," he murmured, urgency evident in his voice.

"I'll be right back," Sin said to Lizzie, tapping the ceiling of the carriage and opening the door. He jumped out. "Wait, young man."

"Oi, guv'na," the young boy blurted out, looking at him with wide eyes. "Me and m' dog was just grabbin' a nibble. We ain't lookin' for no trouble. I swear."

"I didn't think you were looking for trouble, son." Sin scanned the back of Gunter's and glanced at the small hovel the boy had made of discarded crates. "Were you living here?"

The boy's lower lip trembled, and he looked at his dog before answering. "It's just me and Josie here, and we ain't taken nothin' 'cept an occasional sweet roll 'at gets tossed."

Sin considered the structure the child had built for shelter. He'd done a decent job at building it with what was available. But living in a pile of garbage was no place for a dog, let alone a small boy. "You have no home." It was not a question. "No parent or guardian to watch over you?"

The boy shook his head. "Unless you're countin' the bloke who had me crawlin' up them chimneys like a bloomin' monkey. Ain't got no recollection of me pa, and me mum died when my little brother was born."

"Where's your little brother?" Sin asked.

"With the bl…man. I ain't seen Bobby in two years." His eyes welled with tears at the mention of his brother. "He'd be four years now."

"I see." The lads had most likely been sold by their father to a man who used small children to clean out chimneys. It was commonplace. Once the children grew too large to slip up and down chimneys, many were trained to pick pockets or other things, just to survive. It was a despicable occurrence that happened too often in London. Sin planned to do his best to work with his brother-in-law, Lord Armstrong—who saw things as he did on child labor laws—as soon as he completed the Crown assignment he had already agreed to do. In the meantime, the least he could do was find a safe place for the boy and his dog.

"My name is Baron Edward Sinclair, and my home is in Mayfair." Before Sin could say anything more, the carriage door opened, and Lizzie appeared. Titus, his footman—confused over what was happening—hurried to place the step so she could alight from the carriage.

"My name is Mrs. Pritchett. You can call me Lizzie. And I think…" She looked at Sin, who nodded. "I heard your conversation with Lord Sinclair. We would like to do something to help you and your dog. Do you have a name?" Lizzie asked, bending to pat Josie's head.

"The name's Simon—me mum named me fer her pa."

"Well, Simon, there may be a solution that will meet with your approval. Allow me to speak with Lord Sinclair for a moment. We are going to talk quietly. Will you trust us, and stay right there?"

He nodded. "I've got no other place to be."

Lizzie watched as Simon whispered an order to Josie, and the pup sat down next to him.

"Most impressive," Lizzie whispered before turning to Sin. "What do you plan to do?"

"I could give him money, but that's no solution. I'm thinking of taking him to my townhouse and speaking with Mrs. Jones, my housekeeper, who can find a place for him."

"You would do that?" she asked.

"Yes, I would," Sin said. "But I'm not sure he would trust me to go with me, let alone take my offer, after what he's already been through."

"What if you gave him money but bade him stay while we go inside for refreshment?" Lizzie suggested. "We could encourage him to speak to your driver and footman and find out if you are a person worth trusting. It would give him control. He would have the freedom to choose to leave or stay and the additional security of the coins."

"That's very fair, and an excellent idea," Sin said. "Let us put this proposal to the boy." He fished in his pocket and withdrew six shillings. "I can't give him too much, or my footman and driver may demand a raise."

That drew a laugh from Lizzie. He loved the sound of her laugh. He had missed it so much.

Sin approached the boy. "Simon, I live in Mayfair and would like to offer you and Josie a place to live and a position as a valued member of my household. You would have your own room, clean clothes, plenty of food, and time to spend with Josie. We can find a suitable role for you, either in the kitchen or assisting the footmen. I realize you don't know me. And I realize these are just words to you. But I would never harm a child or an animal." He looked at Josie and then back at Simon. "It must be your decision. In the meantime, here are six shillings. They're yours—for you and Josie—whether you agree to this proposal or not. But if you decide to live and work for me at my home, you keep the money and will earn a fair income. If you decide you don't want to do that, you still have six shillings. While we step inside, you can speak with my footman and driver. They can answer any questions you might have."

"You would do that…for me?" Simon asked, his voice filled with emotion. "No one has ever given me so much money in my whole entire life."

"It's yours…yours and Josie's." Sin paused and crouched to meet the boy at eye level. "To be fair, if you decide to accept my proposal, I'd expect you to work—wherever Mrs. Jones, my housekeeper, or Mr. Fringe, my stable master, or Mr. Kingsley, the butler, felt you'd be best. You will earn your keep. But you'll have a home, and you won't have to fear that man hurting you ever again."

"But sir, you don't know me," Simon persisted. "I could rob you blind."

"I don't think you will. And I'm willing to take a chance on you. You have a dog that's taken a chance on you already, and she seems to find you worthy."

Sin held out the coins, and Simon hesitated a few moments and then took them, squeezing them firmly within his grasp.

"I'll talk to 'em." Simon nodded toward the driver and footman, who were observing the exchange with interest.

"Good. I hope you decide to take me up on the offer," Sin said, although he could only imagine what his housekeeper would say when he brought the urchin and his puppy home.

Sin and Lizzie walked into Gunter's and ordered some food and treats for the child and his dog. He courteously held out a chair for Lizzie before heading off with the food to find Simon. He intended for Mr. Rufus to give the boy the food, knowing that the old driver would have an easier time getting Simon to eat.

After handing off the food, Sin returned to find that Lizzie had moved to a spot near a window with a clear view of his carriage and the boy.

"Do you think he'll stay?" Sin asked as they tasted their ices.

"I think…" She paused and nodded to the window, where

they saw Titus and Mr. Rufus talking animatedly to Simon. The boy was nodding in between taking bites of his sandwich. He reached down and handed Josie half of the sandwich, and then whispered something to her. "I think he's made a decision," she finally said. "He just whispered to his dog after he fed her the sandwich."

"How did you become so smart with children?" Sin asked, and then could have kicked himself, thinking he might have hurt her feelings. After all, she had been widowed before she could experience motherhood. "I didn't mean to..."

"It's fine," Lizzie said. "I am not upset. Peter and I had little time together." Her face pinkened. "Anyway, I do love children. I had considered becoming a governess. If it's all right with you, I'd like to tutor Simon—of course, Lady Beadle would have to agree. But I predict that one glance at Simon and you may lose him to her," she teased.

"That is a sound idea, but perhaps we can hold off for now and observe how Simon accepts everything and everyone. That's a lot of change for a boy," Sin said.

"I agree. We can take it a day at a time," Lizzie said. "For now, let's take the boy away from here before that brute finds him."

"Aunt Millie's cats might not appreciate Josie, so we may need to have his lessons at my townhouse," Sin said. "I'm sure they come as a matched set."

"I have a feeling that, knowing your aunt, she would find a way for the animals to get along—no doubt by giving them a stern lecture." Lizzie chuckled.

"This was not the outing I had planned for you today," Sin said after a few moments.

"On the contrary—it has been the most enjoyable afternoon I've had in ages." She beamed at him, making his heart kick into a thunderous beat. Then her eyes suddenly widened. "Look! Simon is climbing up with the driver already. And he's got Josie beside him."

Sin turned and noted his footman had moved to a ledge on the back of the carriage. "Shall we go see what he has officially decided?"

"Yes, please." Lizzie nodded, her lovely green eyes dancing with enthusiasm.

As they exited Gunter's and approached the carriage, Sin noticed Simon was all smiles. And he could have sworn Josie was smiling as well.

"Have you decided?" he called up to Simon. Although the boy's decision had become obvious by the happy look on his face.

"Yes, milord. Titus said your cook makes the best biscuits, and everything she makes is so good that everyone has at least seconds and thirds. Titus and Mr. Rufus both told me that everyone is so very kind at your house. Mr. Rufus said there might be work in the stables. And if I stay there, Josie can stay with me. Your men said you're a decent bloke." Simon sat up and straightened his shoulders "So, I decided to take you up on your offer."

"You've made a fine decision, Simon," Sin said, reaching up and shaking the boy's hand. "I'll meet with Mrs. Jones and Mr. Fringe when we return to my townhouse after we take Mrs. Pritchett home. Then we can make some decisions for you and Josie."

"Ye don't need to hurry on my account. You can take your time escorting Mrs. Pritchett home; she's a true lady of quality, she is," the boy said, nodding at Lizzie, then added, "May I pose another question, milord?"

"Yes, of course," Sin answered, suppressing a smile at Simon's sudden formal tone.

"Do you think this is enough money to hire someone to help find me brother, Bobby?" Simon asked, holding out his open palm with the coins Sin had given him a half-hour earlier.

Sin glanced at Lizzie, whose face glowed with a soft light. Looking into her eyes, he knew that he would move heaven and earth to find Simon's brother.

He cleared his throat and turned back to Simon. "Let us ensure your comfort first. While I cannot make promises that we will discover Bobby's whereabouts, I can assure you we will explore all avenues."

As he assisted Lizzie into the carriage, she gazed up at him and whispered, "If I didn't already have affection for you, what you have done here today would have endeared you to me a thousand times over."

CHAPTER EIGHT

25 Curzon Street, Mayfair
London
The next morning

"AFTER WEEKS OF skies thicker than pea soup, today's sunshine feels like a royal decree from Queen Athena," exclaimed Lady Beadle, her cup of tea rattling with her excitement against its saucer. "I'm tempted to defy convention and venture outside without my parasol! It would be a perfect day to take a hamper and have a picnic."

Lizzie had just been thinking the same thing. It would be lovely to be out of the house. While she was elated about finding Simon and Josie, and bringing them to Edward's townhouse, selfishly, she had been disappointed not being able to spend the day with Edward, as they had planned. However, she would never comment on such a thing. Simon seemed to be a wonderful young boy and his puppy was clearly his best friend. The two were inseparable—and seemed to have their special language. She found herself looking forward to spending time with him. But today, she wished she could rub a magic lamp and see Edward walk through that door.

"Mrs. Pritchett, this just arrived for you from Lord Sinclair," Jenkins said, stepping into the breakfast room, extending his salver with a sealed note on it. "Lord Sinclair's footman is awaiting an immediate reply."

"Thank you, Jenkins," Lizzie said, lifting the note from the salver. With the footman waiting for a reply, could it be something about Michael's whereabouts? Her hands trembled slightly as she opened it.

"My nephew is coming to his senses," quipped Lady Beadle.

Lizzie smiled at the comment. When she opened the note, her eyes widened. She looked up, unable to believe what she was reading.

Dearest Lizzie,

I woke up today to rays of sunshine—a day too splendid to waste. It would be my honor if you would join me today for a picnic so that we might take advantage of what promises to be a sunny day.

I know it's short notice, but I would like to pick you up at 11:00 so that we might enjoy more of this sunny day together.

Yours,
Edward

P.S. Simon and Josie are settling in and are already being spoiled beyond measure by my cook and Mrs. Jones.

Lizzie smiled. "He's invited me on a picnic today—if you can spare me." She could scarcely contain the excitement in her voice.

"We have nothing so important planned that it couldn't allow you time to go on a delightful picnic with my handsome nephew," Lady Beadle said. "What time is he coming to call? Perhaps I'll have a chance to speak with Edward about how the boy is faring… Simon, did you say his name was?"

"Yes, his name is Simon, and Josie is his pup," Lizzie said with a smile. "I too am anxious to know how they are settling in, although Edward did mention in his note that Mrs. Jones and the cook are spoiling the boy and his dog beyond measure! He says he would like to call at eleven—only a little over an hour from now. I'd best reply." She turned to Jenkins. "Would a verbal response suffice?"

"I think it would, Mrs. Pritchett," Jenkins said, with a wry smile.

"Good. Tell him I would love to go," Lizzie said, pushing out her chair to leave.

Lady Beadle smiled. "Eleven o'clock. The boy's wasting no time today. You might consider changing into that buttercream muslin day dress. It's pretty on you with your blonde hair and green eyes."

Lizzie felt a blush heat her cheeks at the compliment. She hadn't taken such care with her appearance since she was being courted by Peter before their marriage. Having spent several years in America with so little funds, Lizzie had become practical in her clothing and hairstyle. She was fortunate indeed that Lady Beadle's generosity had afforded her the luxury of being able to wear pretty frocks, as well as having access to a maid who was skilled in the art of styling hair.

"It is a fine-looking dress and would be perfect for a picnic. Thank you, Millie." Lizzie fled up the stairs to her room. A soft tap at the door preceded the entrance of Lady Beadle's abigail, Doris.

"I've come to help you dress for your outing, Mrs. Pritchett. Lady Beadle wants you to look your best when Lord Sinclair arrives." The maid gave a gentle smile before walking to the armoire and pulling out the pale-yellow dress. "Lady Beadle asked me to have it pressed for you yesterday. My lady is always one step ahead of us," she said with a chuckle.

Doris's laughter was infectious. "Sometimes Lady Beadle feels like a fairy godmother," Lizzie said. It had been a long time since she'd had a mother figure in her life. She had grown to care deeply about Lady Beadle.

A few minutes later, Lizzie smoothed the skirt of her pretty gown, admiring the feel of the delicate material. She stepped over to the looking glass and fought the impulse to twirl. This was one of the colors Lady Beadle had insisted she try—and it looked attractive with her hair and eyes.

Doris deftly twisted her hair into two loose braids, weaving them together to form an elegant crown, tucking tiny, fresh blossoms into the corona, and teasing out a few curls to frame her face. She then handed a small looking glass to Lizzie, who marveled at her reflection.

"I love it, Doris," Lizzie murmured, her gaze fixed on her adorned visage. "You are a true talent. And you were right about the dress."

"It's a pleasure to style your hair, Mrs. Pritchett." Doris beamed. "It complements your complexion perfectly. But time is of the essence; Lord Sinclair will be here soon."

As Lizzie hurried toward the parlor, she caught Jenkins's voice as he greeted their guest at the door on the floor below. With a swift step, she entered the parlor, ready to receive Lord Sinclair.

Lady Beadle, with her customary elegance, said, "Lizzie, your smile could part even the most obstinate clouds to part, my dear." Her tone radiated sincerity. "Doris shall be your companion. Just take care not to lull her into too much comfort after dining, lest she observe with half-closed lids."

Edward entered the parlor.

"Sin, Lizzie told me about Simon and his puppy. I am most excited to meet the young chap and see how we can work to make him feel part of the fold," Lady Beadle said to her nephew.

"Thank you, Aunt Millie," Edward replied. "I knew I could count on your support. The poor lad has had a rough go of life thus far. We would like to make things better for him. Unfortunately, I must leave town for a short duration, and have left Kingsley to coordinate Simon's assignments. It makes me feel better to know you will be lending your assistance. I want him to feel his worth in the household and have left it to Kingsley and Mrs. Jones to determine what job he might perform."

"Of course. Please have them reach out to me if I can be of

any assistance," his aunt said. "Perhaps I can have him over for luncheon—as an opportunity to meet him. Lizzie asked if she could help with his education until you can secure a tutor, and I am thrilled to allow her to be of assistance."

"You are most generous," Edward said. "I will leave it to you and Lizzie to make those arrangements but will let Kingsley know you plan to contact him."

"That's perfect, nephew. Thank you," Aunt Millie said, smiling broadly.

Lizzie grinned. Edward didn't realize it, but Lizzie suspected that Simon was going to have a grand day with his new "auntie."

As THE CARRIAGE awaited, Edward stepped forward, offering his hand to assist Lizzie. A current tingled up her arm and spread an inviting warmth inside her. He also assisted Doris, ensuring her comfort on the opposite side of the carriage.

Lizzie was all aflutter. Taking a deep breath, she was relieved when Edward's deep voice, filled with warmth, broke the silence. "I thought we might picnic near one of the ponds on Hampstead Heath," he suggested, nodding toward the neatly packed picnic basket and blankets in the corner of the seat opposite them. "I asked Cook to prepare a special luncheon for us. Perhaps we could take a ramble after the picnic."

"I confess, I had not anticipated spending this afternoon with you, my lord," Lizzie said. "This will be a delightful way to spend the day."

A man and woman on beautiful mounts trotted past the carriage on Lizzie's side, and she stared after them.

"Do you ride?" Edward asked.

Lizzie looked at him in surprise. "Are we to ride this afternoon, my lord?"

"Not today—but I wondered if it is something you might enjoy. I don't believe we've ever discussed it," he said.

"I do ride, but it's been many years since I've sat a horse. Peter and I used to ride occasionally when we first moved to the colonies. We would borrow a mare from the neighbor for me to ride. And I confess, I never really enjoyed the sidesaddle that I was made to use in England."

"So, you ride astride?" he blurted.

She blushed. "I do. It's how I learned. Occasionally, I would ride when I visited my grandfather's estate. My Uncle Robert was usually there. He was a late surprise for my grandparents and six years older than me. I wanted to ride, so he taught me, and I'm afraid he taught me to ride astride. We would go all over Grandpapa's estate. After I learned, I always rode astride. When Father found out I was riding like a hoyden, as he referred to it, he insisted on proper instruction in *ladylike* riding." She chuckled. "Yet, I must confess, I find riding astride more to my liking; it grants me a sense of command. But now that I am back in England, I suppose I should ride sidesaddle, or risk shocking the *ton*—but I warn you, it is under protest." She winked.

Amusement glinted in his eyes. "That makes sense. I'm not sure I would tolerate riding a sidesaddle, myself."

She laughed and shook her head. "Goodness, it's been a long time since I've given those visits to Grandpapa any thought. I think I was eight. And the visits were sporadic over about three years."

"Was this on your mother's side?" Edward asked.

"Yes. It never mattered to me, since once Grandpapa died, they never contacted us. I don't think we were considered part of the family. The only thing I recall was that the family estate was in Lancashire. It's been so long, and he died many years ago, that my memory is somewhat vague on the details. Mama never heard from her older brother. And then, of course, both she and father passed from an ague."

"So, you are the granddaughter of an earl?" he asked.

"Yes, although the family wanted nothing to do with my mother or father. My father was the son of a merchant and became a vicar because of his true calling to serve the Lord. He was not the typical second or third son of a peer, and when my mother married, she did so after being forbidden by my grandfather. Society no longer accepted her—and by association, my brother and me. When Grandpapa had made peace with the marriage and with my father, he found my mother, and things seemed better for a while."

"How sad for your mother," Edward murmured.

"However, when Grandpapa died, the visits ended. We never heard from them when my uncle became earl," she said, her voice tinged with sadness. "It's something I don't think about. And the lineage wouldn't have mattered where Peter's family was concerned. They were angry and disappointed that their son would marry the daughter of a vicar, whose family owned a mercantile. They had higher aspirations for their son. And I have no aspirations to be a part of a Society that has cast me aside twice."

Lizzie screwed her face up. "Let's just concentrate on today. You told me that any day now you could be called away. It's just nice to spend time together."

"I feel the same way about spending time with you," Edward said. He looked across at Doris. "Doris, I hope you don't mind, but I've had my cook prepare two picnics. One of the baskets is for you and the footmen to share."

Doris blinked a few times, seeming to rouse herself from a semi-dozing state. "Oh, thank you, my lord. That was very thoughtful."

She would probably be asleep within minutes of eating, Lizzie thought with a smile. Not that they planned to do anything more than talk after they ate, but it would lend them privacy. When they were in America, they had been alone for weeks, day and night. She had gotten used to sitting by his bedside, even falling asleep next to his bed. But by the time she realized her feelings for him, he was on the mend, and it was time for him to leave. She had missed him.

Edward lifted the shade and glanced outside. "We're here," he said, tapping the ceiling of the coach. "This is the pond that

Wright and I always race to, and it has a splendid view of the lush meadows down the hill. I believe they named it Wood Pond, perhaps for the wooded area that surrounds it. But this is the uppermost pond."

"It is lovely," agreed Lizzie, looking out the window. Not only was the sun shining, but they had a respite from the ever-present chill that had been part and parcel of the constant, never-ending rain. It was truly a perfect day for a picnic.

Titus set the step and opened the door to the carriage. "My lord, let me know where you'd like the picnic set up."

Edward stepped from the carriage and assisted Lizzie and then Doris. "I've always liked the slight incline of this spot. It allows us to see the pond and the meadows that surround it. I believe that may be the perfect spot for our picnic."

A few minutes later, they were seated beneath the sprawling canopy of majestic oak trees, resting upon a plush blanket amidst a carpet of vibrant wildflowers. Before them, the tranquil water shimmered in the sunlight, billowy clouds reflected on the placid surface.

Tall grasses and reeds bordered the water's edge, guarding a cluster of delicate lily pads that danced on the surface, tickled by the gentle breeze. Lizzie swept her gaze across the picturesque landscape, taking in the tapestry of wooded groves interspersed among fields adorned with an array of blossoms. Goldenrod painted the scene with sunny hues. Wild asters unfolded their charming blue petals and contrasted with the cheerful pink and white blooms of Michaelmas daisies. "This is simply enchanting, Edward," she murmured, her voice barely louder than the rustle of leaves in the trees.

"I thought you would enjoy it," he said, taking her hand and squeezing it, but not letting it go.

"I've never seen anything as beautiful," she said, noticing that Doris had fallen asleep across the field under a neighboring oak tree, having eaten her fill of lunch—a delicious repast of cold meats, cheeses, grapes, and wine.

"I have," he said, pulling her close and tilting her chin up to meet his gaze. Slowly, he lowered his mouth and placed tender kisses along the column of her neck, moving up to her mouth, capturing her lips with his.

Lizzie delighted in his touch. As their tongues intertwined, she felt a rush of longing, and memories flooded her senses— memories of feelings that had begun to blossom in her heart as she nursed him through the yellow jack. She closed her eyes and basked in his masculine scent of leather, sandalwood, and citrus and the feel of his strong arms around her. At that moment, Lizzie realized her attachment to him had started the night she answered her door.

He cradled her face in his big hands, gazing at her with the same intensity as the day he departed from her life. "Lizzie, you *are* special and beautiful. After I left to search for my friend's son, I spent my days cursing myself for not taking you with me and my nights dreaming of you. Though our chance encounter at Celia's ball stands as the luckiest moment in my life, I was determined to find you. I would have spared no effort, scouring every corner of England and Wales until you were found."

Edward looked up at the sky. "I think we might be losing our sunny day to rain." He pointed to the darker clouds beginning to take shape above them. "We should get back before we find ourselves as wet as the pond."

She straightened her clothing and nodded in Doris's direction. "She's not moved since she finished her meal."

"We shall remember that for next time," Edward said with a wink.

They hurried to pack the basket and fold the blanket, just as Titus appeared. "I shall load this into the carriage, my lord, Mrs. Pritchett."

"I'll rouse Doris," Lizzie said, her voice carrying the warmth of the afternoon sun. She turned to Edward. "Thank you," she whispered, her hand tenderly grazing his cheek. "Whenever I conjure the image of the perfect afternoon in the future, it will always mirror the beauty and joy of today."

CHAPTER NINE

Sinclair House
Berkeley Square, Mayfair
The next day

"I FOUND THE latest copy of the *Ton Tattler* and realized we never read the gossip after your sister's party," Sin said. "It's hard to believe we forgot. Kingsley picked up two copies for us, knowing how much I enjoy laughing over it while breaking my fast." He shook the paper and straightened it.

"I'm not sure how they manage to pull so much gossip together regularly," replied Wright. "But each day there is something truly amusing…albeit not very amusing for those featured. And occasionally, it has been my own antics." He laughed. "Looks like Louisa Parker is up to her tricks, again."

"The widow knows the editor and uses every trick in the book to elevate herself," Sin said. "I wish I could say she's harmless. But I know better."

"Well, I'm not sure she'll get away with this one. She's taking credit for your sister's successful fundraising."

"Celia may prickle at it, but she'll likely use it to gain more donations for the charities," Sin said with a shrug. "As long as Lizzie's name isn't splashed across the page, I'm satisfied. I should have paid closer attention to my actions—but the truth of it is, I couldn't resist spending time with her." Lizzie needed to be protected from these social predators in London. She would be vulnerable to their maneuverings. He couldn't bear to have her name splashed across the gossip sheets.

"What are your plans for Simon and Josie?" Wright asked, forking the last of the rashers onto his plate before taking his seat at the table.

"Believe it or not, the boy has already amassed a following in the household. Fringe wants him in the stables, and Mrs. Jones and the cook feel there are many things he'd be good at around the townhouse."

"And to think, only yesterday, his home was a pile of discarded wood scraps behind Gunter's," Wright said.

"Indeed. I've arranged for Fringe to mentor Simon in the stables for the day, assessing where his strengths lie. Meanwhile, Mrs. Jones is organizing suitable attire and footwear for the lad, and she's also preparing a cozy bed for Josie. That little pup has managed to capture the hearts of everyone in my household."

"I remember the dog you had when you were a young lad," Wright said after sipping his coffee. "Wasn't her name Rosie?"

Sin laughed. "Yes. She was a light-brown hound mix with white feet. My parents forbade the dog from sleeping in the house, but each night she found her way to my bedroom and would be there in the morning. Since my parents rarely came to my room, they never realized. I loved that dog."

A quick knock preceded the butler's entrance. "My lord, you've received a dispatch. The messenger asked that you receive it as quickly as possible."

"Thank you, Kingsley." Sin picked the sealed missive from the salver and opened it with his butter knife. He scanned the contents of the note and blew out a breath. "Kingsley, would you ask Reginald to prepare my satchel? We may be leaving shortly."

"Yes, my lord." The retainer gave a slight bow and left the room.

"What is it?" Wright asked.

"From Wellington," Sin stated solemnly, glancing down at the letter gripped tightly in his hand, its contents encrypted. "One of Wellington's top agents took a bullet while intercepting a smuggling operation. Our task now is to rendezvous and pick up where he left off. The agent was on the brink of unveiling the mastermind behind it all before the gunshot rang out."

Wright's expression tightened with worry. "Do we have any leads on the operation's whereabouts?"

"Isle of Wight," Sin replied, his voice tinged with determination.

"I'll get word to my ship. It's in the port, here in London," Wright offered, already moving toward the door. "We can get there quicker than if we take our horses."

"I have a few things to tie up before I'll be ready to leave," Sin said, his mind already racing through the tasks ahead. "What do you say we meet up here around two o'clock? That should give me time to get things done."

Sin rang for Kingsley. The door opened and the retainer appeared as if he'd expected to be called. "Yes, my lord?"

"Have Mrs. Jones, Fringe, and young Simon meet me in the kitchen."

"Right away." The butler started to leave but turned back. "Er...my lord. Do you anticipate being gone for long?"

Sin's brows knitted together in thought. "I'm not sure."

Kingsley was a trusted retainer and watched over Sin's home with an eagle eye. Sin never worried that any matters would be mishandled while he was away. "Usually, these trips take a couple of weeks. I'm hoping it won't take that long. I haven't asked her yet, but knowing my aunt and the way she loves children, I feel sure she will want to participate in Simon's needs. And Mrs. Pritchett has offered to tutor him."

"What time will he go to Lady Beadle's house for tutoring?" Kingsley asked.

"Whatever schedule you and Mrs. Jones work out with my aunt. It's important that Simon feels he is contributing to his and his puppy's upkeep. But as you know, make it something worthwhile that will teach him skills of value. I'm leaving it for you to decide. You know how to reach me if anything comes up. I've replenished the household funds—in case I'm gone longer."

"Yes, my lord. Don't worry about anything here."

"I have complete confidence in you, Kingsley, as always. I will have a missive that needs to be delivered as soon as possible. It shouldn't take me long. And please ask the footman to await a response."

Ten minutes later, Sin handed a sealed sheet of vellum to his butler. "I'll be back shortly. I need to visit my aunt before I leave." His missive was a coded message for his contact at headquarters to investigate Blackwood. The man's interest in Lizzie unsettled him—it was excessive. Sin had been on the verge of interfering, feeling her in need of rescuing. Something wasn't right with the man, and Sin couldn't ignore the niggling feeling that he needed to find out more. Now he was leaving town. As brief as the trip would be, he couldn't get comfortable about leaving her this time.

25 Curzon Street, Mayfair
London

"WHEN AM I going to meet this rapscallion you and my nephew met at Gunter's? Hmm?" Lady Beadle said, peering over the top of the *Ton Tattler*. "From the little you've explained, his story is heart-wrenching. It breaks my heart that children are treated in such a manner."

"Truly, it is heartbreaking, Millie," Lizzie replied, refilling her teacup. "I'm sure Edward is getting him settled. When we encountered Simon, he was sharing a discarded sweet roll with his pup, Josie. He had no home and was hoping to stay out of the clutches of a horrid man who purchased him from his father and forced him to steal and do other reprehensible tasks for him. The child had managed to escape the brute and ended up living in a ramshackle shelter constructed from discarded crates and scraps of discarded wood behind Gunter's."

"That's quite a feat! It's discomfiting to imagine the child living in a pile of rubbish," the dowager said. "I'm so proud of my nephew—he's always had a generous nature. But what if Sin is called out of town, which could happen at any time with his work—and the lad is left alone?"

"No need to worry there. I believe Mrs. Jones has become quite taken with the boy. She and Mr. Fringe have been in a tug-of-war over where the boy will best fit in the household, each wanting him under his or her wing."

Lady Beadle laughed. "That is as it should be. No child should feel unwanted." She stayed quiet for several long moments. "I was never fortunate enough to have children of my own, as you know," she finally said. "My niece and nephew had a wonderful childhood, and I was very much a part of it, but it wasn't the same as having my own child. But..." She fell silent again, a wistful expression crossing her face. "Does it seem silly of me to want a child around this old place?" She dabbed at her eyes with her napkin. "You're as young as you feel, as they say, and having children around certainly helps one feel the joy of youth. To think, Celia is with child. It will be a joy to have a new baby around."

Lizzie watched Lady Beadle, concerned about the older woman's melancholy mood. "Millie," she began gently, "it's not silly at all. If anything, it's lovely. You have so much love to give, and having children around is indeed a joy." She reached out and touched her employer's hand in support. "But have you considered the challenges of adoption?"

"Adoption!" the dowager exclaimed. "My goodness, my dear! Ancient wigs and rouge only hide so many years. I'm talking about being a grandmother or auntie!"

Lizzie covered her mouth with her hands, hiding her laughter. "I apologize. I meant no harm. I misunderstood. I thought you were speaking of a wish to adopt a child."

Lady Beadle threw her head back and laughed. "I can understand your logic, and I know you to be a very caring person who would never hurt my feelings. But you gave me a delicious chuckle, and I thank you."

Lizzie gave in to her own laughter, and they enjoyed a good chuckle. "Simon is such a nice boy with a quick and clever mind," she said finally. "There is so much for him to learn, including how to trust and how to listen and mind his elders. Elders who are trustworthy, that is. I don't know how long he has been on his own with Josie, his puppy, as his only companion. Once Edward's household has everything sorted, I believe Simon would welcome friendly and kind attention from us."

"You make a valid suggestion, my dear Lizzie. Living in Sin's household will allow Simon to learn a great deal of value. And he has his dog, which will continue instilling responsibility in him. Finding him at Gunter's as you did—a young boy living alone on the street—sends me back to the days with the school for the deaf my darling Arthur and I built. For many of the children, it was also an orphanage. They were looked at as different and needed a place to live."

"Generosity appears to run in your family," Lizzie suggested.

"Speaking of my nephew, do you have plans to see him today?" Lady Beadle asked, taking a bite of buttered toast.

Lizzie bit her bottom lip and shook her head. "There are no plans, my lady."

Edward had mentioned he and his friend Lord Wright had some things to check into today. He planned to let his staff decide about Simon. Lizzie longed to check in on the boy, but it was improper for an unmarried woman, widow or not, to visit a bachelor's home, no matter the reason. She would wait for Edward to contact her. "He mentioned he had several matters to attend to, so I don't think so."

"You never know with that one," the viscountess said. "He

needs a family to settle him down." She arched a brow.

"I've been mulling over an idea," Lizzie said. She didn't respond to Lady Beadle's comment about marriage. "What do you think about having young Simon come here and learn his lessons?"

"Could that be possible? At one time, you mentioned that you had considered looking for a governess position. Although, for many reasons, I'm glad you decided to be my companion," Lady Beadle said. "So, were you thinking you might tutor him?"

"Either that or Edward could hire a tutor."

"The idea has merit, my dear—and it would bring a child into the house. Almost like a grandson," Lady Beadle said. "We should arrange for an afternoon outing to take Simon for some new clothing."

"He has never had anyone to care about him. And he has a little brother named Bobby who is lost to him. Although I think Edward will no doubt endeavor to find the boy. It broke my heart when he asked Edward if the money he had given him would be enough to hire someone to find his brother." Lizzie bit her bottom lip to keep from tearing up at her employer's bighearted-ness. "Your generosity may reduce both Simon and me to a sobbing mess, Millie," she said, biting back a smile.

"We don't want to do that. But to think of having a younger sibling subjected to the life he left behind… It would be devastating," Lady Beadle said. "If his brother is out there, I would like to help find him." She stood. "I'd like to meet this young man. Would you like to accompany me?"

One of the things Lizzie loved about Lady Beadle was her inability to conform to what others expected of her. "Yes, I would very much like to visit him with you."

"Excellent! I shall have Jenkins send word that we wish to stop by Edward's townhouse." Giving a very satisfied smile, Lady Beadle departed the dining room. The three cats had been napping near their bowls, but now picked themselves up and trotted after her.

As Athena left, she turned and gave Lizzie a haughty meow before following her mistress with her tail swishing in unveiled anger as she exited.

Did Athena understand our discussion about the dog? Lizzie sighed. *I suppose she won't be watching birds from my window anymore*, she thought as her fluffy duster disappeared into the hall. She laughed. *If they're put out now, wait until Simon brings the puppy with him.*

She would speak with Edward about her ideas. She wondered if the cats could adjust to a young puppy. The boy never left his dog, and if Lady Beadle wanted him here, the dog would be here as well. Simon was very diligent in training Josie. According to him, the dog knew commands, and best of all, she knew she needed to go out to use the bathroom. But it was in Lady Beadle and Edward's hands.

Lizzie decided to have another cup of chocolate. As she moved past the expansive window in the dining room, she stopped and peeked out the curtains. "These sheer curtains let in the sunshine," she murmured. She loved the warmth of sunshine on the really cold days.

England's recent weather hadn't been particularly warm; it was often damp and overcast. The sight of the radiant sunlight streaming in made her yearn for more days like this, especially ones spent with Edward. What she truly craved was to be riding through Hyde Park in Edward's carriage, by his side.

As she gazed out the window, Lizzie was startled to see a man casually leaning against a tree across the street—looking at Millie's townhouse. *He looks familiar*, she thought. *But who is it?* She hastily stepped away from the sheer curtains. A shudder ran down her spine as she remembered who it was.

Baron Percival Blackwood, the odious man who'd cornered her at the Armstrong ball. And those beady black eyes were looking straight at the window where she stood. She shuddered.

Lizzie had to do something. She would speak with Jenkins and ask him to dispatch a footman with a note to Edward.

BEHIND THE CURTAIN, a movement caught Blackwood's attention. Finally, there she was. He had been standing there for an hour, yearning for just a glimpse of her. As he contemplated who might be behind the fabric, his thoughts drifted to Mrs. Pritchett. Privately, Blackwood referred to her as Lizzie, relishing the way her name danced on his tongue.

Yet, despite his advances, she had rejected his courtship in favor of Sinclair. And he hated Sinclair. He took his looks, his wealth, his connections—everything—for granted. *The man will never have to work for his wealth—not like I do.*

Blackwood pulled a small locket from his pocket and opened it up, his eyes watering at the image of his mum. *Mother, this isn't easy for me. But I'm not giving up. I did everything the way you would have wanted. I engaged her in conversation and properly asked her if I could court her.* Although the woman was a widow, she'd looked like an angelic debutante at her come-out. He knew immediately she would be perfect for him—for his needs. He had done it all perfectly, just like his late mother had taught him. But without even a moment's hesitation, Lizzie had rejected him. "But that will soon change," he whispered. "Very soon indeed."

CHAPTER TEN

25 Curzon Street, Mayfair
London

"MY LADY, MRS. Pritchett, Lord Sinclair is here," Jenkins announced with a courteous bow.

"Marvelous! Show him in and do ask the kitchen to send up some tea and biscuits," Lady Beadle replied.

Edward stepped in a few moments later and greeted his aunt and Lizzie. "I'm departing town and wanted to pay my respects before I had to leave. I also want to inform you about Simon and Josie—although I'm sure Lizzie has already briefed you." He cast a warm smile toward her.

Lizzie's throat went dry as soon as Edward mentioned he was leaving. He was *leaving.* Yes, she knew he must have a short assignment, but she kept pushing that from her mind. Now that the time had come for him to leave, she wasn't ready. Yesterday's idyllic afternoon had been perfect, and she'd enjoyed spending time with this man beside her. But here they were, saying goodbye again.

"I look forward to meeting Simon," Lady Beadle said, "although Athena has already advised that we should take our time with a dog, as she isn't fond of them."

Despite the turmoil within her, Lizzie couldn't help but laugh at his aunt's deference to Athena, almost as if she possessed human qualities herself. Admittedly, Lizzie found herself conversing with the cat whenever she visited her room. Then again, Athena did have very expressive eyes that seemed to convey an almost human understanding of things.

"Have you decided about his tutoring?" Lady Beadle asked. "I would be pleased to host him here."

Edward glanced at Lizzie with a curious smile in his eyes.

"I have already spoken to your aunt, and she generously suggested that Simon come here every afternoon for lessons," Lizzie said. "I would be happy to tutor him."

"Indeed, we are happy to help you with the young man's education," Lady Beadle added. "And perhaps a trip to town to gain him suitable clothing is in order. It could be a nice outing—without the dog, of course."

Edward smiled. "Aunt Millie, you are all that is kind. Mrs. Jones has already planned to purchase suitable clothing—but I am certain that as he familiarizes himself with the household, we may find other things he needs. I've left instructions with Kingsley to determine the most suitable assignment for Simon—something that will allow him plenty of time with his puppy—as she is his responsibility." He looked at Lizzie. "Your offer to tutor Simon is kind. And I wholly support and appreciate it. I will instruct Kingsley to organize this in my absence. Simon has never as much as learned to print his name, so lessons will be fundamental."

"It is tragic how these children are forced to live in the East End," Lady Beadle said. "Lizzie tells me the lad has no idea where his younger brother is."

"No, he doesn't. When I return, I will try to locate his brother, Bobby," Edward said.

"Ah, once upon a time, your uncle and I tried to help in a small way."

"It was no small way, Aunt Millie," he countered. "You built a school for deaf children that transformed many lives—lives that would have been cast aside because of their impediment. Your school gave these children a way to communicate, and helped teach us all that being deaf doesn't make one useless."

Lizzie noticed her employer seemed uncomfortable with praise.

"Yes, well, perhaps there is more to do, where that is concerned," Lady Beadle said, studying her ear trumpet. "I just remembered something I need to discuss with the cook for dinner. I'm afraid if I don't tell her now, it will slip my mind, and it is most important. Will you two young people excuse me? I shall return shortly." Without waiting for an answer, she stood. "Perhaps you might enjoy exploring the garden. It's beginning to take on its fall colors and is quite beautiful," she said, leaning on her cane for support.

"Of course, Aunt Millie," Edward said.

A few moments later, Edward and Lizzie were strolling through the garden. Lizzie loved the jasmine and white roses that lined the fence enclosing the garden. Lush clusters of colorful flowers, including pansies and Lenten roses, bordered the gravel path that wound its way through the garden. According to Lady Beadle, the gardener made sure every season was lush with color.

"I've noticed your aunt becomes emotional when speaking about the school for the deaf," Lizzie said.

"Yes. I've noticed, but it's always been so. Her schools were very instrumental in helping deaf children leave a bad situation for a brighter future—all over London. Many would have been sold into hopeless situations."

"I can't fathom the desperation that would lead a parent to consider selling their child," Lizzie whispered, her voice heavy with sorrow. "It's a profound cruelty inflicted upon both parents and children alike. As a society, we must strive for better, to protect the most vulnerable among us."

Gravel crunched beneath their feet as they walked to the long wooden swing in companionable silence. Edward held it while Lizzie sat down and adjusted her dress.

"I step out here now and then to smell the roses and enjoy the tranquil oasis." She pointed to the trellises that covered the lattice surrounding the swing and the fence, both full of white and pink roses. "Their scent is heavenly." The autumn hues were beginning to show themselves, and birds flitted about preparing for migration.

"Are you leaving?" she inquired in a hushed tone, her voice barely above a whisper. Seeing the garden gate ahead of them brought back memories of when she bade farewell to him a little over a year ago.

Edward stood in the doorway with the strap of his satchel thrown over his shoulder. His horse waited patiently tethered to a post. "I am hopeful I can be back within a month. I need to find my friend's son—whether he is dead or alive. But I promise to return, Lizzie."

The sight of him leaving made her heart catch in her chest. "What if you don't find him?"

"I will still come back for you. You are the best thing that's happened to me in a long time, and I don't want to lose you." He pulled her close, his gaze locking onto hers. She hoped he would express his true feelings for her. Yet the words her heart yearned to hear remained unspoken.

"My friend could die before he ever sees his son again," he continued. "I can't let that happen—not if there's anything I can do to bring him home safely. But time is of the essence, I fear. There is speculation the British may be pulling away from Louisiana, and that will make returning him to his father more difficult." He leaned in and gave her a deep kiss. "I meant what I said, Lizzie. I will be back for you."

She choked back the lump in her throat and blinked away the tears that threatened her.

"I'll be here." Then he left. She watched him until he disappeared from her view completely.

For more than a year, she had never thought to see him again. Would this trip be different? Would he return?

"Yes. Unfortunately, I've been called away on an urgent matter. I hope to be gone no longer than a fortnight. But it might be a little longer." With his strong arm around her, he tugged her closer and lifted her chin. "Upon my return, I plan to whisk you away to the theater, or the park, or Gunter's—anywhere you fancy. Perhaps even fishing in one of those ponds, like the one we picnicked near yesterday!"

"Fishing? My goodness, it's been ages since I've cast a line. Michael used to take me to a quaint creek behind Father's vicarage. He taught me to bait my hook, though he always handled the fish. Eventually, he taught me to swim. It was our little secret. Michael believed it was important for me to learn," she reminisced fondly.

"You think of him often, don't you?" he gently inquired.

Tears spilled from her eyes. "I wish I knew where he is," she confessed softly. After a moment's pause, she added, "I have this terrible feeling he needs me."

"If something had happened to your brother, I feel the Admiralty and Marine Affairs Office would have alerted you. Did you inform them that you live here?"

"Yes, although I don't have much confidence in them. It was almost like they were covering something up the last time I stopped by to inquire about Michael," she said.

"Lizzie, why do you say that?"

"The young man in the front office seemed ready to tell me something. Instead, he excused himself and brought his superior officer out to speak to me. They told me nothing. I know in my heart that there is something they are keeping from me, and I fear it has something to do with a dangerous assignment that Michael is on. Otherwise, why would they be so secretive and evasive?" She swiped at her face and turned away, embarrassed by the tears she couldn't control. "Forgive me, Edward—it's just that Michael is the only family I have left. The only person who has always been there for me."

"Lizzie, I promise I will inquire about your brother on your behalf. Please trust me. But he's not *all* you have. You have me."

He pulled her close and cupped her face in his hands. "Lizzie, I know it seems like history is repeating itself, but trust me. I'll be back."

Her mouth suddenly felt like it was full of cotton. She simply nodded.

"You must promise me one thing, Lizzie. If you leave the house, promise you will take a footman with you. I couldn't bear it if anything happened to you."

Lizzie struggled to find her voice. "Do you think Blackwood is dangerous?"

"I don't know, but I need you to promise. I will feel better if I know someone like Reggie will be with you, should you go out," he said.

"I promise," she replied. Blackwood frightened her. What Edward asked was reasonable. "Just hurry back, Edward." *Hurry back to me.*

He leaned in and covered her mouth with his, and his touch ignited an overwhelming need within her. Lizzie moved her hands around his neck and fingered the hair at his nape, pulling him closer, while their tongues met in a tender exploration of each other's mouths, tasting and feeling every nuance. Their heartbeats became one as they poured their very essence into that moment. When the kiss ended, Lizzie touched her lips, determined to remember the taste of him.

She wanted to believe that one day they could share a future, but Lizzie doubted that could be her reality—even as Lady Beadle had assured her that, as Peter's widow, the *ton* would welcome her. Peter's parents hadn't seen things that way. To them, she was the daughter of a vicar whose family had owned a mercantile. Because of his lineage, her father wasn't a gentleman in the eyes of the *ton*, and Lizzie wasn't what they wanted for their son. She couldn't risk the scorn of Society. Never again.

Two days later
The English Channel outside of the Isle of Wight

AS THE BOAT approached the Isle of Wight, the first glimpse revealed rugged limestone cliffs standing supremely above cerulean waters, their appearance battered by centuries of waves and wind. Seabirds circled overhead, while the breeze carried the salty tang of sea spray and the faint scent of seaweed.

As the brigantine drew nearer, the landscape unfolded into verdant hills dotted with quaint villages nestled among rolling emerald fields. The harbor town of Ryde came into view, bustling with activity as colorful ships of all sizes bobbed and swayed in the gentle swell of the waves.

"I see the caves you were telling me about," Sin observed, folding the telescope. "I agree. They are well hidden. Without your guidance, I doubt I would have found them. I hadn't realized that the island had become such a hub for smuggling."

"Yes, since the war, the heavy taxation has pushed people to seek desperate measures for survival," Wright explained. "Some men on my crew have family involved."

"Does this assignment pose a problem? Our mission is to locate Captain Michael Robinson—"

"Mrs. Pritchett's brother," Wright interjected.

"Yes. Lizzie isn't aware of my true purpose here. I only informed her I would be away for a few weeks," Sin said.

My God! I love her. Why didn't I tell her? Instead, he'd merely said he cared deeply for her. Even so, she said little in return—nothing about her affection for him. Had he fooled himself about the depth of her feelings? He didn't know. But he planned to see her as soon as possible when he returned, and he would make sure she knew *his* feelings.

"She knows about your allegiances?" Wright raised an eyebrow.

"Lizzie knows I serve the Crown and, lately, Wellington. She's aware that my previous assignment in America was driven by friendship. But she knows nothing of my assignments," Sin assured his friend. "However, I had a high fever for weeks and have little recollection of what I said. But I've never worried about her loyalty."

Wellington's coded missive had informed him that Captain Michael Robinson was a prized agent and a courageous man, and they needed to do their utmost to find him. He should have asked Lizzie more about Michael, but he didn't want to reveal his assignment and didn't want her hopes up. Instead, he'd met with his sister after he told Lizzie goodbye. Celia gave him a description of Michael and a little more. His coloring was like Lizzie—blond, tall, green eyes, charming. Celia said the ladies were wild about him. However, the mamas wanted a title for their daughters.

At least Sin wouldn't need to marry for convenience to secure his legacy title. He had made peace many years ago with the decision to allow the title to pass to one of the other men in his family. He had no plans to marry unless it was for love.

Unless it is Lizzie.

"Put the red ensign flag up. Let 'em think we are a British merchant. And watch for the usual traps. Remember, we are on a rescue mission," Wright told Manson, his first mate. "Dock in Ryde—but once the sun goes down, everyone needs to be back on board."

"Aye, captain," Manson said. "I'll give the order for the men to be on alert for problems and keep drinking to a minimum."

"Good man. Thank you," Wright said.

Sin and Wright went below deck to Wright's cabin while the men readied the boat for docking.

"Once we rescue Robinson, we can find out what he knows about the leadership in this smuggling operation," Sin said. "You know more about the smuggling trade than I do. What are the odds he'll be alone in the cave—or with minimal guards?"

"There's a good likelihood," Wright said. "But it depends on what they are smuggling. If we can get in there at dusk, that would be best. If he's guarded lightly, the smugglers will likely be at the local pubs. They believe in intimidating those around them, although it's unnecessary, given that most of the villagers turn a blind eye to what they see whether for fear or support of the smuggler, something that frustrates the revenuers and customs officials." He slipped his spyglass into his belt. "Let's go to the kitchen and get something to eat. The crew will be back shortly, and we'll need to get underway."

THE RECONNAISSANCE WORKED. An hour later, Manson returned and found Sin and Wright up on deck. He informed them that he'd overheard the owner of the local tavern arguing with two men, saying they needed to get back to the cave before "the Man" arrived. The men pushed back, arguing that the prisoner was near death and in no shape to escape, and they would take their time eating the only meal they'd gotten that day. It seemed the prisoner was a surprise catch. And the smugglers assumed they would no doubt be rewarded. Manson thought that if the prisoner was Robinson, he would be guarded lightly.

"The sooner we can rescue Robinson, the less likely we will run into whoever is organizing this operation," Wright murmured.

"It's nerve-racking to know someone is diverting all the ammunition and guns," Sin said. "That can only turn out badly. Our orders are only to rescue Robinson, but I have a sneaking suspicion we'll be back to enjoy the beauty of this lovely island."

He focused on the spot he had seen earlier when he had searched for the cave opening with the spyglass, using a large rock he had seen as a landmark. In the moonlight, the white, jagged edges of the rock formation lent a strange beauty to the coastline. The back of his neck prickled with awareness. He checked his boots, feeling for the blades he usually packed on these missions.

Dressed from head to toe in black, Sin and an extra man, McDougall, climbed down the ship's ladder, where Wright waited in the small black boat below. As they rowed toward shore, the area of the cave's entrance became more visible, nestled within the folds of the rocky terrain, seamlessly blending with the surrounding landscape. Vines and cascading branches attached to the rock formations hid the opening. It was still well hidden—even as close as they were. He noticed an outcrop of chalky rock that had formed above the entrance and appreciated having the landmark.

Sin hoped their intelligence reports were correct. The sooner they rescued Robinson, the sooner he could get home to see Lizzie, tell her about her brother, and *hopefully* discuss their future.

CHAPTER ELEVEN

Isle of Wight

NIGHT HAD CLOAKED the entrance to the cave by the time Sin and Wright arrived, their lanterns extinguished to avoid detection. They stopped when they heard voices. If Robinson was in the cave, he wasn't alone.

"How long do you think we have before the next high tide?" Sin whispered to Wright. He noticed the floor of the cave was smooth from all the waves that had pounded it over the years. It was still damp, with a few scattered puddles, from the previous high tide, and Sin began to worry about where Robinson was being kept. If the man wasn't on high enough ground, he would be engulfed by water. If he were fevered from injuries, that could make matters much worse. According to intelligence they'd received, Robinson had been captured eight days ago. "I hope we aren't too late."

"We may have a couple of hours before high tide returns. Not much more than that. There's a watermark from high tide earlier today." Wright pointed to the wet line on the cave wall, a foot and a half up.

Sin hoped Robinson was on higher ground. At least he and Wright had time before the water flooded the cave floor once more. They made their way deeper into the cave's tunnel, and the sound of raised voices made them stop and listen.

"Ye think ye're so tough, my lord! We'll see about that."

The voice could only be one of the smugglers.

A groan echoed back to them.

They exchanged a glance. Sin could read the expression on his friend's face, and he felt the same way—he wanted to charge in there and beat the smugglers to a pulp. But they couldn't risk alerting them.

"Dickie, what are ye doin', man?" another voice said. "This poor sod is already half in the grave. If ye want to stay and beat up on the poor bastard, it'll be you that answers to the Man. As fer me, I'm headin' to the Eagle Eye. I ain't gonna waste another night watching the tide roll in here when I could be ridin' Molly's sweet thighs."

"Aye, I reckon ye're right, Joe," the man named Dickie muttered. "Besides, this one ain't goin' nowhere. Maybe I'll set my sights on the barmaid with the red hair."

"Well, what are we waitin' for? I got a thirst for a few tankards of ale and my Molly."

The two men continued to extol the virtues of the curvaceous barmaids as Sin and Wright waited for the sound of their shuffling footsteps to fade away.

"According to the intelligence from Manson, there are several side tunnels that go all the way into the town," Sin whispered. "Let's hope we can get Robinson back to the ship before any smugglers return."

"Well, I'm always up for a good brawl," Wright said with a grin.

"Yes, but I doubt Robinson is," Sin replied.

Further into the cave, they rounded a corner to discover Lizzie's brother trussed up and anchored to an overturned chair, lying in a shallow puddle of water. His blond hair, so much like Lizzie's, was matted with blood, and his shirt and breeches were stained, most likely from blood as well. He groaned. They'd gotten there just in time. Given the overturned chair, it was likely he would have drowned when the tide flowed back in.

"Robinson," Sin said as they righted the chair. "I'm Edward Sinclair, and this is Asher Wright. We're going to get you out of here."

The captain nodded, cracking open bloodshot eyes glazed with fever.

As they sliced through the ropes that bound Robinson's arms and legs, they noticed two dirks sleeved on the inside of his boots.

"Hard to believe the blundering idiots didn't find those fine blades," Wright quipped.

"Was trying to reach for my dirk and toppled over," Robinson said in a half chuckle, half moan.

"Can you tell us where you're injured?" Sin noted the jagged cut marring the side of the younger man's face. The wound was swollen and red, pus oozing from the deep gash.

"Shot in the left leg," Robinson rasped, barely getting the words out. "Knifed right side."

"I have a physician on my ship," Wright said. "He'll tend to your wounds."

"Th-thank you," Robinson said.

"You're welcome," Sin said. "Now, let's get you up and out of here."

He and Wright stood on either side of Robinson, their shoulders bracing the younger man under his arms as they helped him stand.

Robinson clenched his teeth as they began their trek back to the ship.

The moonlight was both a blessing and a curse. It provided enough light to guide them, but also illuminated them for the smugglers. Sin hoped they could get back to the ship without alerting them, or they would have a fight on their hands. If they were forced into battle, Robinson might not survive.

They stayed in the shadows as much as possible. Robinson went in and out of consciousness and occasionally uttered a groan as they made their way to the beach. McDougall, who'd been guarding the dinghy, helped lift the wounded man into the boat.

"We were fortunate. The intelligence from one of your men

said you were close to Ryde," Sin said as he and Wright pushed the dinghy into the water and then hopped in.

"Did Vic survive?" Robinson muttered, his swollen eyes regarding Sin.

"I'm sorry to say Vic died from his injuries. You are the only survivor," Sin said.

Robinson muttered a curse and swiped at his eyes. "All brave men… Good families. Vic's last mission." His head dropped.

They fell silent as Sin, Wright, and McDougall swiftly rowed back to the ship. They understood all too well, as they too had lost many friends over the years—good men who'd fought alongside them in battle.

Sin's thoughts turned to Lizzie… *Lizzie.* How he missed her. After spending time with her since the night of the ball, he could not believe how foolish he was to have left her behind in Boston a year ago, something he regretted every day. When they got back to London, he would do everything he could to convince her of his feelings and to make up for the past. But for now, he needed to get her brother to safety.

He glanced at Robinson, who seemed to have fallen into a feverish doze. *I promise to bring him home to you, Lizzie.* "Do you have any other wounds?"

"Just a few," Robinson whispered, rousing slightly. "I'm glad to see you. Thank you for coming for me."

"It's hard to believe we are getting away without a shot being fired," Sin said as they pulled up next to the ship.

"Manson's information was helpful. They were more interested in their food and comforts than in the valuable prisoner they had," Wright said.

"I'm almost sorry we won't be there to see the looks on their faces when they realize you're gone." Sin chuckled.

McDougall grabbed the boat winch and secured the dinghy to a rope hanging from the side. Wright picked up the end of another rope that his men had thrown down.

Taking off his coat, Sin wrapped it around Robinson's midsection and secured it to cushion the man's wound. Robinson's eyes flickered open as Wright tied the rope into a slipknot around his waist and hips.

"Can you grab hold of the rope?" Sin asked. "It will take pressure off your wounded side."

"Aye." Robinson nodded. He grunted as he wrapped his hands around the rope.

Wright signaled his men to hoist Robinson up. He managed to hold on to the rope as the sailors worked swiftly to pull him up. In a matter of moments, they eased him safely onto the ship's deck.

Sin blew out a relieved breath.

"McDougall, you go next," Wright said as the sailors threw a roped ladder down.

They held the ladder taut as McDougall scrambled up. Sin glanced over his shoulder, marveling at their luck. The smugglers had referred to their leader as "the Man," but not by name. Whoever he was, he was in for a surprise when he found out his men had allowed a high-level naval officer to escape thanks to their eagerness for bedding barmaids.

"You go next," Wright said.

"Nay, you go," Sin countered.

"I went first last time," Wright said, crossing his arms over his chest.

Sin rolled his eyes, but he respected Wright's code of honor, for it matched his own. He climbed up the ladder and leaped onto the deck, then turned and watched his friend practically fly up the ladder, marveling at his agility. The man was a giant and yet moved with the grace of an acrobat.

Sin remained on deck as they set sail, breathing in the salty sea spray. The wind had begun to kick up, and the waves were lapping against the side of the ship.

"Our friends have returned from the pub early," Sin said as Wright joined him.

"Mayhap the barmaids were already tucked in for the night," Wright said, chuckling as he pulled out a spyglass to observe the smugglers.

They watched the men run back out of the cave, shouting curses, their swinging lanterns casting shafts of light left and right.

"Poor fellows," Sin quipped.

"Well, that was certainly a first. It was almost too easy," Wright said as the brigantine sailed away from the Isle of Wight.

"Yes, but not so easy for Robinson," Sin countered. "I doubt he would have survived much longer."

"Bronson is cleaning and wrapping his wounds. He'll try to get some beef broth into him."

"He needs a healer," Sin said, knowing how crucial it was to have someone dedicated to Robinson's care. If it hadn't been for Lizzie, Sin would have likely died from the yellow jack. Just as their friend Romney owed his life to Bethany, who was knowledgeable about plants and herbs.

"We had planned to take him to my estate, but I think he would be better off sailing to Romney's," Wright said, seeming to echo Sin's thoughts. "Lady Romney has a real talent for herbal medicine."

"You're right. Robinson seems to have only grown weaker since we picked him up. His wounds are festering, and the next few days will be crucial. How far is Romney's estate?"

"Folkestone, Kent," Wright replied. "Just a few hours away. And we would not have to travel far by land after we dock. Whereas my home is farther inland."

"A sound decision," Sin said. "If memory serves, I think Bethany is not due to give birth for a few weeks yet."

"Aye, but knowing Lady Romney, she would no doubt be stubborn enough to care for Robinson even with a babe in her arms," Wright said.

"Aye, Romney is a blessed man to have Bethany," Sin said. "The toughest part is yet to come—keeping him alive." Fortune had been on their side when they rescued Robinson. But they had to make sure they didn't lose him.

"It's settled. We'll send a rider ahead of us as soon as we land," Wright said. "I'll check on Robinson."

CHAPTER TWELVE

25 Curzon Street, Mayfair
London
The next morning

LIZZIE PLACED HER hands on her hips and took a step back to admire the transformation of the small classroom before her. Excitement bubbled up within her. Simon would soon arrive for his first lesson. Lady Beadle's equally unwavering enthusiasm for the boy had brought a smile to her face. It was the dowager's idea to convert one of the spare upper rooms—likely originally intended as a nursery—into a cozy classroom suitable for two boys.

With Reggie's assistance, they had painted the walls a cheerful, pale yellow, hung matching curtains on the window, and laid down a rug with a pleasant blue and yellow pattern, accented by subtle streaks of pale reds and browns. The room was warm and inviting.

"You mentioned that Simon has a younger brother," Lady Beadle had said. "We shall need the extra room when Sin finds him—and I have the utmost confidence in my nephew's abilities. I want the young man to know that education is important." She insisted the room be outfitted appropriately, and had made certain a large chalkboard was installed to take up most of one wall. She'd also ordered enough supplies for an entire school, along with reading primers and two children's desks, along with a desk for Lizzie.

Millie had also insisted on purchasing clothing for Simon, despite Edward having informed them that Mrs. Jones would take care of that. "I believe the boy will need a few extra items—in case my nephew wants to take him to church."

There was no talking her out of it.

Lizzie chuckled as she made her way downstairs to the parlor. She was certain Simon would not leave Josie at Edward's and recalled her earlier conversation with Lady Beadle about the dog.

"We cannot have the dog running loose and chasing the cats while young Simon is here—how will he be able to learn his letters and sums if he must constantly chase after the dog? I will think of a solution."

And she had. Lady Beadle had conceived of a clever idea to keep the pup both contained and comfortable at the same time. She'd instructed Reggie and Thomas to build a large crate for the dog—painted yellow, of course—while the housekeeper and a maid sewed a plump pillow for Josie to nap on, along with several chew toys from scraps of cloth to keep her engaged while Simon was having his lessons.

The crate Lady Beadle had ordered was perfect, and Lizzie couldn't imagine Josie not loving her new space. She smiled as she remembered her employer's enthusiastic applause when she beheld the completed crate.

Her thoughts were interrupted by Jenkins's stepping into the parlor.

"My lady and Mrs. Pritchett," he announced. "Master Simon and, er, Miss Josie have arrived. The puppy is leashed."

Lady Beadle stood. "Excellent! Show the boy in. But please have Reggie attend us."

Jenkins cleared his throat. "What about Miss Josie, *the dog*, my lady?" the butler asked in a whisper, eyeing his mistress's three cats, who had all raised their heads.

Lizzie could have sworn it was the word *dog* that had drawn their attention.

Before they could address the butler's concerns, Simon walked into the parlor, with Josie trotting beside him. "Good morning, milady. Good morning, Mrs. Pritchett. I have a new leash for Josie."

Lady Beadle leaned forward on her cane. "I see you have, Simon. And it matches that smart red collar, too."

"She likes to go on walks," Simon explained.

"Excellent idea!" exclaimed Lady Beadle. "Reggie, please make sure to escort Josie to the mews to allow her to attend to her, er, personal business, while Simon is having his lessons."

Simon giggled as Reggie entered the room at the mention of his name. "That's what Mrs. Jones says when Josie has to pee and poo!" the boy said.

Lady Beadle turned to Lizzie and gave a wry smile. "I believe you will have several good lessons to impart to this handsome lad."

Reggie reached for the leash as Josie wagged her tail excitedly. At the same time, Athena leaped down from the back of the settee. She arched her back and hissed, then whirled, scaling to the top of the window valance.

Oh dear, thought Lizzie. The cat was clearly outraged at Josie's presence.

Venus, usually a placid cat, emerged from the corner where she had been watching warily. She arched her back, puffed up her fur, and hissed as well. The cat's ears flattened against her head, and her tail became noticeably bushy.

Meanwhile, Zeus, who was sleeping on the other end of the sofa, lifted his head, sniffed, settled back down, and promptly fell asleep—oddly unperturbed by the dog's presence.

Josie jerked her leash loose from Reggie's grip and bowed her front legs in Venus's direction.

"Milady, Josie wants to play with your cat," Simon said, stepping forward. Venus, however, flew across the room and out the parlor door. The puppy bounded after the frightened cat, clearly mistaking her fear for fun, happily barking.

Reggie ran after the dog, followed by Simon.

"Oh goodness!" Lady Beadle said, wearing a look of horror. She rose from the settee and rushed after them, thudding her cane on the floor.

Lizzie followed but stopped when she heard the clanging and banging of pots and pans, followed by Cook's scream. The chaos had moved to the kitchen. She entered the room to pandemonium. Cook was on the floor, cake batter dripping down her face. The broken crock had landed next to her. The cat was on the worktable, directing a withering glare at everyone before leaping down and scurrying away. Meanwhile, Josie was enthusiastically lapping up the cake batter that had puddled on the floor.

Reggie and Jenkins helped the stout woman stand as Lizzie took a clean cloth, dampened it with fresh water, and proceeded to wipe the batter off the poor woman's face and smock.

"Come on, Josie," Simon said, leaning down and picking up the leash, gently tugging Josie away from the unexpected treat. "I'm ever so sorry, Lady Beadle." His shoulders quaked and his bottom lip trembled.

"My dear boy," Lady Beadle began. With her chest still heaving from exertion, she sat in the chair closest to her. "This isn't the worst thing that could have happened. The animals are fine, and Cook can make more batter. How is dear Cook, by the way?" she asked over her shoulder.

"She'll be right as rain," Lizzie said, handing Cook a dry cloth.

"Very good. Cook is made of stern stuff, she is." Lady Beadle turned back to Simon and waved him toward her. "Simon, dear, please don't fret. Many successes begin with small mishaps. Josie is like a child and must be taught how to behave. We shall all endeavor to help you in this process. In the meantime, what do you say we allow Reggie to take Josie for a brisk walk? Then she'll be ready for a nap, I'll wager."

"G-good idea, milady," Simon agreed. His slumping shoulders straightened.

"Wonderful. I am so pleased to have you here," Lady Beadle exclaimed, patting him on the head. "As soon as we check on the kitties, what do you say we take a short excursion to a few shops? There are a few things that I think you will need."

"Y-you want to buy me stuff?" Simon said, his eyes wide.

"Well…of course! We thought you might like a few things to wear to places like church," Lady Beadle offered gently.

"Ain't never been to church, 'cept to clean the chimney. And that weren't no fun," Simon said, shrugging his shoulders.

"Our church does not need for you to clean the chimney. And I can assure you that you will not be sweeping any more chimneys," Lady Beadle said with a firm nod. "The only requirement is that you listen to a fine sermon every Sunday and perhaps participate in the children's nativity play at Christmas. But that won't be for a while yet."

"But won't Josie and I be learning lessons today?" he asked.

"Yes, of course," she said.

"I'll take you upstairs to the classroom, Simon," Lizzie said, reaching for his hand. "Lady Beadle wants to make sure it has everything you need. After a brief first lesson, we shall go into town."

"But don't I need to get back to Lord Sinclair's house?"

"Today, you will spend the entire day with us, and join us for tea," Lady Beadle said.

"That sounds like fun!"

"And we already spoke with Mr. Kingsley," Lizzie added. "He said to take your time today. So that we can all become better acquainted."

"He's a right nice man, if ye ask me," Simon said.

"Er…yes. I believe he is very good friends with our butler, Mr. Jenkins, isn't he, Jenkins?" Lady Beadle turned to the butler.

"Indeed, my lady," Jenkins agreed.

"Very good. Now off with you, young Simon—enjoy your lesson with Lizzie."

Lizzie hid a smile as she led a bemused Simon away. Oh, what a story she would share with Edward when he returned. Her heart swelled as she pictured him throwing his head back with laughter at the antics of Josie and the cats. She hoped, wherever he was, that he was safe. She was eager to see him again, eager to spend time with him. And she hoped that by the time he returned, he would have some information about her brother.

WIDE-EYED, SIMON LOOKED around the classroom. "Is all this for me?"

"Lady Beadle was very enthusiastic in her efforts to set up a suitable classroom for you and"—Lizzie pointed to the second desk—"your brother."

"You people have been nicer to me than anyone in my life."

"Simon, you are a good boy and very deserving of a chance in life. Lady Beadle and Lord Sinclair want you to have that chance."

"I'm not going to let you down—not any of you," he said, swiping at a lone tear.

AN HOUR LATER, following a brief lesson on writing his name—a skill Simon was eager to acquire—they set off for town, bound for the tailor and milliner.

Simon, who sat across from Lizzie and Lady Beadle, his back straight and his hands on his knees, leaned forward slightly and confessed, "I'm not accustomed to riding inside carriages, milady."

"What do you mean?" Lady Beadle inquired, her curiosity piqued. "Were carriages a rare sight in your previous life?"

Simon shook his head. "Not exactly. But I've never been in one. I was supposed to ride in a carriage...once. The Man, he was in charge of us boys. He took those of us too big for chimney sweeping to a town far away. Promised we'd meet pirates. But there were none." His expression soured at the disappointment.

Lizzie's heart ached as she imagined the hardship this child had suffered. "Children have no control over their fate," she murmured.

"The first day in that town, they had us dig a tunnel, even as water flooded in," Simon continued. "None of us could swim. It was so slippery that it was hard to stand. One day, I escaped by hiding in the tinker's cart."

"Do you remember the name of the town?" Lizzie inquired.

"No. But we slept in a barn behind a public house called the Eagle's Claw. The owner's wife was kind to us and gave us extra food when her husband weren't looking," Simon recalled.

"Thank goodness you managed to escape," Lady Beadle said.

"Did you find Josie in that same town?" Lizzie asked.

"No, ma'am. I found Josie in another town. By then, the tinker had seen me, but he were nice and said he'd take me to London. Some boys were tormenting her outside an inn. I snatched her away. Lucky thing, the tinker was finishing up his ale inside. I snuck Josie into his cart and off we went." Simon's infectious giggle made Lizzie smile.

He was such an adorable child. Even after everything he'd gone through, he was sweet and possessed a big heart. Simon reminded her so much of Michael when he was a boy.

Lizzie blinked back sudden tears at the memory of her brother. She hadn't seen him in more than six years and wondered what he looked like, if war had changed him. She hoped not. Michael had been her hero growing up. He was five years older than her, and she had always looked up to him. "Josie is indeed special. Like family," she said in a soft voice.

Simon nodded. "My only family, besides my little brother Bobby. Only I don't know where Bobby is no more. No one can make me laugh like Bobby."

"Well, Lord Sinclair plans to help you find him," Lady Beadle said.

"You think he will do that? For me?"

"Of course he will. He will do his best," Lizzie said, her heart wrenching for the missing boy. Surely Edward, with all his connections, would be able to find him. Bobby *and* Michael. If the past five years had taught her anything, it was never to lose hope. After all, it had been Michael who made it possible for her to meet Lord and Lady Armstrong, secure employment with Lady Beadle, and then meet Edward again.

"We'll talk about it when Edward returns," Lady Beadle added, echoing Lizzie's thoughts.

"Oh, Lady Beadle, I ain't never met no one so good as you."

She cleared her throat. "Well now, perhaps you could call me Aunt Millie," she suggested gently. "Aunts are family too."

Simon's face lit up. "I never had no aunt before. I bet Josie would love it too."

Lady Beadle chuckled. "I'm sure, although we'll have to work on helping Josie and the cats get along. And what about riding inside the carriage?"

The young boy leaned back against the leather squabs and smiled. "I think me and Josie like it. There's no hay in our hair and it doesn't smell like paint and other things the tinker carries in his cart."

They entered town and the traffic picked up, forcing the carriage to slow. A few minutes later, it came to a stop next to a row of shops in Mayfair.

"I know this won't be as exciting as visiting a sweet shop, but you might be just as pleased with the outcome," Lady Beadle said as Reggie helped her alight from the carriage.

Simon's eyes lit up, and a smile spread across his face as they approached a tan brick shop. The name, Swagger & Stitch, was painted on a jaunty sign above the door. "You're taking me to a real tailor?" he asked eagerly.

"What other kind is there?" Lady Beadle's eyes twinkled. "And he'll measure you for breeches, jackets, some nice cotton shirts, shoes, and a lovely coat. Perhaps we'll even find some ready-made clothes in your size."

Simon's grin widened, his excitement palpable. "I can't believe I'm getting new clothes. I've never had anything new in my life."

Lizzie felt a warm tug at her heart. She reached out, gently squeezing Simon's shoulder, and offered him an understanding smile. She knew the feeling well—the joy of something new and unexpected. Memories of her mother stitching together clothes from scraps flooded her mind. Or when an older woman who lived near her cabin in Boston helped her clear a small swath of land behind her cabin and gave her seeds and instructions to plant a vegetable garden. She'd also taught Lizzie a few recipes that Peter had loved. When she'd agreed to marry him, her skills were very limited. It thrilled her to show him what she had done. When she became a widow, gardening and sewing were essential to her survival.

Simon ducked his head and swiped the back of his shirt across his eyes. "I wish I'd always had an aunt like you. I wish we could find Bobby so he can have an aunt, too."

"You sweet boy," Lady Beadle murmured.

The doorbell jangled as they entered the shop and were greeted by the proprietor, Mr. Finley Sewell, a tall, slender man with a balding pate and kind blue eyes. "Lady Beadle and Mrs. Pritchett, how nice to see you again." He turned to smile at Simon. "And who do I have the pleasure of meeting?"

"Mr. Sewell, allow me to introduce Simon, my nephew. He will require everything for a young boy, of course—breeches, shirts, vests, coats, etc. And if you have any ready-made pieces, so much the better."

Mr. Sewell's eyes twinkled. "Mr. Simon, if you will allow me to take your measurements, we have several handsome ensembles that can quickly be altered to the necessary specifications."

TWO HOURS LATER, the bell rang again as the small shopping contingent exited Swagger & Stitch. Simon wore one of his four new outfits. He and Reggie placed several packages in the boot of the carriage.

"That was so much fun. Mr. Sewell promised to deliver the other two outfits to us in a couple of days," Lady Beadle declared, rubbing her gloved hands together. "But now I feel in need of a slight pick-me-up. Does anyone besides myself crave a hot cup of tea? Mayfair's Sweet Shoppe is two doors down, and the aroma has beckoned me since our carriage stopped. They've made quite a name for themselves with their delicious sticky buns."

They entered the shop, ordered, sat back, and waited for their drinks. Lizzie noticed Simon staring out the window, his eyes riveted to something, or someone, across the street. "What is it, Simon?"

"It's *the Man*."

"The Man?" Lizzie asked.

"That's what he's called by all of us boys who have to work for 'im." The boy shivered. "He's standing there and staring at the shop."

"You worked for him?" Lizzie asked.

"I don't know his name, but that's the man who made me clean chimneys and sent me to dig the tunnels," the boy said tremulously. "And he's the man who has Bobby."

Lizzie looked out, waiting for a carriage to rumble past so she could describe the horrid man to Edward. Recognition shot through her, and she gasped, accidentally knocking the silverware to the floor.

"Who is it, my dear? You look like you've seen a ghost," Lady Beadle said, turning to see for herself.

"L-Lord Percival Blackwood," Lizzie whispered.

CHAPTER THIRTEEN

The southern shores of Kent

"MANSON, DO YOU have a reliable messenger that can take this missive to the Romney estate in Folkestone, ahead of our arrival?" Sin asked. "Their estate is Graceview Manor, and it's only a few miles inland. We'll make our way there once we dock but will be slower because of Robinson's condition. I don't want to surprise Romney...not totally," he added said, handing Manson a sealed sheet of vellum. No matter how he handled this, there was no way to avoid intruding on his friends during what should be a private time.

Manson turned to Wright. "Captain, we have a loyal crew, but I can't guarantee—"

"It's coded and sealed," Sin interrupted, his tone harsher than he'd intended. He prayed silently that the adage that "first children arrive late" held some truth. While he hated to wish any delays on Romney and his wife welcoming their first child, selfishly, he needed Bethany's extraordinary skills to keep Robinson alive.

The man's fever had worsened in the few hours it took to sail from the Isle of Wight to the shores of Kent. Robinson had endured hell while doing his duty, losing all his men in the bargain. If they could not save him, at the very least they could do their damnedest to keep him alive long enough for Sin to bring Lizzie to see him one last time. He couldn't bear the thought of telling her they had lost her brother.

"If we are double-crossed by someone in our crew, you know what happens," Wright said, his words nudging Sin back into the conversation going on around him. "They'll end up on a small and intimate island."

Manson nodded. "I'll send Rodgers. He knows the area and can rent a horse as soon as we dock."

"Good. We will be a few hours behind. Hopefully, it will give them enough time to prepare for our arrival," Sin said.

"Understood, Lord Sinclair. I will see it done." Manson left the deck and retrieved Rodgers.

The brigantine docked with little fanfare, and Manson was left to manage a short leave for the crew. Sin and Wright quickly located transportation. They secured a decent carriage and driver to convey Robinson comfortably, and two good horses for themselves.

Folkestone had much more to offer than Sin had anticipated. He had expected the coastal community to have adequate resources as the home of an influential peer of the realm, but was pleasantly surprised at its much larger presence. Folkestone was a bustling town, replete with merchant ships and fishing boats, as well as a popular seaside resort. He immediately understood the attractiveness of the area to the Romneys, and would remember its amenities as a place he might like to visit with Lizzie. Directly across the English Channel, one could even see the cliffs of Dover.

Sin and Wright rode as outriders for the carriage, unwilling to take any chances should highwaymen be about.

As Sin glanced over at Robinson stretched out on the carriage seat, worry gripped him. They had covered him with blankets to keep him warm, but he had been weakened by his week in captivity in a dank, cold cave. He'd also lost a substantial amount of blood from his wounds, and his complexion was pallid, his body consumed by fever. Each labored breath was a reminder of Sin's vow to ensure the man's survival and reunite him safely with his sister.

He was banking on Bethany's skills in healing to aid their cause, having witnessed her abilities firsthand in America, when she saved the life of a wounded Romney. He was left blind and forsaken amidst a heap of presumed British casualties, but his desperate cries were heard by Bethany's dog, Dandie, who, in her way, demanded they rescue him.

"How do you think he's doing?" Wright asked from the other side of the carriage.

"I hope he's not getting any worse," Sin replied. "Your ship's doctor gave him laudanum to manage his pain, and cleaned, stitched, and bandaged the wounds. But the fever is coming from somewhere. Fortune was on our side when we rescued him. The toughest part is yet to come…keeping him alive." As soon as they made it to Romney's, he would send a dispatch to Wellington to let him know the success of the operation. With any luck, they would soon be able to tell the duke a more hopeful account of Robinson's health.

As they continued their journey, a gentle breeze carried a floral waft, blended with the tang of the sea. Sin thought he could detect a hint of jasmine and roses. It took him back to the walk he had taken with Lizzie the day they went on a picnic, shortly before he left. The look on her face when he'd told her he would return in two weeks made him think she still had little confidence in a future together. Peter's family, curse them, had hurt her deeply, scorning the marriage of their son to the daughter of a vicar. He could not understand their contempt on any level, especially considering Lizzie's maternal grandfather was an earl. On top of that, as a widow in America, Lizzie found herself alone and adrift, with little to no support from Boston society.

Sin would never forsake her. Never abandon her. Now he had to convince Lizzie of that. He had never wavered from his determination to work under Wellington. And now he would apply that same determination to winning Lizzie's heart.

My God, I love her.

With illuminating clarity, he realized he'd been in love with her since the first moment he stumbled into her cottage and gazed upon her angelic face. *Why did I not tell her?* His declaration would be the first words from his lips the next time he saw her.

Thirty minutes later, they arrived at Graceview. Crushed oyster shells provided a firmer surface for the carriage and the horses, the crunching sounds heralding their arrival as they made their way along the main driveway toward the manse. Lights illuminated the white, four-storied home made of limestone, with large white columns supporting a covered piazza that extended across the front of the home. Potted plants, hanging baskets, and lanterns offered an additional welcoming warmth. Sin smiled as he beheld several rocking chairs, which had been popular in America. No doubt due to Bethany's touch.

It appeared their luck was continuing, as Sin spotted Lady Bethany and Romney standing on the front steps. Her dog Dandie stood calmly beside his mistress. "That bodes well for Robinson," Sin commented. Thank goodness!

"Wright, Sinclair, welcome," Romney said as they approached.

Sin and Wright dismounted, and two grooms stepped forward to take their horses. The carriage came to a stop in the curve of the driveway in front of the house.

"We asked your man Rodgers to stay, in case you needed him for anything further," Bethany said. "He is in the kitchen taking a meal. Our cook insisted. But we let him know you had arrived. Ah, there he is now."

They turned to see Rodgers approach from the side of the house. Sin and Wright both nodded a greeting.

"Let us help with Robinson," Romney said as he signaled two footmen who carried what looked like a stretcher. "My clever wife suggested we use a door and wrap it in a thick blanket with pillows."

The footmen carefully slid the makeshift stretcher into the carriage next to Robinson's unconscious form. Then Sin and Romney climbed onto the wagon and carefully, doing their best not to jostle the wounded man, slid him onto it.

They slid the stretcher out of the carriage and into the care of the two footmen, who slowly made their way up the steps into the house.

"We've prepared a guest room on the first floor—to make it easier for Bethany, who will be tending Robinson," Romney said as they entered the house. "And Dr. Fox is also on his way. He has been visiting Bethany daily."

"We apologize for the intrusion," Wright said. "But Lady Romney's skills can only help—if she feels up to the challenge. We realize this isn't the best time for her. But by the time we were able to rescue him, he'd been held for at least a week, and it looked like he received some level of daily torture. We haven't been able to speak much with him. The ship doc did his best, but he only cuts, cleans, and stitches."

"I thank you for your faith in me," Bethany said.

"You will rest, my dear, should it be required," Romney said to his wife. "You promised."

"I promise, husband." She smiled and waved, then walked toward the room housing Robinson with a footman by her side.

"Has Robinson been able to convey what happened to him?" Romney asked as he ushered them into the library. Dandie was on his heels and settled next to her master.

"He's communicated very little," Sin said, sitting across the desk from Romney. "His wounds and fever have left him in a near stupor."

"And the fever got worse during our journey here," Wright added from the chair next to Sin.

"I have heard rumors about a smuggling ring being led by Blackwood," Romney said. "While I have no direct proof, rumors suggest several other lords, although I have heard no names, have similarly gotten over their heads in debt and are providing their support—much of it in the form of information on shipments of munitions and guns being returned from France to England."

"Can you pen a report to Wellington to update the general on the situation?" Sin asked.

"I will, but at this point, it has only been chatter and speculation. I have no names except that of Blackwood," Romney said.

Sin's unease deepened at the repeated mention of Blackwood's name. Despite his prior request for a report on the man before departing London, nothing had prepared him for the staggering magnitude of Blackwood's possible criminal activities. He penned three missives—one to Wellington to go along with Romney's. In it, he described the rescue of Robinson, including the cave and its location. He also penned one to his sister and brother-in-law, asking them to escort Lizzie and Lady Beadle to Romney's estate. And finally, he penned one to Lizzie and Lady Beadle, informing them that he had rescued Robinson and brought him here. He decided not to elaborate on the details, but informed Lizzie of his message to Armstrong to escort her to Romney's estate. He had hoped to deliver her brother to her safe and healed. But if Robinson didn't survive this, Lizzie might never forgive Sin if she didn't get to see her brother one last time.

AN HOUR LATER, Romney escorted Sin and Wright upstairs to Robinson's room, where Bethany was checking the patient's pulse as the maid, Louisa and a footman were gathering up soiled linens.

Bethany turned to the maid. "Louisa, please ready another tray of clean cloths and rolls of bandages. Ask Cook to prepare a tray with oatmeal and willow bark tea. And have a footman bring up a pot of boiled water."

"Yes, milady," the petite maid said with a quick curtsey.

"Do you have my sewing kit?"

"Yes, milady, I already placed it in the room."

"Thank you, Louisa."

Sin and Wright exchanged bemused glances as Bethany continued to give orders to her staff like a seasoned field general.

She turned to them. "Do you recall when he had laudanum last?"

"Just before we disembarked from the ship," Wright replied. "We thought he would need it on the journey here."

"Good, then he should be fine for another few hours. I must leave you gentlemen to tend to Captain Robinson. Please take time to rest and make yourselves at home. My husband will see to your comfort. In the meantime, we've readied chambers for both of you. I will inform you of Captain Robinson's condition as soon as I can."

"I think we've been given our orders," Romney said, chuckling. "I have some brandy in the library." He turned to his wife. "Remember your promise. Louisa will be my eyes."

Bethany stood on her tiptoes and kissed Romney's cheek. "I promise."

Sin thought about Lizzie and felt his heart wrench. He admitted to himself that he envied the Romneys' relaxed affection and hoped with all his heart that he and Lizzie could share the same in the future.

"Lord Sinclair…" Bethany began in her soft, melodic voice.

"Sin. Please. We are old friends now. And I'm here to help," he said.

"Sin," she amended with a smile. "Before you leave, can you point out the locations of his stitches? I want to make sure I understand the injuries."

"Certainly." He showed her where the knife wound was, as well as the gunshot wound. "He seems to have suffered some torture. I saw small gashes on his arms, but they didn't appear to be infected."

AN HOUR LATER, Sin checked on Robinson and was surprised when he saw the transformation in the captain. He had been bathed, his beard shaved, his wounds cleaned, and he was, for the first time, resting comfortably. Sin exchanged a glance with

Wright, whose expression of surprise matched his.

"You have accomplished a feat in such a short time," Sin said.

"My wife is incredible," Romney said, stepping into the room behind them.

Bethany blushed as she explained the use of the willow bark tea and the poultices she would apply to his wounds. "The most important issue is to battle infection, and hopefully we can accomplish that," she said. "The main wounds are in his ribs and his leg, as you no doubt have already observed. His left leg is riddled with fragments."

"The ship's doctor said he had gotten the ball, but suspected there were fragments that he had been unable to find and dig out," Wright said.

"This is why his leg wound had begun to fester," Bethany added. "There are red streaks, and a putrid smell is emanating from his wounds. Given he was shot and stabbed more than a week ago, I was surprised that his leg was not worse. As you can see, the redness has already begun to abate after two of our footmen bathed him."

"He was facedown in water when we found him—and I fear he spent a lot of time in water during high tide," Sin said.

"Goodness! Where was he?" Bethany gasped.

"The Isle of Wight, tied up in a cave. The ground was high enough. But when we arrived, he was tied to a chair and pushed into the rising water," Wright added.

Bethany's eyes widened even more.

"What it is, darling?" Romney asked.

"The water may have inadvertently prevented a severe infection," she said. "Knife wounds are difficult to clean because they are narrow and deep."

Another maid arrived carrying a tray filled with additional cloths, bandages, and oatmeal.

"Thank you, May. Please place the willow bark tea on the side table to cool."

Sin recognized the aroma from his time recuperating under

Lizzie's care. It was the same tea she had spoon-fed him night and day. His chest ached at the memory. He'd been in just as bad condition as Robinson, but Lizzie had not given up on him. And nor would they give up on her brother.

"Thank you, Louisa and May. Please place the willow bark tea on the table to cool just a bit," Bethany said.

"Where is Dr. Fox?" Romney asked.

"He sent word that Mrs. Lambert was in labor," Bethany replied as she arranged various supplies next to the bed. "He said in his note that he did not think it would take long, since it is her third child. I'm certain he will be here soon."

"What can we do to help?" Romney asked.

"Two of you can hold him down, and one of you can hold this lantern above the wound."

They helped Bethany ready Robinson's leg, placing a towel beneath and holding him steady as she poured a liquid that made everyone's eyes water over his wound.

"Is that vinegar?" Wright asked.

"Yes, I distill it with various herbs to cleanse wounds," she said. Bethany took a pair of small tweezers and began to dig into the various gashes in his leg where the gunshot had exploded.

Robinson groaned and tried to kick out, but Sin and Wright held him down while Romney held the lantern over the leg.

An hour later, Bethany dropped a fifth metal fragment into the bowl. This one was the biggest yet, and the most deeply embedded. "There now," she said with a sigh. "I think we have all of our culprits."

"You need to sit down, darling. In this, I must insist," Romney said, pulling out a chair and helping her sit.

Bethany sat and lifted the hem of her gown. "My feet have begun to swell."

"I think it's time for you to lie down."

"Darling, we still have to suture his wounds."

"I can do it, milady," Louisa said, stepping forward.

"Well, I can get this cleaned out if you can help me with the stitches, Louisa," Bethany said. "I don't think I can bend over too much longer, but I want to clean this once more." Pouring hot water and the vinegar solution over his wound, she carefully cleaned it with a clean cloth. Looking up at Sin and Wright, she said, "This can be gory."

Sin laughed. "I hope you appreciate your wife's sense of humor."

"I do," Romney said, chuckling.

Once the leg wound was cleaned, Bethany sat down and let Louisa take over. The maid withdrew the silk thread from the sewing kit and began to make small stitches along the gash. When she'd finished, she moved back so Bethany could see them.

"They look perfect, Louisa," Bethany said. "Now we must see if we can get Captain Robinson to eat some of the oatmeal. Otherwise, his stomach could add to his problems—all the laudanum and tea could be disquieting."

Robinson began waking from the laudanum. They fluffed pillows and coaxed him to eat a few bites of oatmeal. With no small effort, Louisa convinced him to drink the willow bark tea. He was still moaning and groaning in pain.

"I feel better about things than I did earlier," Bethany said, pointing to Robinson's leg. "He may still have a fever for a few days. But I hope we've managed to stem any serious infection."

Dr. Fox chose that moment to arrive, escorted by their butler, Jeeves.

He greeted everyone and examined the patient. Stepping back, he commented, "As usual, you have outdone yourself, Lady Romney. I try to keep your talents hidden so that I can keep my employment in these parts."

"You flatter me, doctor. If not for you, I don't think my husband would have survived this pregnancy," Bethany teased.

"Since you are here, would you mind checking Bethany?" Romney asked.

Dr. Fox chuckled. "I will be happy to, of course."

"You seemed much more relaxed in London, Romney. What changed?" Sin asked.

"She's closer to her due date," Romney said with a wry smile.

"I'm fine, Matthew," Bethany said. "I promise. My feet are a little swollen, but I've been sitting and following the doctor's orders. Besides, there are two more weeks before this baby is due."

"Your husband may be more relaxed on the second child. But you do need to prop up those legs and rest the ankles," Dr. Fox said. "They are very swollen. You've been on them too long."

"Yes, doctor," Bethany said. "I promise."

"Come, darling, I'll escort you to our chamber," Romney said, placing his arm around his wife's delicate shoulders. "Will you fellows be fine here with Robinson?"

"Yes, of course," Sin replied. "Thank you, Bethany—you have conjured a miracle this day."

"I don't know about that, but we can certainly pray for one," Bethany said, blinking back tears. "I wish we could guarantee he will survive. Fever is a nasty foe. But we will do our best."

"Thank you again," Sin said, hoping that Robinson was strong enough to fight his fever and live to see his sister again.

CHAPTER FOURTEEN

25 Curzon Street, Mayfair
London
The next day

"GOOD MORNING, MRS. Pritchett," Simon said, taking one of the seats and withdrawing his small chalkboard.

"Good morning, Simon. Are we ready to learn?" Lizzie asked.

"Yes, ma'am!" the young boy said, thumbing through the supplies at his desk. "I even have books! I ain't never owned a book."

"You have never owned a book," Lizzie corrected him.

"No, never!" he responded enthusiastically.

Lizzie laughed. "Simon, when I said you have never owned a book, I wasn't agreeing with you. I was correcting how you said it—as an example of the correct way to say it. You are living in the home of a baron and must learn to speak properly."

Simon cocked his head and stared at her. "But did you understand what I said?" he asked.

"I did," she replied.

"Then wouldn't that mean I said it correctly?"

Now it was her turn to cock her head. Her lips twitched at his clever retort. He was such a bright boy, but he had also never had the opportunity for an education, so she would have to clarify the reasons why they said or wrote something a certain way. She recalled when she and her brother were growing up, Michael had an informal way of speaking with his friends that was different from the proper way of speaking to their father or with other adults. She explained her theory to Simon, and his eyes widened in comprehension.

"Therefore, if you are speaking to Baron Sinclair, for example, you would speak to him in the proper way as I have just described," she added. "If I correct some of the more blatant errors, my hope is you will learn to rephrase and speak them correctly."

"I think I understand, Miss Lizzie," he replied. "I'm supposed to pay 'tention to what you are sayin' to me so I will learn to pronounce the words correctly. I will talk proper-like with grownups like you and the baron, but maybe with Josie I can talk regular-like."

Josie gave a soft woof from her crate as though in agreement.

Lizzie threw back her head and laughed. "Yes, I think that would be fine, and I'm sure Josie would appreciate that."

"But what if I forget? Will I get in trouble? Seems like there are a lot of rules in Proper Society."

"I promise, you won't be in trouble if you make a mistake. One of the ways we learn is from our mistakes." Lizzie understood all too well how stuffy and judgmental *ton* Society could be. "I have an idea that will help you remember…by using *repetition*."

"*Repe*—who? I don't know him," he said, smiling up at her with a mischievous twinkle.

Understanding dawned, and Lizzie chuckled again. Simon was such an adorable child. "I have a feeling that tutoring you will teach me a few things too."

"I have some big plans after I'm done learnin'," he said with a sly smile.

"After you're finished *learning*," she emphasized. "Remember that speaking properly means saying the complete word. So instead of *learnin'*, we say *learning*."

"Learn-ing," Simon repeated.

"Very good. Now, I'd like to begin with the vowels—what they are and how to pronounce them," she said. "That will make it easier when we move into spelling. We'll start with letters that are vowels, and then we'll move to the rest of the alphabet." Lizzie had written the vowels on the large slate board before the lesson. She picked up her pointer and tapped each vowel, saying it aloud and asking Simon to repeat it.

Josie barked from her crate, drawing their attention once more.

"Josie says she likes her new bed," Simon offered.

"She does appear to enjoy the space," Lizzie observed. The dog was stretched out behind the door to the crate. "I declare! She seems to be growing. We'll have to get her a bigger crate soon."

"Yes, ma'am. Since she's been eating regular-like, she's been getting bigger," Simon agreed.

"She's likely to be a big dog, judging from the size of those paws," Lizzie murmured. "Has Kingsley said anything about her sleeping in your room?"

"He likes Josie. She follows him 'round, 'specially when she gets tired of sleeping while I'm doin'—*doing* chores."

Lizzie nodded at his self-correction and hid a smile over his other speaking errors. It would take time, but Simon was bright and clever, and most of all, he seemed to love learning. "What does Mr. Kingsley think about Josie following him around?" Lizzie asked. She couldn't imagine the efficient and practical Kingsley feeling comfortable with a pup dogging his every step, but it seemed one never knew.

"I think he likes it. He reaches in his pocket and gives her a treat when he thinks no one is looking," Simon said with a grin.

"Does Mr. Kingsley know you found out his secret?" she asked, arching an eyebrow in amusement. She would enjoy sharing this tidbit with Edward as well.

"I don't think so. He had his back to me. When I saw him do

it, I had to watch 'im again to be sure I saw what I thought I saw. And another thing… Lord Sinclair's cook is making the treats for him."

A smile stretched across her face. "I see that you and Josie are gaining ground in both houses, it seems."

"What does that mean, Miss Lizzie?"

"It means we are all becoming attached to you and Josie. Honestly, Lady Beadle was thrilled when she saw this crate and its beautiful bed."

"After Josie chased that cat yesterday, I thought we'd never be allowed to come back," Simon said, glancing down and plucking a thread on his new breeches. "But Lady Beadle told me she looked forward to seeing me again."

"I'm glad to hear it," Lizzie said, knowing Lady Beadle was already very fond of Simon. It was hard not to love the little boy—he was all heart. "I'm certain that in time we'll figure out how to make peace between the cats and Josie."

"I'll make sure to teach Josie everything I learn."

"I would like you to practice the vowels for one hour before bedtime. Remember, *practice makes perfect*. That way, we can start to learn to spell and write your name sooner." She reached down and unhinged Josie's cage.

"Josie, stay," Simon commanded. The dog came to his side and sat. "She didn't hurt the cat, but I'm sure she scared her."

"Yes, dear. Venus is dear to Lady Beadle's heart. You will need to demonstrate control over your puppy. She has a great deal of energy and can cause havoc when she gets loose. My suggestion is you keep her on a leash while she is in the house until you have total control," Lizzie advised.

"Practice makes perfect," Simon repeated. "I like that, Miss Lizzie. I promise I will practice every night."

"Very good, Simon."

Simon packed up his reader and his slate and secured them with a leather strap. She recalled her brother had used one of those with his books years ago. "Where did you get that?"

"Kingsley gave it to me. Said it were his when he was my age. He thought it might be useful," Simon explained.

"He said it *was* his," Lizzie corrected her.

Simon opened his mouth to give a rejoinder but closed it and smiled. "You are correcting me, right?"

Lizzie smiled. "You are catching on. Eventually, it will become second nature."

"I'm not sure what that means, but I hope learning will become easier," Simon said. "I'm gonna try real hard, Miss Lizzie." He snapped the leash on Josie and pulled her close to him.

"I know you will," she said.

"Shall we see you tomorrow, Simon?" Jenkins asked.

"Yes, sir. I'll be here." The young boy tapped the bundle hanging over his shoulder. "I've got a lot to learn."

"Very good," Jenkins said with a nod.

Lizzie accompanied Simon and Josie to the waiting carriage that would convey the boy and his pup back to Edward's townhouse. "I'll see you again tomorrow, Simon. Have a good afternoon."

"Thank you, Miss Lizzie." Simon hesitated, and then he rushed forward and wrapped his arms around Lizzie. "I'm so happy you're teaching me things."

Lizzie blinked back tears as she hugged him back. "I'm so happy too," she said, her voice thick with emotion.

She watched the carriage drive away, breathing a deep sigh as the truth dawned on her—she was happy. She hadn't been this happy in a long time. She was so thankful for all the good and kind people who were now in her life. Once more she vowed to speak to Edward, when he returned, about finding Bobby and Michael. Yes, it would be a challenging task, but if anyone could accomplish it, Edward could.

"LADY BEADLE IS in the dining room, Mrs. Pritchett. She wishes to serve luncheon once you have finished the boy's lessons."

"Thank you, Jenkins," Lizzie replied. "Please let Cook know we are finished for the day."

"Outstanding, Mrs. Pritchett." Jenkins gave a quick bow and left the room.

Lizzie walked into the dining room and found it empty. As she waited for Lady Beadle, she wandered to the window and peeked out from behind the curtain. She'd found herself doing that constantly since seeing Blackwood staring into the house from across the street, and after their excursion to the tailor's, when Simon spotted "the Man." Lady Beadle had wanted to storm out of the Sweet Shoppe to give Blackwood a piece of her mind. But Lizzie had convinced her otherwise. Simon had been frightened enough, and she did not want to add to his fear. Yet she would have sworn it was she that Blackwood was watching, not Simon.

Even so, they'd escorted the boy back to Edward's town-house, spoken with Kingsley, and explained what had transpired.

"Do not let this child out from under your watchful eye," Lady Beadle had told the butler.

"I promise we will watch over Simon and Josie with the utmost care," he'd replied. "I will speak with the entire staff and inform them of the gravity of the situation. If we see the blackguard lurking, we will send word."

Lizzie trusted Edward's staff. They were used to their master's dangerous assignments and were mindful of the safety and security of his home.

She scanned the environs once more and then, heaving a deep sigh, let the curtain fall back. Like most days, she saw no one. But the man she saw watching Lady Beadle's house days ago had *not* been a figment of her imagination, as she had initially tried to convince herself. It had been Lord Blackwood. And the frightening man had been watching Lady Beadle's dining room window. He'd been watching *her*.

Was he watching her even now, from somewhere she couldn't see? Lord Blackwood had been watching her while they shopped in town yesterday, but why? And how would he know they would be in town shopping unless he'd followed them? A shiver skittered up her spine as she realized the strange man must have been watching the house longer than she'd initially suspected.

Edward had wanted her to have a male escort whenever she left the house, and she promised she would. But even with Reggie in attendance yesterday, the man had boldly stared at her from across the street. But what had truly set off her alarm bells was what Simon had told her about Blackwood. The child had called Lord Blackwood *the Man* and asserted he was the one who'd made him and Bobby, and countless other little boys, work in the chimneys. Blackwood was the man Simon had escaped from. The reason why he'd been living out of a crate behind Gunter's the day they found him. Simon had been afraid of the Man, but it didn't appear that he thought he would be recognized. Were there so many children that the Man wouldn't know one from another?

She shuddered. Edward had only been away four or five days, but it seemed like weeks. Lizzie felt watched every time she went out—even when she walked in the garden, with Reggie just a few feet away, she'd begun to feel a terrible dread, like an ominous, dark cloud was hovering over her. Not even as a widow, living alone in Boston with armies battling miles from her home, had she felt this fearful, as though the devil himself were stalking her. Edward was the only one who made her feel safe.

"I will see Lady Beadle gets this right away," she heard Jenkins say, closing the door downstairs.

A messenger? What if it is bad news? Oh God! Her heart began to pound. *Calm down!* The missive wasn't for her—it was for Lady Beadle, who had all sorts of engagements and friends in the *ton*.

"What is it, my dear? You look stricken," her employer said.

Lizzie took a deep breath to ease the constriction in her

throat. "A message came for you. It just reminded me that I've heard nothing from Michael."

"My lady, a missive just arrived for you," Jenkins said, stepping into the dining room and handing the note to Lady Beadle.

She arched a brow. "Don't be such a worrywart, dear—it will give you premature wrinkles. It's probably a message about an upcoming social gathering. You know they come at all hours."

"Yes, of course you're right."

"As it happens, it looks to be from Celia. I recognize her handwriting," Lady Beadle said as they took their seats at the dining table. Breaking the seal, she scanned the note. "Celia is asking us to have tea with her this afternoon. At three. She says it's important."

"Are you going to reply?"

"Yes, my dear. It's most unusual…I will admit to that. But that doesn't necessarily mean something bad." Lizzie saw a flicker of worry cross Lady Beadle's expression. "Perhaps she's finally told William about the baby and wants to talk to us about planning the nursery." She chuckled. "Now, that will be a pleasant diversion! I'll send a footman straight away to tell her we will be there."

"Yes, that would be pleasant indeed," Lizzie said, schooling her features into a smile. And yet she couldn't shake the feeling that something was wrong. *Very* wrong.

LIZZIE AND LADY Beadle arrived at the Armstrongs' promptly at three. Lizzie had managed to calm her nerves, trying to convince herself that they were there to celebrate an official birth announcement. But the two faces that met them in the parlor looked subdued. As Lizzie and Lady Beadle took their seats, the door opened and a maid entered, pushing a small silver tea cart.

"William, Celia, is something wrong?" Lady Beadle asked. "I

confess, I expect happier faces when news of a little one is announced."

Lord Armstrong looked questioningly at his wife, who shook her head and shrugged slightly.

Lizzie bit back a smile as she watched Lady Beadle observing her niece with shrewd eyes.

Lord Armstrong drew a deep breath. "I'm afraid this isn't the best news."

At once, Lizzie's stomach clenched.

"We received an urgent message from Lady Bethany Romney earlier," he began. "It seems she had an unexpected visit from Lord Wright and Sin. They have your brother with him."

Lizzie gasped. "Is Michael… Is he all right? Is he—is he dead?" She had had the persistent feeling that he needed her.

"No, Lizzie, dear. Michael is not dead," Lady Armstrong said, moving to sit next to Lizzie and squeezing her hand. "He is injured. And it is very serious." She handed a sealed missive to Lizzie. "This note arrived with the message for William and me."

With trembling hands, Lizzie turned over the message before opening it. Then she began to read.

Dear Mrs. Pritchett,

Minutes ago, we received notice that Lord Sinclair and Lord Wright will be arriving shortly with your brother, Captain Michael Robinson. First, please let me reassure you that your brother is alive, but according to what my husband and I have been informed, he has been badly injured and maintains a significant fever.

I cannot tell you more at this time. But rest assured, we will give him the best care possible.

I know how I would feel if a family member of mine were missing or injured, which is why I took the opportunity to write to you before Lord Sinclair, Lord Wright, and Captain Robinson arrive.

I extend an invitation to you and Lord and Lady Armstrong. Lord Armstrong is quite familiar with the location of Graceview Manor, and I am certain he can convey you here within two days.

Graceview is but a few miles inland from the coast of Kent, near the town of Folkestone. It is a lovely area. I only wish your visit was under better circumstances.

Sincerely,
Lady Bethany Romney

"It was thoughtful of her to write us about your brother. I'm sure Sin didn't find out until after the letters were sent," Lady Beadle said. She arched a brow. "You know how secretive he can be." Looking at Lizzie, she asked, "What do you want to do?"

Beads of sweat formed above Lizzie's brow. Michael was injured. Something had happened to him, just as she'd feared. "I must go to him at once. I will hire a carriage."

"Nonsense. We would never let you take that trip alone. I will go with you. We shall take two footmen to assist us."

"Anticipating your answer, we have readied a carriage and hired outriders," Lord Armstrong said. "We have a two-day trip ahead of us. We cannot chance traveling without them."

"That was very thoughtful," Lady Beadle said. "Your carriage will be far more comfortable than mine for such a trip."

Lizzie turned to her. "You plan to go with me?"

"Of course! I have no intention of letting you travel alone. And I'm certainly not staying home twiddling my thumbs."

"And I have no intention of allowing you ladies to travel alone—certain stretches of the thoroughfare are notorious for highwaymen. I will accompany you," Lord Armstrong added.

Lizzie trembled at the mention of highwaymen.

"I've also sent ahead to secure rooms for us at an inn halfway there. We'll set out first thing in the morning," the viscount said.

"William, that would be most appreciated," Lady Beadle said before Lizzie could respond.

Lizzie's stomach was in knots. "Do you think Edward knows

we are coming?"

"I'm sure he did not know of Lady Romney's messages until they were already dispatched. But I'm certain he knows by now." Lady Armstrong chuckled. "Lady Romney knows my brother quite well from their adventures in America and would have anticipated his penchant for secrecy."

"True," Lady Beadle agreed. "We must take our leave and prepare for the journey. Thank you, my darlings."

Lizzie hugged Lady Armstrong. "I don't know what to say except thank you." She looked up at the viscount. "Thank you both, my lord."

"I pray that you arrive to see your brother looking hale and hearty," Lady Armstrong said, squeezing Lizzie's hand.

LADY BEADLE WALKED up the steps to the front door of the townhouse. The door opened, and she handed her pelisse and gloves to Jenkins. "Jenkins, we must travel to Kent in the morning. Lord Armstrong has already arranged for us to travel with him. We shall require provisions for the journey—the usual fare. We will be traveling to Folkestone—to Graceview Manor, Lord Romney's country house. Mrs. Pritchett's brother has been injured and was conveyed there by my nephew and Lord Wright."

"Yes, madam. I understand perfectly and will see it done." Instead of leaving the room, he held up the salver. "An urgent missive from Lord Sinclair arrived for Mrs. Pritchett only moments before your return."

Lizzie froze and turned to Lady Beadle. "Do you think Michael has passed?"

"Nonsense, girl. Were that the case, my nephew would be standing here before you instead of Jenkins. Would you rather I read it?"

Lizzie shook her head. "No, it's all right. I'm jumping to conclusions. It's just that Michael is all the family I have."

"Not true, my dear," Lady Beadle said firmly, looping her

arm through Lizzie's. "I am your family as well. You are as dear to me as Celia, Edward, and William." She took the note from the salver and handed it to Lizzie. "Thank you, Jenkins. Please send word to young Simon that his lessons will resume upon our return."

"Very well, my lady," Jenkins said before excusing himself.

"Do you think he is…gravely injured?" Lizzie asked as she fumbled with the missive in her hand.

"Open it, my dear," Lady Beadle insisted.

Lizzie broke the seal.

My Dearest Lizzie,

I could not share this with you before I left, but my mission was to rescue your brother, Captain Robinson. We were successful in our mission; however, he is badly wounded. Because I knew of Lady Bethany Romney's skills as a healer, and given that Graceview was only a few hours away by ship, Wright and I decided it would be best for your brother if we came here.

Thus far, Lady Romney has already made a significant difference in Captain Robinson's condition. Their family physician has also examined your brother and will continue to oversee his care along with Lady Romney.

I assume you have already had word from Lady Romney. She informed us of her message to Lord Armstrong upon our arrival at Graceview. By now, Lord Armstrong has received my other missive asking him to escort you here.

Please be safe.

Yours,
Edward

Lizzie had suspected that Michael had been on a dangerous assignment, but the Admiralty Office would not tell her anything. And Edward hadn't told her his mission was to search for

Michael. On the one hand, she wished he had trusted her enough to tell her, but on the other, she understood why he had not. She could not be angry in any case. If there was one thing she'd learned from her time in America, it was that one's life could change in an instant and love should never have conditions.

"Do you think we will get there in time, Millie?"

"My dear, knowing William and his love of fine horseflesh, we will arrive as swiftly as if we'd flown there in Zeus's chariot. Given that both Lady Romney and Edward wrote to you, it must be serious. But let us think positively. And pray."

Chapter Fifteen

25 Curzon Street, Mayfair
London
Dawn, the next day

"**A**RE YOU SURE you have everything, Doris?" Lady Beadle asked. "I don't imagine we will be gone more than a fortnight, but to get to a strange city and find you are missing something most important is disconcerting."

"I used the list you gave me, my lady," Doris said. "I checked everything—twice." The maid spoke loudly and carefully enunciated, as was her custom when her mistress was not using her ear trumpet.

Lizzie stayed quiet while Lady Beadle and her maid finished the packing. She hoped she had everything but was mostly concerned that she get there for Michael. *Please, God, keep him safe for me.*

Then it struck her. "Lady Beadle," she said, standing beside her employer.

Lady Beadle gave no reaction to having heard her. She was still arguing with Doris—now over what color dresses were packed.

Lizzie stepped around Doris and looked at her employer. "Lady Beadle, did you pack your ear trumpet?"

"La! That's what I'm missing," the older woman cried out. "Doris, it's next to the settee in the parlor. I had it yesterday when I entertained for tea."

"I'll get it, my lady," Doris replied, barely dipping a bow before leaving to retrieve the hearing apparatus.

They were supposed to have left already, but it appeared Lord Armstrong had been detained. Although Lizzie was curious as to whether Lady Armstrong had discovered she was *enceinte* yet. Or maybe she knew it but wanted to wait until after the first trimester. That was what some people did, she understood.

Lizzie had long ago given up hope of having a child.

Thinking about children made her think about Simon. "Millie, did you ask Jenkins to send word to Simon that we would not be here for a couple of weeks?" Lizzie hoped their absence wouldn't discourage the young lad. He had such a thirst for knowledge, and she looked forward to working with him more. The small schoolroom Lady Beadle had created was delightful, one of the most generous gestures she could imagine. No wonder Lady Armstrong and Edward adored this woman so much. She, too, had become fond of her over these past months.

Lady Beadle looked up. "Of course, my dear. I asked Jenkins to handle that for me. And I never have to ask him to do something twice. I'm certain it was done."

For reasons she couldn't fathom, Lizzie felt chilled. Bumps covered both arms, the hair on the back of her neck stood, and a feeling of unease swept over her. Warily, she slowly scanned the area in front of the townhouse, taking in each home nearby, the trees and shrubs—anywhere a person could hide. It was early, just breaking dawn, and the sun had not completely penetrated the shadows. While Lizzie saw no one about, she was certain he was out there. She could feel it. He was staring at her...from *somewhere.*

She wished Lord Armstrong would hurry. She was ready to go—anything to get away from that dreadful man and his lifeless black eyes.

"JOSIE, WE CAN'T let them leave us behind. They don't know how bad the Man is. We got to protect 'em. Lord Armstrong's carriage is here. He's the man we heard Lady Beadle ask Mr. Jenkins about. Let's you and me hide inside it so we can go with them and keep her safe." The Man was watching Miss Lizzie—*not me*, Simon thought. It was the same thing he did when he snatched children from the East End. Simon had seen it often enough.

He cocked his head and looked at the little brown dog. "I don't think the Man recognized me, girl. Probably because I growed taller. Or maybe because I've got you, Josie. He wouldn't be looking for *his boys* to have a dog." He looked down at his clothes and smoothed the small waistcoat Lady Beadle had purchased for him and stood a bit taller. "Or maybe it was my nice clothes." Simon reached down and gave his dog a pat on her head and a piece of the cheese he had taken from the larder at Lord Sinclair's. "The cook told me to get whatever I wanted," he told Josie, looking at his jacket before picking a piece of thread off the sleeve.

Cautiously, Simon scanned the area around the carriage. Activity was bustling, but no one was paying attention to the carriage, where he and his little dog wanted to be. They edged closer. He heard the driver and two footmen arguing behind the carriage over where to put the food hampers and trunks. The men on horseback were joking about someone they met at a pub. Everyone was busy, but no one saw him sneak up to the side of the coach. Quietly, Simon opened the door on the side away from the townhouse and climbed in. Josie jumped in behind him.

Hastily, he scanned both benches. "Lord Armstrong sure has a nice carriage," he whispered. "It's very big. And both benches have plenty of holes to breathe. We should be comfortable." Quickly, he opened the lid of the bench that faced the driver and spread out one of the blankets. "Hurry, Josie. They'll be leaving soon." The dog hopped in, and Simon tucked in right behind her. He pulled the bench lid down and shifted around until he and Josie became comfortable. "It'll be a long ride, Josie, and we'll have to be quiet."

As if in answer, the puppy gave a light yip of understanding.

Graceview Manor
Folkestone, Kent

SIN SAT UPON Romney's large white steed and surveyed the coastal community of Folkestone below. He turned his head at the sound of horse hooves coming up behind him and saw Wright approaching on a large black mare.

"You're riding like you have a burr under your saddle," Wright said. "I never mind a morning ride, but I had no idea you meant it to be a race."

"I cannot get Lizzie off my mind. And I find myself constantly going over everything in my head. At least her brother seems to be out of danger."

"You've sat vigil for two nights," Wright said. "He's made an amazing recovery, considering his difficulties when we found him."

"I agree. My fear was she'd arrive and he'd be worse, or even dead," Sin said. "Robinson looks much better this morning. He's still feverish, but we spoke briefly, and he seems more lucid."

"Well, I'm no doctor, but that seems like the right direction," Wright said. "What do you think about taking a trip into town and nosing around? Romney's information hints that Blackwood is connected. But we need proof. I'd like to have a pulse on whether he's here yet, or when he's returning."

"That's a good idea." Sin gave a quick shake of his head and sat up straighter in the saddle. "Sleeping in a chair is not recommended." He stretched his arms. "I hadn't intended to sleep in the chair in Robinson's room last night. I must have fallen asleep after Dr. Fox left. Fatigue and brandy are a potent combination."

"I agree. On my way out, I passed the maid named May, and after asking about Robinson, she mentioned that she was getting ready to bring him oatmeal." Wright chuckled. "He probably won't want to see a hot bowl of oatmeal for a long time after he makes it through all of this. I know I wouldn't."

Sin laughed heartily. "When his sister gets here, he may find himself eating more than he thinks. She believes the stuff has many medicinal qualities. Lizzie told me often that oatmeal reduces anxiety and has anti-itch effects—among other things. When I had yellow fever, she made me eat a lot of it, always reminding me how it helps with inflammation around wounds. I ate a *lot* of oatmeal."

Wright laughed again. "You may be right. Perhaps we've not given Mrs. Pritchett her due. She seems to have quite a knowledge of natural remedies herself."

"I hadn't thought of that, but you're right. Speaking of Lizzie, I'm sure she's on her way. I wrote to her and asked her to come." Sin wondered how things were going with Simon's lessons. He had a feeling they were going well, and wished he were there. More and more he was realizing that his work for Wellington was coming to an end. He wanted more from life than traveling from assignment to assignment. He wanted a family, he wanted to plant roots, and most of all, he wanted Lizzie.

"Your aunt will be with her," Wright said.

"Yes, you are right about that. I cannot imagine Aunt Millie staying behind."

"I quite like your aunt. You're lucky to have her, you know. She keeps things interesting," Wright said.

Sin smiled. "She's always been that way. Celia and I loved to stay with her when we were children. Nothing seemed off-limits. And that attic of hers has a treasure trove of clothing from the past."

"Have you forgotten? I was at the dance in Bath. I noticed the orange wig," Wright said with a grin. "So, when do you want to ride into Folkestone? I thought a drink at one of the local pubs might give us a little information."

"That's not a bad idea. But let's break our fast and perhaps ask Romney's advice on where to go. He knows the area better than we do," Sin said. "Let's head back."

SIN AND WRIGHT found the Romneys in the dining room breaking their fast.

"Good morning, Lord Sinclair, Lord Wright. Did you sleep well?" Bethany asked, her eyes sparkling with laughter.

"I did, thank you, Bethany," Sin said.

"I've asked our cook to prepare more bacon for you, Sin. I know it's one of your favorites," she said, taking a bite.

At that moment, the dining room door opened, and a footman entered carrying more eggs and bacon.

"Just in time," Sin remarked before filling his plate. He took a seat across from Romney. "I have a favor to ask."

"Name it," Romney said.

"I sent a note to Armstrong and Lizzie. I have no doubt she's on her way here, but probably won't arrive until tomorrow. I asked Armstrong to come with her. In the meantime, you mentioned your suspicions that Blackwood is leading a smuggling operation. Wright and I want to find out more about his operation, and we would be grateful for any tips you can give us—like whom to speak with, that sort of thing. And do you know where the man stays when he's here?"

Romney put down his fork and wiped his mouth, then leaned back in his seat. "First, I don't need to remind you to be careful. Blackwood's become a problem around these parts over the last two or three years. Before that, we had nary a whisper about smuggling here. Now I understand it's become a major, but hushed, topic of discussion—although I've seen no evidence that the people farm our land aren't loyal to my family."

"Of course," Wright said.

"He has two lieutenants—mean individuals, in my opinion. One runs his smuggling operations while he's not here, and the other… Well, there are whispers that he buys children from poor families and uses them as chimney sweeps. The man is a monster."

"I would love to beat him to a pulp," Wright said. "Pardon me, Lady Romney,"

"No offense taken," she said. "I completely agree with you."

"What have you heard about Blackwood in this area?" Sin asked.

"I've been listening to the scuttlebutt, and I intend to put a stop to it. If a family doesn't have enough to put food on the table, I want them to come to me, not sell their child," Romney said, his face flushed with emotion.

"I have taken a child into my home who was cleaning chimneys for someone called *the Man*. A coincidence? I think not. I'm inclined to think 'the Man' is the same one who controls the smuggling ring in this area. And we all know it can be none other than Blackwood."

"If our intelligence is correct, Blackwood runs a cloak-and-dagger operation," Romney said. "We should probably speak with Robinson if he's up to it—before our reconnaissance. Learn what he knows first."

"Good suggestion," Wright said after draining his cup of coffee.

Sin finished his own coffee and stood. "Let's speak with Robinson."

"I'll go with you," Bethany offered.

"No, darling," Romney said. "You've been on your feet enough. I'll accompany them. May is still up there, isn't she?"

"She should be. If she hasn't changed his bandages, please ask her," Bethany said.

Fifteen minutes later, the three men walked into Robinson's room and found the captain sitting in his bed while May fed him oatmeal. When the door opened, the pretty young maid stood.

"My lords. I was helping Captain Robinson with his meal."

"Yes, I see that." Sin bit his bottom lip to keep from smiling. "I was thinking your injuries were to your leg and midsection, Robinson. I was unaware you had injured your arm."

"Considering the extent of my injuries, I thought it was important to keep my arm healthy and strong," Robinson said with a sly grin.

"May, Lady Romney wishes for you to change Captain Robinson's bandages—but can you wait until we speak with the captain? We shouldn't be more than a half-hour."

"Yes, my lord," the maid said, bobbing her head.

"Thank you, May," Robinson said, his lips curved in a crooked smile.

The young maid blushed and curtseyed, holding the breakfast tray as she scurried from the room.

"Robinson, tell me I don't need to have you chaperoned," Romney said, arching a brow.

"Of course not," Robinson said. "I promise to behave."

"Good." Romney drew up a chair. "Sin and Wright want to do some investigation in town. But I suggested we find out what you know about Lord Blackwood."

"The smugglers revere him. I believe he's in charge of everything but have limited evidence. And a few lords are reputed to be aiding him—Lord Pattison, Lord Pegram, and Lord Nesbitt are names I've heard."

"I know of them," Romney said.

"According to our intelligence, they were feeding information about the arms being sent back to England," Robinson said. "But our evidence is limited. We thought we had the right cave but took a wrong turn in one of the tunnels. They discovered us. There's also a house in Folkestone he inherited from an elderly uncle. It's not in great shape, but we were going to check it out. We just never made it," he lamented.

"Your captors didn't know who you were, did they?" Wright said. It was more of a statement than a question.

"No. They called us revenuers and beat us with their pistols, fists, and whatever was handy. It was almost as if they were more interested in thrashing us than learning who we were." Robinson's voice cracked.

"You were lucky. Had they known who they had, who knows if we would have found you alive," Wright said.

"I know we're peppering you with these questions, but did you hear them refer to 'the Man'?" Sin asked.

"Many times…and whoever it is, they were afraid of him," Robinson said. "While I had my suspicions it was Blackwood, we never learned who it was for sure."

"Who do you think it is?" Wright asked.

"I think it's Blackwood," Robinson replied.

"I sent word to Lizzie and asked her to come," Sin said.

"Bethany sent word, too. She felt it was the right thing to do," Romney said. "I've no doubt the woman is on her way."

"She mailed me and told me she'd run out of funds and needed to return," Robinson said. "So I'm glad to hear she's back in England. I couldn't wait for her to arrive, so I left a note for her at the Admiralty and Marine Affairs Office."

"She's taken a position as companion to my Aunt Millie," Sin said.

"As in Lady Beadle?" Robinson asked, sounding surprised. "I left word for Lizzie to contact Celia and William for help, knowing they would assist her in getting settled. But goodness! I never imagined her as a companion—to Lady Beadle, no less." He chuckled.

"Lady Beadle will most likely be with her when she arrives," Wright added. "They appear to have grown quite close."

"I'm pleased to hear that. It's been several years since I've seen or spoken to Lizzie—except for the odd letter here and there. It's strange to hear myself say this, but I miss her. With our parents gone, we're all each other has."

The remark rankled Sin. Lizzie had him, too. *But didn't Michael say he hadn't spoken to her?* He cleared his throat. "Then you don't know about my relationship with her."

Robinson turned to Sin and narrowed his eyes. "What rela-tionship?"

"Relax," Sin said. "I had yellow fever and stumbled upon your sister's cabin in the woods near Boston when I was at my worst. I was in America to find Romney—who, you have probably heard, had gone missing after the Battle of New Orleans. Lizzie nursed me back to health. I left to find Romney—and by the time I got back to Boston, she was gone. We ran into each other at Celia's ball—what a surprise that was!"

"I can only imagine," Robinson said, smiling.

"She was upset that the admiralty office would tell her noth-ing of your whereabouts, terrified that you were injured or worse. And I couldn't tell her I was coming to find you—but I can tell you, finding you alive was a balm to my heart."

"That's my sister," Robinson said. "Did you develop feelings for each other?"

"Yes. And fool that I am, I've not told her how I feel," Sin said.

"Which is?" Robinson asked.

"I love her."

CHAPTER SIXTEEN

"Josie, you have to quit moving," Simon whispered as he tried to keep his pup from squirming. "Settle down and get comfortable, girl. We have t'be very quiet, Josie. Miss Lizzie needs us, so we need to stay close to her. Shh! I hear voices. They're coming."

The little dog seemed to understand his plea and, after spinning around once, finally curled up next to Simon's head and placed her head protectively over his. They stayed as still as they could while the carriage groaned and moved as people climbed aboard. "I love you, Josie," Simon whispered. "You're my best friend."

As though she could comprehend, the little dog licked his ear. It tickled and made Simon bite his lip to keep from laughing. Josie loved to lick his ears. He probably had the cleanest ears of anyone he knew.

With his head up against the front of the box, he could see Miss Lizzie's booted feet through the decorative holes in the bench. He was relieved, as all the holes made it easier to breathe. Miss Lizzie was sitting on the bench next to Lady Beadle, opposite where he and Josie were hiding. It wasn't the most comfortable way to ride in a carriage, but at least he'd be dry. He thought back to when he rode in the back of the tinker's wagon to get away from the Man. It had been his only chance to escape, and he had been cold, wet, and hungry. And determined.

The Man hadn't recognized him the other day when Simon saw him across the street from the Sweet Shoppe, nor did the Man spot him that morning, which gave Simon hope he would continue to have good luck. He needed to watch out for Miss Lizzie because the Man had been staring at her. Simon had seen a wolf look at a rabbit like that once. He didn't know *why* the Man wanted Miss Lizzie, but he had seen him snatch his brother and other children to work in chimneys. They had no choice but to go.

The Man was the meanest person Simon had ever known. He didn't care about what he did to others or how many of Simon's friends died in the chimneys, or under rocks when a tunnel collapsed. The small boy sent a silent prayer to God to watch over his baby brother, Bobby. Not a day went by that Simon didn't think of Bobby. No way would he have left his brother behind, but the Man had separated them. Simon didn't know where the Man had taken Bobby. But he knew he had to stay alive to find his brother. After seeing all the boys who died because of the Man, he knew he had to save himself.

But one day I will find you, Bobby, and I'll get you away from the Man.

⋙✕⋘

LIZZIE SETTLED IN her seat and snugged her pelisse closer around her neck, hoping they had bright sunshine on their trip. The black coach wouldn't draw too much attention. And she liked the midnight-blue color of the leather seats and the four small lamps, two on each side. Having light while traveling early in the morning or after sundown would be nice.

She moved the black curtains aside and glanced out the window at the dreary clouds lining the sky and noticed the sun peeking from behind them. She hoped it would make a full appearance. She loved sunny mornings, although snuggling under a warm blanket with a cup of chocolate and a book on a cloudy morning was a cozy way to spend an hour or two. Lizzie hated traveling during a rainstorm, fearing the winding roads and the mud could slow them down, or worse, lead to an accident or a loose wheel. A shudder shook her.

"You're cold. Take more of this blanket, my dear," Lady Beadle suggested. "We have a long ride ahead, and you must take care of yourself. The last thing you need is to catch a fever on the journey to Lord and Lady Romney's house. How will you care for your brother if you are ill?"

The carriage opened on the other side, and Lord Armstrong climbed in. "I apologize for my tardiness."

"Don't give it a thought, William. But we are glad to get underway," Lady Beadle said.

"Ah, well, you know how insistent my darling Celia is," he said, adjusting his coat beneath him. "At the last minute, she insisted I add lemonade and her favorite oatmeal and raisin biscuits to the hamper. The biscuits are fresh from the oven. I'll admit…they are good."

"It won't be long before I'll be wanting one or two of those," mumbled Lady Beadle. "Your cook uses those plump, sweet raisins. I can almost taste them."

"We anticipated that," Lord Armstrong said. As if summoned, one of the footmen opened the door and handed him a small wicker basket. "Thank you, James." The footman nodded and closed the door.

Lizzie couldn't help but laugh. "I've never tasted oatmeal biscuits, but they sound delicious."

"Ladies, we have a footman and four outriders, so don't be alarmed to see men on horseback around us," Lord Armstrong said. "I wanted to ensure we had no trouble on the way to Folkestone."

All Lizzie had thought about since receiving Edward and Bethany's letters was her injured brother—she could think of nothing else. But as the carriage lurched forward, signaling the beginning of their trip, she couldn't shake the unease that enveloped her. The Armstrongs' carriage was new and plush inside, and without the kind of flashy monogram that was on many of the aristocracy's carriages. She was grateful for that, because highwaymen targeted the fancier carriages. Despite the armed outriders, she wanted to ask Lord Armstrong if he too was armed, but held her tongue. She was being ridiculous. This was not the first trip he had arranged. And he had taken their safety very seriously—much more seriously than *she* could have arranged. She had been prepared to take a mail coach to reach her brother if necessary.

"What do you think, Lizzie?" Lady Beadle asked, bringing Lizzie's focus back to the conversation.

"I'm sorry. I suppose I was woolgathering. Forgive me," Lizzie said.

"We will travel as far as is reasonable but will need to stop for the night to rest the horses," Lord Armstrong said. "I sent a footman ahead to make arrangements. We were discussing having a short stop in a few hours and having refreshments. Would that suit you?"

"Oh, yes. That would be lovely. I would like nothing better than to stretch my legs in a few hours."

"Excellent," the viscount said, withdrawing a small book from his pocket. "I brought along some reading material and hope you won't find me rude if I read it. It's research for a bill I plan to propose in Parliament when I return."

"Certainly. I brought a book along, too. I was hoping it would take my mind off worrying about Michael," Lizzie said, withdrawing her copy of *Emma* and opening it to the beginning, determined this time to read past the first chapter. Despite her efforts to like the heroine, thus far, Lizzie found her unlikeable because of her snobbishness. After what she had been through with Peter's family, she had little patience for the narrow-minded elite. Had Lady Beadle not purchased it for her, she might have discarded it.

"Oh, wonderful. You brought *Emma*. I thought the book had considerable merit. I don't want to spoil it for you, but I quite liked the way the heroine finds her way," Lady Beadle said. "I hope you don't mind." The older woman lifted a small satchel. "I brought my satin pillow, just in case the stimulating conversation fails to keep me awake."

Lizzie snorted as the carriage hit a bump. "Oh dear! I apologize. How unladylike of me." She could feel the heat making its way up her neck. However, thinking again of Lady Beadle's comment made her smile. "My apologies, Millie. I just realized how it must have seemed when I pulled out my book. Of course, I'd find conversation much more fun, but I assumed everyone would want to read."

"Pish!" Lady Beadle said, laughing. "Besides, I almost brought a book. But each time I try to read it, I fall asleep. So I decided to bring a pillow instead." She gave a sly smile.

Lord Armstrong and Lizzie laughed.

A thumping noise followed by a muted whimper beneath Lord Armstrong's bench drew their attention.

"Shh. Hush, Josie. They'll hear us."

Lady Beadle narrowed her eyes and nodded toward the bench, where the thumping had resumed. "I think we have visitors."

Lord Armstrong tapped on the ceiling, and the carriage stopped. He stood and lifted the bench, and Josie hopped out, followed by Simon, who stood and brushed off his waistcoat and pants.

"Simon! What are you doing here?" Lizzie exclaimed.

"I'm sorry, Miss Lizzie, but we snuck in when I saw the Man watching you this morning. He was watching you like he did others before he took 'em. Me and Josie was walking this morning and saw him. I couldn't let 'im hurt you."

Lizzie hugged Simon. She *had* felt as though someone was watching her this morning as they were loading things into the carriage. But from where? She had hoped this trip would take her away from the ghastly Lord Blackwood and his lifeless eyes.

She could have kissed Simon for his courage and bravery, even though he was sneaky about it. His admission made her feel that she wasn't imagining things, that Blackwood had indeed been spying on her. Surely she could now leave that nightmare behind.

"That's quite a story. Do you happen to know the name of this individual who was watching Mrs. Pritchett?" Lord Armstrong asked.

"He's the Man. That's all anyone ever called him. He took my brother and made him work in the chimneys. Took those of us who got too big to slip up the chimney and made us dig tunnels. Two of my friends died when the tunnels collapsed. He didn't care. And when he looked at Miss Lizzie, it was like she belonged to him. The same way he looked at Miss Lizzie this morning. I couldn't let him take her." Simon's voice broke. "Lady Beadle, please don't be mad at me and Josie."

"Why didn't you tell someone you saw him staring at Miss...Mrs. Pritchett this morning?" Lord Armstrong asked gently.

"Mostly because I was thinking I needed to find a way to go, and I was studying the carriage."

"Sweet boy. We aren't mad at you," Lady Beadle said. "I do wish you had let us know. Mr. Kingsley will be worried. But we would enjoy your company on our trip. I'll have to send word as soon as I can."

Lizzie saw tears welling in Simon's eyes, but he brushed them away. "He's not making this up," she blurted. "I felt someone staring at me this morning but tried to tell myself I was imagining things. I looked around but didn't see anyone...this time."

"Were there other times, Lizzie?" Lord Armstrong asked.

She nodded. "I saw him staring up at the dining room window after breakfast."

"He was staring at us while we were shopping—from across the street," Lady Beadle added.

"No, I saw him. The Man was staring at *you*, Miss Lizzie," Simon said.

Lizzie shuddered.

"Did you recognize him when he was watching you?" Lord Armstrong asked.

Lizzie nodded. "Lord Percival Blackwood."

Lord Armstrong blinked. "Are you certain?"

"Yes," Lady Beadle said. "I saw him too. And don't forget, Lizzie, he also accosted you the night of the party."

The viscount ran his hand through his hair. "I wish I had known about this. Unfortunately, I can do little about it until I return to London."

Simon shook his head. "You don't understand. The Man doesn't only live in London. He also lives near the water. That's where the caves are—where he made us build tunnels. I ran away. That's why I was on my own with Josie. I had no place to go—and I didn't want the Man to find me."

Lizzie couldn't shake an impending feeling of dread. She glanced out the window, thankful for the outriders and Lord Armstrong's presence, and was also glad Simon and Josie were safe with her and Lady Beadle. But despite the added protection, she was worried—and she couldn't help but shake the sense of fear that had permeated her to the core. She prayed they would get to the Romney estate and Edward and Michael without delays. Edward, Lord Armstrong, and their friends would know what to do about Blackwood. And she could remain at Graceview helping Bethany tend to Michael with dear Lady Beadle, Simon, and Josie safely with them.

CHAPTER SEVENTEEN

Later that day
Somewhere on the road to Folkestone, Kent

"WILLIAM, I WONDER if we could find a place to stretch our legs," Lizzie said, bending back a page in her book and placing it next to her. In truth, she had hardly read it in the past several hours. Only one chapter. All she could think about was Blackwood. Hopefully, once she saw Edward and Michael, these ridiculous fears would go away. Besides, they were at least three hours out of London, and the man was far behind by now.

Lady Beadle smiled at Simon and Josie across the carriage from her. "I'll bet you are as hungry and parched as I am, hmm? It's high time I gave these old legs a bit of exercise and found something to nibble on before I waste away. Thankfully, pleasant weather has accompanied us on this trip."

"I'm starvin', and so is Josie," the boy replied. "We could do with one of them oatmeal biscuits you mentioned this mornin'— that is, if it's all right with you, Lady Beadle and Lord Armstrong."

Lizzie smiled. Simon was trying his best to pay attention to his diction, and she was proud of his efforts as a lad that had spent his whole life in the East End of London. He also took his responsibility for Josie seriously. The puppy lay close to his legs and didn't crowd the other passengers.

While Simon's obvious affection for her was heartwarming, hearing why the two of them had stolen aboard the carriage had upset Lizzie more than she had first thought. Guilt tugged at her. When she started the trip, her thoughts had been of helping Michael and seeing Edward again. Now, all she could think of was the beady eyes and long, unkempt hair of Lord Blackwood. Never had a person so unnerved her. She thought back to his efforts to gain her attention the night of the Armstrongs' party. Lately, the man seemed to be everywhere she turned. She couldn't help it—he frightened her to death.

"I agree. It's a good idea to stop and stretch," Lord Armstrong said, reaching up with his cane and tapping the ceiling of the coach. When the coach stopped, he stepped out and spoke to Henry, the footman. They were so close, Lizzie could hear their conversation.

"According to *Patterson's Roads*, there's a nice park less than a mile ahead, my lord," Henry said.

"Excellent choice. If I'm not mistaken, Lady Armstrong and I stopped there on our way back from the coast not too long ago. It's a nice place to stop, stretch our legs, and have a bite to eat," Lord Armstrong said.

"I'll see it done, my lord," Henry said.

As the door closed behind him, Lord Armstrong sat and smiled in Simon's direction. "Does Josie enjoy chasing sticks?"

The boy nodded vigorously. "Yes, milord. My Josie loves to run and play. But I don't always have a ball. They are hard to come by. So sometimes I tug on the stick, and we act like we are fighting over it. She growls at me, but she's just funnin'."

Lizzie made a mental note to purchase or make some leather balls for the little dog.

"Excellent. Perhaps you would allow me to participate. It's been a while since I was able to play with a *real* dog and not one of those fluffy lap dogs—no offense, ladies," Lord Armstrong said, laughing.

"Nephew, there is none taken," Lady Beadle replied. "After all, *I* have cats. And you see, my dear, cats possess a simple elegance that cannot be rivaled by the boisterous antics of a dog. It takes an insightful eye to appreciate their elegance and independence, much like the flair for interesting conversation in polite Society," she said, wearing a satisfied smile. "And should they engage a tree, it would be to climb, rather than to carry parts of it in their mouth."

Simon seemed puzzled. "I ain't never seen cats do nothing but chase mice, run from dogs, and eat and sleep."

Lord Armstrong chuckled.

Lizzie winked at Simon in a subtle effort to applaud his clever response. "It's lovely how you play with Josie. I've never had a dog of my own and fear I've missed out on something very important. Perhaps we can find a ball and you can show me some of your games."

Simon smiled at her. "I'd like that so much, Miss Lizzie."

Before the conversation could continue, the coach pulled into a shaded area near a babbling brook. The door opened, and Henry placed the step down. "If it pleases you, my lord, we will set up a small picnic site on the grassy spot beneath the tree."

"Perfect."

As Lord Armstrong helped Lizzie from the coach, she scanned the area, looking for anything that resembled Blackwood. Thankfully, all she could see was the breathtaking view in front of her—a beautiful babbling brook, a meadow of purple and white crocuses woven into green grass and shaded by large beech and fir trees.

"I don't think we could have improved on this spot if we tried," she said as she watched Henry withdraw the hamper and picnic cloth from the boot of the coach. She helped Lord Armstrong spread the cloth to create a comfortable picnic spot for the four of them.

Ten minutes later, the sound of horses' hooves drew everyone's attention as the outriders circled back. Lord Armstrong walked over and spoke with them. It appeared that he had encouraged them to take a break, because the four men became all smiles and walked their horses to a shady spot nearby, where Lord Armstrong's staff had already begun to share a large basket of food and drink.

"When we finish our refreshments, we can find a nice stick for Josie to play with," he suggested, fishing out finger sandwiches, meats, cheese, fruit, and oatmeal biscuits from the hamper. "My cook also sent along her delicious, pickled cucumbers and onions. I confess they're among my favorites."

"It's a good thing I didn't know they were in the food hampers, or we'd have stopped much earlier," his aunt said, spearing a few pickles for her plate. "Those are delicious. I much prefer a salty taste to a sweet taste. Have you ever tried these, Simon?"

"No, Lady Beadle," the boy replied.

"Pish, please call me Aunt Millie. Now, try one. I've always thought pickles were among the best picnic flavors," she said, as she stabbed a small, pickled cucumber and held it up.

Simon took the pickle and, making a face, downed it, obviously expecting to find it distasteful. Lizzie laughed with Lady Beadle when he opened his eyes with wonder. "That was good. I never knew cucumbers could be good like that. They mostly don't have a taste."

"My dear, cucumbers are a very versatile vegetable," Lady Beadle informed him. "And they have many restorative properties. They are a staple in my house, especially during the summer months."

"I will never forget how good they tasted pickled, Aunt Millie," Simon admitted. "But I don't think it's something I can share with Josie."

"I imagine you are correct about that, my dear," Lady Beadle conceded.

Lizzie enjoyed the break. Simon and Lord Armstrong played with Josie, each taking turns tugging the stick from the dog's mouth. The viscount had a great time and even promised to take Simon fishing when they returned, which delighted the boy, as he had never been fishing before. Despite his difficult childhood, he had a gentle and loving attitude, especially toward his pet and those he deemed his family. Lizzie wanted to remember this spot, and would mention it to Edward and Michael on their return to London. It felt like heaven on earth to her, and she knew they would both enjoy it.

As Sin rode alongside Wright into Folkestone, they noticed that the townspeople seemed preoccupied and barely noticed their arrival. "Do you think something is going on? Perhaps the regent is coming into town?" He said the word *regent* slowly and gave Wright a knowing look. He wondered if this concern they witnessed had anything to do with Blackwood returning, but didn't want to use the man's name for fear of being overheard.

Wright nodded in understanding. "You may be onto something there," he said. "The regent tends to stir things up when he arrives. We should keep our ears open to anything about his lieutenants."

Several workers rushed from a pub nearby carrying large pots of something that smelled like stew and placed them in the back of a wagon. A middle-aged woman hurried out behind them and helped them cover the wagon with a tarp. "He never warns us he's coming," she complained bitterly, clearly not caring if anyone overheard.

"Did you hear that? I wonder if she's speaking of the regent," Sin said.

"A large group is expecting to be fed somewhere," Wright observed. "Stew seems an unusual food selection for a party…but not for workers."

"She barely noticed us watching her," Sin muttered. "No one

protested when she grumbled—which I took as general agreement."

"You could be right on both counts. She didn't even glance our way. Certainly an oddity," Wright said. "What do you say we enter the pub she just left and enjoy an ale? Who knows what we may hear."

Sin nodded. "Probably a good idea. I'm glad we ate before we left. I hate drinking ale on an empty stomach."

Wright grinned. "I think they either water down the ale in these small-town pubs or don't change out the stale stuff. My stomach always suffers when I drink it. The only reason I continue to do so is to provide cover."

They walked into the dimly lit pub and headed to the back, where they could see everyone. Wright took the seat against the wall in the back, and Sin took the one to his right.

"I hate to be surprised," Wright said.

"Understood," Sin agreed.

There was a single sconce on each wall to light the room, which left it dark, making the patrons' eyes adjust to the poor light. To make it worse, old bits of food, drink, and dregs of vomit covered the floor in places, forcing the patrons to trod through or over them.

"Look at the candles," Wright whispered. "They're already drooping in their sconces, as if surrendering from a night of heavy drinking."

"A buxom barmaid is heading our way. Think you could turn on the charm?" Sin asked.

"I'll try to hold back and not overdo it," replied Wright, grinning.

"M'name's Brandy. How can I serve you?" the red-headed barmaid asked, leaning over Wright's lap so he could get an eyeful of her charms.

"How about starting with a glass of ale for the two of us?" he said, plunking down a shilling.

"Right away, handsome," she said, smiling broadly as she

scooped up the coin and tucked it into her bodice. She was back a few minutes later with two large glasses of ale. "There's more where that comes from, my lord, if ye get my meaning."

"I do," Wright assured her, wearing a tight smile.

Voices rose when two men entered the pub and took two empty barstools in front of the barrel of ale. The buxom barmaid stepped around the bar and made herself comfortable on one of their laps.

"It appears you have competition," Sin teased.

"Then I shall do the gentlemanly thing and step back," Wright replied.

"Do they look familiar? They've certainly caused the place to buzz with excitement," observed Sin.

"Possibly, but in this light, it's hard to be certain. Do you think they could be someone's lieutenants?" Wright asked.

"I suppose anything is possible. They do seem to hold some sort of influence."

Wright set his empty glass down. "Why don't we go find the house that Robinson told us about?"

"That might be a good idea. Did you by chance get an address?"

"Robinson told me it's on Hugo Street, on the south side of town," Wright said.

Sin set his glass down. "Let's go. I need to smell fresh air again."

Settling into their saddles, Sin and Wright headed south. "Folkestone is small enough. We should stumble onto the right road, I think," Sin said. "Something's happening, but no one was saying anything loud enough to make sense."

They had gone about ten minutes when they found Hugo Street. Turning onto Hugo, they noticed a wagon coming right toward them. "Isn't that the woman that came out of the pub?" Wright asked. "She looks upset. Maybe the stew sloshed out of the large kettles."

Sin smiled. "I'm sure that would upset her. But the wagon

seems much lighter, so she must have dropped it off somewhere."

Both men tipped their heads as the wagon passed, but again, the woman didn't seem to notice them. Instead, she coaxed her horses to go faster."

"Is that the house?" Sin asked, slowing and peering down a rut-filled driveway leading to a two-story wood structure. The house was nearly hidden from view by overgrown shrubs and trees. He slid from his horse and stood where he could see it better.

"Had the drive not been there, I might have missed it. It appears rather run-down. Not exactly where I would expect a baron to live," Wright said, tethering his horse to a nearby branch.

At that moment, the door opened, and a small blond boy stepped out and walked to a well on the right side of the house. He paused and stared at the two men as they stood partially hidden behind the overgrowth of trees, but a man yelled from inside, and he quickly lowered a bucket into the well.

"The boy didn't appear troubled by our appearance," Wright observed. "I couldn't make out what was said, but whoever was inside the house, the child immediately became anxious. Maybe it was his father telling him to hurry."

"Perhaps—but he acted more scared than obedient." Sin shook his head. "We should go back and talk to Robinson and Romney about what we saw. Maybe they can add their insights to it. I feel we've stumbled upon important information, but I should want to interpret it fittingly."

"I agree. As we've sometimes seen, important clues are occasionally hiding in plain view," Wright said.

CHAPTER EIGHTEEN

Sheep's Head Inn
Ashford, Kent

L IZZIE EXHALED A breath she hadn't realized she was holding when the small convoy pulled into the Sheep's Head Inn in Ashford. It was late in the evening, and despite the comfort of the carriage, she was tired of riding in it. She needed rest and a way to force Blackwood from her consciousness. But until she saw Edward and Michael, she doubted that was possible. "What time will we be departing tomorrow?"

"Plan to leave at six o'clock," Lord Armstrong said as he assisted her from the carriage. "If we leave on time, we should arrive around midday. We've covered two-thirds of the trip and have about twenty-five miles left to go. Once you are refreshed, I'll meet you in the dining room—it's reserved for us."

"Do we have a room together?" Lady Beadle asked.

"Not unless they are short on rooms. I requested individual rooms, thinking everyone would appreciate the privacy."

"You have always been a thoughtful man," Millie said, smiling at her nephew-in-law.

"Lord Armstrong, what about me and Josie?" Simon asked, tugging the dog's leash close. "We don't mind sleepin' in the stable with the horses."

"Nonsense. You will have a bed, just like the rest of us. Right, William?" Lady Beadle asked.

Lizzie couldn't bear this little boy being separated from his dog or sleeping in the stable. She wouldn't be able to sleep a wink. "I would be happy to share a room with Millie if that helps secure a room for Josie and Simon," she said. Lady Beadle snored…loudly, but for Josie and Simon, Lizzie could endure it for one night.

"Simon, we did not expect you on the trip, but you have been a most welcome addition," Lord Armstrong said. "You won't be sharing the stable with the horses. Lizzie, your offer is appreciated, but there will be no need for that. Simon shall stay in my room."

The young boy brightened. "And Josie?" Simon asked, looking up at Lord Armstrong. "Will she have to sleep in the stable? If she does, I should sleep with her because she will be frightened. And I promised her I would always take care of her."

"Of course Josie will sleep in our room. She is the best-behaved dog I've ever met." Lord Armstrong reached out and patted the boy on the shoulder. "I hope you and Josie have a big appetite, son."

Simon straightened. "Yes, sir! Since I've gotten used to eating regular-like, my stomach complains when I don't."

Lizzie laughed and swiped at a rogue tear. "Simon, we shall do our best to keep your stomach from complaining."

AFTER TAKING THE time to relax and refresh in her room, Lizzie decided to lift her mood by changing into one of the dresses designed for her by Lady Beadle's modiste. This time, she wore a pale-yellow muslin with white lace trim around the sleeves, collar, and empire waistline. After quickly readjusting her chignon, she felt presentable and went to gather Lady Beadle.

An hour later, she and Lady Beadle walked down the stairs to the dining room, where they found Lord Armstrong, Simon, and Josie waiting for them.

"Josie couldn't wait," Simon said, indicating the dog, who was enjoying a bowl of scraps provided by the cook. "I told her it was rude to eat before everyone else, but she didn't listen."

"We'll overlook it this one time," Lord Armstrong said with a wink.

"I apologize for keeping you waiting," Lady Beadle said. "I had to send one of the footmen to the carriage to find my ear trumpet. I simply cannot hear without it."

Lizzie bit her tongue to keep from laughing. By now, she was certain her employer read lips—not a word escaped her notice.

"We've only been down here long enough to order food," Lord Armstrong said. "The kitchen staff just brought it. I'm looking forward to a pleasant dinner and a good night's rest for our early start tomorrow."

"Did you have any trouble with Simon's accommodations?" Lady Beadle asked.

"Not at all. The innkeeper brought a comfortable cot into my room for him and a large pillow for Josie, who promptly dragged it to the front of the fireplace," Lord Armstrong said.

"Oh, I am pleased to hear it. Most inns don't allow pets. How did you manage it?"

"It wasn't hard when the innkeeper began to calculate the amount of money he would not make if I decided to move us to the Swan, which is only a few miles down the road."

Lady Beadle chuckled. "Clever man. I wouldn't have wanted to separate Simon from Josie."

"Josie and I both appreciate it." Simon grinned. "Since we moved into Lord Sinclair's house, Josie discovered she likes fireplaces, especially when they're lit. It was hard to stay warm in our shelter behind Gunter's. This is ever so much better. I appreciate the warmth of a fireplace, but after having to climb up and down so many to do the cleaning, I'd rather sleep in my bed, away from them."

"I can understand that, son," Lord Armstrong said, reaching down and scratching Josie behind the ear. "I'm glad Lord Sinclair and Mrs. Pritchett encountered you that day. You're a good lad."

It pleased Lizzie to see the acceptance and display of affection Lord Armstrong had for the boy. She was fond of him herself.

Dinner was delicious and filling. The lively conversation lasted only a few minutes as travel fatigue wore down their little group. Lizzie enjoyed a hearty meal of roast lamb, potatoes, asparagus, and plum pudding before finally retiring to her room. Despite her fears brought on by Blackwood lurking outside the townhouse that morning, she felt herself finally relaxing and feeling more comfortable. They were but a few hours away from Michael and Edward, and Lizzie was confident that once she arrived at Graceview Manor tomorrow, they would find a way to stop Blackwood's harassment of her.

The rooms were clean and comfortable, with goose-down comforters and freshly washed linens. After spending the entire day in the carriage, Lizzie practically melted into the sheets. Her room was next door to Lady Beadle's, and even without visiting her friend's room, she knew that the bed was against the same wall as hers, as she could hear Lady Beadle's familiar loud snores coming from the other side. She was so tired that her eyes closed the moment her head hit the pillow. Her last thought was her growing excitement of finally reuniting with her brother and praying that he was on the mend and seeing the man who'd made it all possible—Edward.

Wearing a smile, and despite the snores from next door, Lizzie fell into a deep slumber.

Just before dawn

MOONLIGHT STREAMED THROUGH a crack in the faded white curtains when Josie began licking Simon's face. Opening his eyes to a squint, Simon saw it was still dark. He stretched his arms and legs and groaned. "Can you hold on a little longer, Josie? When the sun shows itself, that's when we need to get up. It's just a little longer..."

Another whimper—this time louder—confirmed what Simon already knew. She had to poop...and soon. He glanced at Lord Armstrong's bed and saw the man was still in a deep sleep. "Gosh, girl. We gotta wake him and let him know we're gonna have to go outside. The last thing Lord Armstrong told me was to not leave the room, that inns could be dangerous. Are you sure you can't hold it a wee bit longer?"

As if in answer, the little dog jumped from the bed and slapped her paw on the door.

"Fine. I'm up," Simon grumbled. He never wanted Josie to think he was mad at her—even if he could have used a little more sleep.

The smell of sausage wafting in beneath the door made Simon's stomach growl. "We gotta hurry. It'll soon be time to eat." He put his legs over the side of the bed and pulled on his shoes and socks. Out of an old habit, he had gone to bed with most of his clothing still on. He grabbed the little hat Lady Beadle had insisted they buy when they shopped for clothes and slapped it on his head. "Can you smell that, girl? Sausage! We're lucky we don't have to look for our food no more, Josie. We just follow the rules, learn the ways of the gentry, and show up for meals," he murmured, picturing a hearty plate of sausages, fried eggs, and toast smothered in jam.

The puppy whimpered and stepped over to the bowl of water sitting next to the door where Lord Armstrong had placed it last night. She lapped up a few mouthfuls, then picked up her favorite stick between her teeth.

"Not too much, or we'll never make it outside before you go," Simon admonished her.

A grunt sounded from the other bed. "Simon, is that you?" Lord Armstrong sat up. "What's the matter?"

"Beg pardon, milord. It's Josie. She has to go out. She usually doesn't wake me like this, but maybe her stomach is feeling poorly."

"That's understandable, lad. She probably isn't used to riding all day in a carriage. And the food may not have settled well. I'll get dressed and follow along with you shortly. Stay close to the inn and don't venture far. Be aware of your surroundings."

"I promise, milord," Simon said.

"Call me William. We're friends."

"Thank you, Lord…William," Simon said almost reverently. He vowed never to take for granted his good fortune. He finally had what he'd always dreamed of…a family.

Josie whimpered again, reminding Simon she couldn't wait longer. "I need to take her, sir."

"Yes, of course. Go on. I'll be right behind you, lad."

The boy and the dog quietly made their way down the stairs and through the pub, where the aroma of sausages and fresh bread made Simon's mouth water. Josie lifted her nose to sniff, momentarily distracted from her immediate dilemma. "It'll be there when we get finished—I hope. Let's hurry, Josie."

After a few minutes of sniffing around the sparse bushes in front of the inn, Josie finally settled on a place to do her business, making Simon smile. "Just hurry, girl. It's chilly out here." *I've never had anyone make sure I had a bed to sleep in or food in my belly. Or clothes that didn't smell or have holes. Our lives got better when we met Miss Lizzie and Lord Sinclair.* And he had always wanted a dog he could love and who would love him in return. In Josie, he had that. They looked out for each other. She needed him and he needed her. The only thing missing from his life was his little brother. Simon wanted to find Bobby before something happened to him. Lord Sinclair said he'd help. *But where to look?*

Simon had seen two of his friends die when the big rocks in the tunnels they were digging fell on them. He heard them scream, and then nothing. Hiding in a crevice, he'd heard the Man tell his people to get rid of the boys as if they had meant nothing to anybody. He watched the men shove his mates into a boat and then row it out to sea, unable to do anything or risk losing his own life. Deciding then and there he had to escape, or he too would come to the same end, he ran away and was thankful for finding Josie—his best friend.

"Goodness, Josie, how much you gotta do?" he whispered, irritated. A sudden noise nearby told Simon that he and Josie were no longer alone in the yard. Could it be Lord Armstrong? Heavy, clomping footsteps and a muffled curse made him realize that it was not the kindly gentleman but two strangers.

"Be careful, you dolt," a rough voice muttered.

Quickly, Simon picked up Josie and stepped back into the shadows. He got her attention and put his finger over his lips—his signal for her to be quiet. He had trained her to do this shortly after finding her because their lives sometimes depended on slipping by unnoticed. From the shadows, they watched two men making lumbering motions toward the stable yard.

The men were carrying something wrapped in some sort of blanket or rug. As they drew closer, the shorter man tripped. The taller man sounded angry as he complained, "Did you hear how the bastard spoke to me? Smugglin' is one thing, but he ain't payin' us enough to kidnap some chit. What's the lass ever done to his lordship?"

The smaller man stumbled, nearly knocking them both off their feet. "Sorry, Spike. Good thing we didn't drop her. The Man would get mad about that."

"What the hell did I tell you about sayin' my name when we're doing a job?"

"Sorry, Spike. I won't say your name no more."

"For the love of... Just keep your trap shut."

As they walked past, a shaft of moonlight illuminated their bundle. The burlap blanket had slipped, forcing Simon to smother a gasp. The slender arm of a lady covered in long, flowing locks of glistening blonde hair was hanging from the opened flap.

That's Miss Lizzie! No one could have hair as pretty.

Simon watched as the men hefted her up, shoved her inside a carriage, and slammed the door.

"Careful, you dolt. You're going to damage the goods, and then he won't pay us. He's always looking for an excuse not to pay," the taller one said.

Simon's mind began to whirl. They must have hit her on the head to knock her out, otherwise Miss Lizzie would be fighting and screaming for help. He had to do something. *But what should I do?* Lord Armstrong still hadn't come down from the room. Most likely, there would not be time to run up and get him.

Remembering a piece of paper he had in his pocket from dinner, when Lizzie was helping him with his letters, Simon pulled it out and took Josie's stick. He pushed the stick through the paper and, hurrying from his hiding place, dropped it and his hat just behind the carriage. Helped by the light of the moon, he and Josie managed to wiggle into the boot of the carriage in the nick of time. After closing it, he shrank to the bottom and hugged his beloved puppy tightly.

"We just made it, Josie. It's up to you and me now." He prayed that Lord Armstrong would be out soon and find Josie's stick and the hat.

LORD ARMSTRONG STEPPED out of the inn and looked around, puzzled. *I asked him to stay close. Where could they be?* When he spied a stick stuck through a piece of paper and a hat in the middle of the yard, a chill ran down his spine and a sick feeling formed in his stomach. He examined the paper and realized it was Simon's handwriting from the impromptu lesson Lizzie had given him during dinner. William also recognized Josie's stick and Simon's hat. *My God! They've been taken. I shouldn't have let them go out without me.*

At that moment, the window to Lizzie's room on the second floor opened, and Aunt Millie's voice pierced the morning mist with a shrill scream. "Lizzie's gone. Someone's taken my Lizzie!"

CHAPTER NINETEEN

Graceview Manor
Folkestone, Kent

"MY GOD! WHAT do you mean they are gone? Gone where?" Sin asked, his eyes nearly bulging as he struggled to maintain his temper. *Dammit.* He would have never asked her to come if he knew he was putting her in danger. Lizzie could be anywhere by now. *His* Lizzie. He would find her—he had to. There was still so much left unsaid. He loved her and couldn't live without her. Sin rubbed his hand through his hair.

"Simon and Josie are missing too," Aunt Millie cried, twisting the hat that Armstrong found in the inn's yard. "The dear boy may have seen what happened to her. It would be like him to steal away…just like he did on our trip here."

"Wait! What happened on the way here? Simon stole away in the carriage to protect Lizzie? From what?" Sin looked in Armstrong's direction. "Do you think he's stolen away…again?"

"I think it's a possibility. The stick and the hat were placed there on purpose—I believe by Simon."

Sin crouched down in front of his aunt, looking up at her. "Aunt Millie. We will find all of them. But I need you to tell me everything you know."

She dabbed at her eyes and straightened her shoulders. "I'll do anything to find my Lizzie and that darling little boy. Shall I tell you everything that I know that has to do with Lord Blackwood?"

"Yes and no. I want to hear about anything unusual that has happened of late to Lizzie. And if it has to do with Blackwood, tell me anything you heard him say, anything that you saw, and anything that Lizzie said."

The older woman exhaled a shaky sigh and began. "The night of Celia's charity dinner was the first time I noticed anything. I saw Lord Blackwood following her, and he wouldn't leave Lizzie alone. But she seemed to manage his attentions well enough, so I didn't interfere…at first. But Lady Pemberly told me that Baron Percival Blackwood practically accosted Lizzie."

She continued to recount every odd encounter with the man, including the trip to town when he stared at her from across the street. Sin found it difficult to listen to, but he decided to ask questions when she'd finished, lest she forget something.

He would recall his questions. When she got to this morning, the hairs on the back of his neck stood.

"The man's been stalking her. He seems obsessed with her. Why?" Wright asked.

Sin thought back about any romantic interest Blackwood may have had but could think of no one. "I agree, but I cannot even recall his mentioning a romantic interest. Never—as far back as I've known him."

Wright placed his hand on Sin's shoulder. "We will find her."

"I blame myself for this. I should have anticipated this," Sin said. He looked at Armstrong. "William, you must take your time. And tell us everything you know."

"You can't be more upset with me than I am with myself," Armstrong replied. "We had outriders. I took every precaution, only to have them strike in the cover of darkness while we slept. This morning, Simon woke me because Josie needed to go out. I let him go but told him I'd be right down. I should have been there."

"Start over—but start from the beginning, including what happened *before* you left for the trip here," Sin said.

Sin listened to every word. When Armstrong finished, he nodded. "Perhaps Wright and I should lay out what we know. It might help to say it all out loud and put this whole thing together. Wright and I rode around the town, following a lead from Romney, and finally found the house that Blackwood inherited. It's in Folkestone, but we had to look down a drive to see it. It's set back from the road and is rather neglected. But from what we heard, he stays there when in town."

"There was a child there...a blond boy," Wright said, turning to Sin. "I feel like there's something I missed about the boy. Something I should have noticed—a familiarity...or something." He shook his head as if to clear it. "It's probably nothing."

"He was a handsome young boy—seemed to be about four years old, adequately fed, although his clothing seemed rather small for him," Sin added.

"He seemed sad," said Wright. "I don't know why that would have struck me. Young chaps get into trouble."

"If that is Blackwood's place, perhaps he is one of those children who misses his family," Bethany said. "I mentioned before that he's rumored to buy small children from families down on their luck."

"Despicable thing to do," Aunt Millie said, shaking her head. "How could someone blessed to have a child sell it? If that is, indeed, what happened." She swiped at tears that had continued to roll down her cheeks since her arrival.

Sin realized every parent who sold a child justified it to themselves, but in his mind, nothing could support that horrible abuse of a child. "I don't know how to answer that, Aunt Millie. But perhaps you should lie down. You've had a bad shock. We will find Lizzie and Simon—I promise."

"Nonsense! I would do nothing but think about it. There must be something I can do," his aunt said.

Armstrong leaned over and ran his hand through his hair.

"Who are these blackguards? We questioned the innkeeper and his wife, and they knew nothing. We notified the local magistrate, and they promised to send word if they learned of anything."

"I know who's responsible for this," Sin said.

"Who?" William asked.

"Blackwood."

ONCE THE CARRIAGE pulled off the road onto a gravel bed, Simon poked Josie. "Josie, girl, we have to be ready to hide when this carriage stops. They'll be getting Miss Lizzie out, and it's up to us to help her. But we have to be smart and do our best not to get caught by him, because he's mean, and I know what he'd do to us. And it wouldn't be good."

Josie whimpered her understanding.

"We have to be quiet."

The dog tucked her head in his lap. They were going to find Miss Lizzie. He knew the Man had her. Simon had worked in the chimneys or, when he got too big, on the streets in the East End picking pockets. He hated picking pockets and preferred to do things to earn his money. The toffs paid him to watch their horses. Some paid him to deliver things. But whatever he earned was never enough for the Man. He sneered at the effort and told Simon to stop wasting his time because he planned to send him back to the tunnels.

When the carriage stopped, Simon lifted the lid just enough to see. When he was sure the men had taken Lizzie away, he eased out and then lifted his puppy from the boot. The two of them hid behind some crates and barrels next to a shed. When the door to the shed opened, Simon peeked between the barrels and saw a young, blond-haired boy with a slight limp walk into the shed.

Immediately he came out of hiding and embraced his brother.

"It's me, Simon, Bobby." Wiping away the tears, he introduced Josie. "I found her when I left. She's been my best friend."

"I love doggies. She's so pretty, Simon," Bobby said with his slight lisp as he petted the dog's head. "But you must hide. The Man just got here. And they brought a pretty lady in yellow."

"That's my Miss Lizzie. She rescued me from sleeping in the trash behind a building—me and Josie. We've got to rescue her."

"Follow me. I know a secret way," Bobby said.

Simon stopped his brother and hugged him. "Bobby, I love you and I've missed you. When we leave, you're coming with me. I know Lady Beadle would want you to live with us. And Lord Sinclair said he'd help me find you. And if they don't, we will go somewhere. But I'm not losing you again. Promise me that you'll stay close."

Bobby nodded, and for a moment he stayed quiet. "Nobody knows about my secret passageway except me. I've never showed anyone. I think we can hide there. But it's small. I don't know about the lady in yellow. She was rolled up in a large blanket when I saw her, so I don't know if she'll fit." He looked around. "We need to get out of here before he sees us. He's planning to take a bunch of us to work in the tunnels tonight."

Simon followed his brother, stepping back as he moved three pieces of wood in the floor of the cabin, uncovering a hole that led to a secret passage.

"Go ahead. We have to get in the hiding place and be fast," Bobby said. "There's a secret room I'll show you. If we get in trouble, meet me back there. I've been smuggling food and water down there."

The two boys and the dog stayed quiet in the opening beneath the floor as a large man opened the door and stood above them, looking around. "I saw the boy headed in here. I sure didn't see him leave. Damn! Maybe he took the potatoes inside to the cook," he muttered. Shrugging, the man left.

"If I show up without the potatoes, I'll be beaten," Bobby whispered.

Simon's heart squeezed. He wouldn't leave Bobby behind. Never again. Somehow, they would get out of here. He wasn't sure how, but he was going to get help. "Show me how to get to Miss Lizzie."

Bobby showed him through a very narrow passageway. It wound around and took them to the second floor of the house. Bobby listened at the wall before opening the cover for the passageway. After checking the hall, he stepped out and indicated Simon should follow. "She's in that room. Be quiet. Maybe I should keep Josie with me in here until you get in there."

LIZZIE OPENED HER eyes to darkness and found herself alone on a pallet on the floor. The blanket smelled musty. She groaned and lay there, thinking and staring up at a ceiling she didn't recognize. The taste of laudanum nearly overwhelmed her. Someone had poured an excessive amount of the drug down her throat. She raised her arm and could smell smoke on her clothing. Suddenly, the memories came flooding back.

She recalled being back in her room at the inn and hearing someone cough. It sounded close to her. Slowly, she roused herself from her sleep. It was still dark outside, and as she adjusted her eyes, she gaped at the faces of two men she'd never seen before. When she opened her mouth to scream, the shorter man shoved a cloth into her mouth.

"Don't be afraid, milady. The Man has weird ideas, but he doesn't plan to hurt you. But if ye scream, I'll be forced to knock ye out, because there won't be time for the laudanum to work," the taller one whispered.

Tears welled in her eyes, but she nodded, and the man had eased the cloth away and poured laudanum down her throat. She recalled almost choking on it. Her last thought had been of Edward. *Somehow, he will find me*, she remembered thinking.

Suddenly, she heard the scratching. At first it sounded like a mouse, but as it went on, she realized it was outside the door. Then she heard a voice she recognized.

"Miss Lizzie, can you hear me?" Simon whispered. "Are you awake?"

"Simon. Is that you?" Lizzie rasped. She sat up and did her best to stand on shaky legs. When she finally stood, she tried the knob, but the door wouldn't budge. "It's locked. Look around and see if you see a key."

"I will, Miss Lizzie."

SIMON LOOKED UP and noticed the skeleton key hanging on a hook at the top of the doorframe. "I see it, but I can't reach it. Wait." He scooted back to the opening he had crawled out of, where Bobby waited with Josie. "Bobby, I need you to get on my shoulders and reach the key. It's too high for me."

"Will Jothie stay quiet?" Bobby asked.

"As a mouse." Simon got Josie's attention and put his finger in front of his lips. Josie immediately lay down and looked up at Simon. "Climb on my shoulder, Bobby."

After two tries, Bobby was finally sitting on top of his brother's shoulders.

"Reach as high as you can and see if you can grab that key," Simon said.

"Got it," Bobby said, passing the key to his brother.

Once Bobby was off his shoulders, Simon unlocked the door and then turned to close the entrance to the passageway. The three of them then scooted into Lizzie's room.

"Oh my God! He looks just like you," Lizzie whispered. "Just half your size and blond."

"And I limp and talk funny," Bobby said. "The men that tell me what to do make fun of me."

"You've always had that limp," Simon said. "Don't pay them no mind."

"I agree, Bobby. And there are ways to overcome a lisp. We can work on your ability to say the letter *s*," Lizzie said, wrapping her arms around both boys. Josie squeezed her nose in between them. "Thank you both for risking everything for me. But boys, we've got to find a way to escape." She locked the room from the inside and dropped the key into her bodice.

"All the bad men are eating and drinking in the kitchen. They might go to their favorite place and drink after they eat," Bobby said.

"And where would that be?" Lizzie asked.

"It's a pub above the tunnels near the water," Bobby said with a shiver. "It's scary to work there."

"Do you think she could fit in the secret passage?" Simon asked.

"Secret passage?" Lizzie asked. "Out of here?"

"Kinda. We can hide in there until we can get away from here," Simon said.

"Me and Simon got here in the secret tunnel without being seen," Bobby said. He looked at Lizzie and then nodded. "I think she can."

"Who else knows about the secret passage?" Lizzie asked.

"Only me," Bobby said. "But we betta hurry. If they don't go to the pub, they could be up here."

Both boys put their ears to the door. When they heard nothing, Lizzie unlocked the door and Bobby opened the door to the passage. Just before she stepped into the passageway, she locked the door to the room. When Lizzie stepped into the passage, Bobby pulled the cover to the passageway closed.

The dark passageway lightened when they found their way to a small room. "We can have light in here," Bobby said, lighting a lamp that was hanging on the wall. "We should stay here until it gets dark. There's food and water," he said, pointing to a stack of vegetables and a jug of water. "And blankets." He nodded toward a stack. "It gets cold in here."

"I confess to being overwhelmed and confused by everything that's happened to me. I wonder if we can sit for a little while?" Lizzie asked.

Bobby nodded, and both boys made a pallet and placed it on the dirt floor.

Lizzie sat down and patted the pallet. Both boys sat, and Josie wedged her nose in between them. "The only thing I know is the little I remember. Can the two of you tell me what you know about how I got here?"

CHAPTER TWENTY

Graceview Manor
Folkestone, Kent
Evening

S IN SADDLED HIS horse, preferring to do it himself. His head
pounded with frustration and worry. He needed to keep his
hands busy and keep his mind focused as they readied to leave.
Hearing voices, he glanced over his shoulder and saw Romney
and Bethany walking closely together, hands clasped, approaching the barn. He knew Bethany well enough to know she would
want to go. She was capable and courageous, and had she not
been pregnant, keeping her here would have been next to
impossible. But as much as he knew this, he also knew that
Romney would never allow her to go in her condition.

Sin contemplated everything that had gone wrong since the
moment he encountered Lizzie at the Armstrong ball. He should
have realized what Blackwood was capable of. He should have
known that a man like that would never let go of an obsession.
And he was clearly obsessed with Lizzie. Why had she not fully
confided her fears to Sin? Was it because she didn't want to worry
him? Was it because she was so used to fending for herself and
thought she could somehow cope on her own?

Sin could kick himself for being so blind to what had been

right in front of his nose all along.

In addition, he could have been honest with her about his mission. It could have given her hope and reinforced her faith that he truly did care about her concerns about her brother. Of course she would have wanted to know the truth about his mission. It would have cost him nothing and meant everything to her.

He shook his head as he cinched the leather straps of the saddle. What a fool he'd been. All for the sake of duty. The importance of following protocol. Nothing was more important than Lizzie. Besides, deep down, didn't he relish the thought of being a hero in her eyes? By saving Michael and returning him safely, Sin would bask in the light of her gratitude and love.

He scoffed at his own selfish pride. He had failed Lizzie. Had failed to protect her. And now she could be lost to him forever, kidnapped by a lunatic. And each minute that ticked by was another minute that bastard could do something to hurt Lizzie, Simon, or Josie.

"There you are," Romney said as he and Bethany reached his side. "Jeeves said you had gone ahead. Armstrong and Wright will be here in a few minutes. Armstrong sent word for his outriders to join us. And Wright sent word to his men aboard his ship."

"We were worried you'd gone ahead alone," Bethany said.

Sin arched a brow. "I thought about it." He knew better than to leave without reinforcements. He planned to save Lizzie and Simon, not put them in more danger.

"We just came from seeing Michael," Bethany continued. "Despite his stubbornness, we managed to convince him that Lizzie would not want him risking another fever should he become hurt."

"Luckily, Lady Beadle was most insistent on sitting with Michael and telling him all about her adventures with Lizzie," Romney added.

"My aunt is one of a kind," Sin said with a faint smile. "I thank you both for speaking with Michael. For everything you've both done for him, for us."

"You crossed an ocean to save me," Romney said, clapping Sin on the back. "It's the least we could do."

"We're ready," Armstrong called out as he and Wright strode toward them. "Between my outriders and Wright's men, we'll easily overtake Blackwood and his thugs."

"Aye, we'll be done and back in time for dinner." Wright grinned.

"We have no idea what we're going to find at Blackwood's," Sin said. "The place is set a fair distance from the road. I regret we didn't get a better look at the house and property when we were there. It's of a significant size and shrouded by trees."

"But we'll have plenty of men to spread out," Armstrong said. "We'll get them out safely, Sin."

Sin prayed his friend was right.

LIZZIE AWOKE FROM a light doze to the sound of thumping from above. The heavy footfalls of what sounded like many men moving were enough to cause dirt to sprinkle down onto her head in the small underground room. She glanced around and saw the boys and Josie huddled together, still asleep. She continued to listen to the thudding, her instincts suddenly on high alert. Something was wrong. The sounds and shouts seemed more than just a group of rowdy men eating and drinking and contemplating a night on the town. There was something else that had woken her up.

A faint, acrid smell reached her nostrils, and she glanced around the small space and noted the two tallow candles they'd placed on a low bench. The flames had all but petered out. But the smell was too strong to be coming from the candles.

Lizzie's eyes suddenly widened in panic. *Fire!* The house was on fire.

Grabbing Simon's shoulders, she shook him and then Bobby. "Get up, boys. The house is on fire. We must escape this tunnel, or we'll suffocate from the smoke."

Simon stood and roused Josie. He sniffed the air. "That fire is a big one. It's spreading fast."

Bobby sniffed the air. "Smells like something caught fire in the kitchen. It's close. We should go to the shed. I'll show you the way," Bobby said in his gap-toothed lisp. "It's the same way I brought Simon down here."

"Good boy. We must make haste," Lizzie said. The smell of smoke was becoming stronger, and she could see it swirling above their heads. She held Josie to her chest as she watched the boys grip a large, heavy piece of wood, revealing a narrow tunnel with a low ceiling.

Bobby led the way, followed by Simon and Lizzie, who kept Josie cuddled in her arms as they made their way through the dark tunnel.

"We're almost there," Bobby said over his shoulder. "We'll have to crouch down and crawl the rest of the way, Miss Lizzie, or you'll hit your head."

"Thank you, Bobby," Lizzie said. "How far away is the stable? We'll need a horse to help us get away faster."

"The stable is next to the shed," he said.

The small group made their way carefully through the tunnel. Lizzie could feel the air growing hotter, realizing they must be passing underneath the blaze. Although she knew dirt wouldn't catch on fire, the place would heat up and the smoke would smother them if they didn't get out in time. Peter had explained so much to her before he set out to join his battalion when they lived in Boston. He'd spent hours teaching her so many practical things she would need to know to manage on her own.

Despite the growing heat from the fire over their heads, she felt a surge of determination course through her. She hadn't thought about her late husband in a while, but in that moment, she could have sworn she felt his presence.

"You can do this, Lizzie…"

How many times had he said those very words of encouragement when teaching her how to properly chop wood or wield a hammer?

"You never know when this will come in handy," he'd remind her.

Peter had even taught her how to load and shoot a pistol. She'd kept one beneath her bed—until she had to sell it to buy food.

Despite her determination, her fears became more urgent as Simon and Bobby began to cough. She said a small prayer of thanks as they had to crawl on their knees. It meant they were nearing the end of the tunnel.

"We're here," Bobby whispered, reaching up and unhooking a trapdoor.

"Thank goodness we've made it," Lizzie breathed, handing Josie to Simon.

She placed her ear to the door of the shed and could hear distant screams and shouts. Slowly opening the door to the shed a crack, she peeked out. It was dark, well after sundown, and the air was full of smoke. "You boys stay here with Josie while I slip into the barn and check for a horse. Keep a sharp lookout."

"We can go with you," Simon said. "Maybe we can take two horses or a carriage."

"I'm sure the three of us and Josie will be fine on one horse," Lizzie reassured him.

"You know how to ride a horse?" Bobby lisped. "I like horses. They are always nice to me."

"Horses are very nice creatures," Lizzie agreed. "And yes, I learned to ride at my grandfather's house. If I hurry, I can saddle a horse and we'll be off in no time."

She wrapped her arms around the boys and hugged them both. "Thank you for coming to the rescue. You're both very brave boys. But I want you to stay hidden from those bad men until I give you a signal."

"How will we know what the signal is?" Bobby asked.

"I'll whistle." She smiled as the boys exchanged a look, their faces showing surprise and a little awe. She'd clearly impressed them.

Peter had taught her a lot, but so had Michael. She was eight years old when her brother showed her how to whistle using her thumb and index finger under her tongue on a fishing trip at the local pond on their grandfather's estate. What a wonderful day it had been.

She blinked back sudden tears. She prayed she would succeed in getting the boys safely to the Romney estate. How she longed to reunite with Michael. And Edward—God how she missed him. There was so much she wanted to tell him. So much she wanted to share…

Lord Armstrong and Lady Beadle had no doubt reached Graceview and informed Edward about the kidnapping. Knowing Edward, he would have immediately organized a search party. But would they know where to look and who was behind it all? She couldn't afford to wait. She had more than herself to think about. She had to keep the boys safe.

"You boys stay hidden. I'd rather you stay here where it's safe, but if something happens, I'll yell, and I want you both to run away as fast as you can."

"Don't worry, Miss Lizzie," Simon said. "I'll watch over Bobby and Josie."

"And I'll watch over Simon," Bobby added.

Lizzie's heart tugged as the little gap-toothed boy hugged his big brother close.

Simon slipped his arm around Bobby's narrow shoulders as he kept a tight grip on Josie's leash. Thankfully, the dog understood the need to be quiet. Simon had done a good job training her.

Lizzie crept out of the shed and made her way to the barn. She stopped just inside, waiting for her eyes to adjust to the darkness within. Scanning the interior, she spied a large horse already saddled. Relieved, she approached the horse and murmured soothing words to the animal as she reached for the reins. "Good boy," she whispered as she patted his flank.

She was about to turn and lead the horse out of the barn when she felt arms snake around her.

The point of a cold steel blade pricked the skin beneath her throat. "Do not scream, or I'll slice your pretty little neck," a raspy voice breathed into her ear. "I thought my chance to have you had slipped away," he said. "You're a clever girl, Lizzie. It's something I had not anticipated. But no matter. I've waited a long time to taste your charms. I can't wait to do what I have planned… You'll never guess all the tricks I've learned over the years," he said, pressing himself against her back. "Unfortunately, it will have to wait until we're far away from this dank hellhole."

Swallowing her revulsion, Lizzie did her best to maintain a calm façade. Out of the corner of her eye, she saw the boys poking their heads out the door of the shed. She hoped it was too dark for them to see, or they would no doubt rush to her rescue. *Think, Lizzie! Think!*

"Let her go or die," a deep voice called out in the darkness.

Edward! She almost sobbed her relief.

"I'm afraid you hold no power here," Blackwood said, laughing. "She's mine." He swung Lizzie around and pressed the point of the knife deeper, causing a warm stream of blood to run down her neck. Her knees trembled so badly she thought they would buckle beneath her. She kept her breathing shallow—she feared a deep breath would push the blade even further.

Lizzie met Edward's across the stable yard. His eyes burned with a fury she'd never seen before.

"I'm giving you one more chance to let her go, or you will die where you stand," he said, his voice lethal.

Frantically, Lizzie tried to think about how to escape before a flash of memory stirred her. She recalled Peter's lessons on how to fight and defend herself. He'd warned of renegades on both sides who would think nothing of assaulting a woman. She could hear his voice in her head. *"Try to remember these things, Lizzie. I don't want to leave you, but more than that, I don't want to leave you vulnerable."*

Closing her eyes, she pictured Peter showing her what to do.

"With the heel of your boot, stomp as hard as you can on top of his foot. You'll break most of the bones and be able to get away..."

Biting her lower lip in determination, she calmly counted to three and lifted her right leg, then drove her heel into the top of Blackwood's foot.

His shrill scream pierced the night, and he dropped his knife. When he released her, she ran toward the boys and embraced them. She turned just in time to see Edward leaping through the air, a battle cry roaring from his throat, and toppling Blackwood to the ground.

Punch after punch, Edward pounded and pummeled Blackwood's face and chest. Lizzie hesitated, not knowing what to do. Blackwood was an evil man, but she didn't want his death on Edward's conscience.

Just then, shouts reached her ears and Wright and Romney reached Edward's side, each hooking an arm around him to pull him away from Blackwood.

"Stop, Sin," Romney bellowed. "He's still a peer. You don't want his blood on your hands. And he'll feel the hangman's noose soon enough."

"I don't care," Edward growled as he struggled against his friends.

"Think, man!" Wright shouted. "We need to bring him in alive to question. We need to find out about the extent of his operation. And dead men can't speak."

"All right!" Edward barked. He shook off his friends, scanning the yard. "Lizzie!"

"We're here, Edward."

He spun about, and his eyes met hers, his chest heaving. He strode toward her, his eyes never leaving her face. Her vision blurred with tears as he reached her side.

"Lizzie," he breathed, and wrapped his arms around her.

A sob escaped her as she hugged him tight. "I love you, Edward, and I'm so happy to see you," Lizzie said, gazing up into his face.

⇶⟩⟩⟩✕⟨⟨⟨⇷

"I LOVE YOU, Lizzie. And I'm so happy to see you too," Sin said.

She was alive and safe and in his arms. He would never let her go.

When he saw the knife pressed against her throat, he'd fallen into a black haze of fury and heard a roaring in his ears as he launched himself at Blackwood and began to pummel him. All he wanted was to punish the bastard who'd caused so much pain, death, and destruction.

But it was over. It was finally over. He could breathe again as he held the woman he loved more than life itself.

"Are you all right?" He pulled out a handkerchief and gently dabbed at the blood still streaming from the wound on her neck. "My God, when I saw his knife against your throat, I almost lost my mind."

"Hush, it's all right—just a scratch, see?" she said, taking the handkerchief from his hands. But you, on the other hand, have quite a few scratches and bruises." She laid her hand against his cheek.

"You are the bravest, most courageous woman I have ever known," he rasped, his voice breaking.

"And you are the most wonderful man. I love you, Edward Sinclair."

A bark from Josie made them both chuckle.

"And I see young Simon has perfected the art of sneaking onto carriages," Sin said.

"I'm sorry, milord. But I had to be sneaky to help Miss Lizzie," Simon said.

"These boys are heroes," Lizzie said. "They rescued me from a room where Blackwood was holding me prisoner."

"How did you all manage it?" Sin asked. "We searched the house from top to bottom and couldn't find you. We had a devil of a time when one of the thugs caused a fire in the kitchen."

"They took me through a narrow tunnel and hid me until we could escape through a trapdoor in the shed."

Sin crouched down and smiled at the boys. "I'm sure Kingsley gained a few more gray hairs when you took off, son. But I am grateful to you for your courage in protecting Lizzie." He squeezed Simon's shoulder.

"Thank you, milord, but it was my brother Bobby here who did most of the work. He led us through the tunnel."

Sin turned to Bobby and held out his hand. "I thank you for your courage. It's a pleasure to make your acquaintance." The little boy looked like a smaller version of Simon.

"I missed my brother," Bobby said, looking up at Sin with wide eyes. "Can I come home with Simon and Josie?"

"You certainly can! I would be delighted to have such brave boys living in my home." Josie barked as though indignant at not being part of the conversation. "And Josie, of course—we would never forget such an important member of the family." Sin chuckled, scratching Josie behind the ears.

Hearing Armstrong call out to him, Sin stood and turned. Armstrong and his men approached on horseback, each carrying one or two young boys. The youngest looked to be barely three years old. The children were all thin, wearing dirty, shredded clothing that barely kept their emaciated bodies covered, and some were crying, no doubt from fear and hunger. "The children were being loaded onto a wagon bound for the tunnels—the same place we found Robinson."

"We'll take them back to Graceview," Romney said.

Sin noted two of Romney's men were standing guard over an unconscious Blackwood, his arms and legs tied with rope.

"From what I've been told, there are many more that could

use our help," Armstrong added.

"Did you round up all of Blackwood's men?" Sin asked.

"Yes, my lord," one of the outriders responded. "The magistrate and his men have arrived and are loading them onto the wagons."

"Well, you can take Lord Blackwood along to the magistrate as well. Make sure he has at least two men always guarding him."

"Yes, milord." Armstrong's men nodded and then hefted Blackwood onto the back of one of the horses and led him away.

"Those poor children," Lizzie whispered beside him, reaching for his hand.

Sin turned to look at the woman he'd loved from the first moment he'd stumbled into her small cottage back in Boston. "We'll make sure they will all be cared for. I'm certain Celia will know of families who would open their hearts and homes to the children."

Lizzie nodded, wiping tears from her eyes.

"I'd best get you all back to Graceview," Sin said. "I'm certain Michael is impatient to see his beloved sister again."

"Bethany had a few things to say about his trying to come with us," Romney said. "And just before we left the manor, a messenger arrived with something from Wellington for him. I'm anxious to find out what it was."

"And dear Millie?"

"I'm sure she's impatient too," Armstrong said. "Last I heard, she'd misplaced her ear trumpet."

They helped the orphans into the back of a wagon and covered them with blankets to keep them warm. Sin and Armstrong assisted Lizzie, Simon, Bobby, and Josie into the wagon.

Romney was sitting in the driver's seat, holding the reins. Wright and the other men had mounted their horses, ready to depart. Armstrong sat astride his horse, holding the youngest boy protectively in his arms.

Sin hopped into the back of the wagon and settled himself next to Lizzie. "It's going to be a long journey for these children," he whispered, taking her hand in his.

"We'll help them every step of the way," she whispered back, laying her head on his shoulder.

"Lizzie, I have a lot to make up for. But I plan to rectify that very soon." Sin kissed her on the cheek, gently wiping the fresh tears that tracked down her lovely face.

"As long as we're together, that is all that I could ask for," she said.

Sin still couldn't believe how lucky he was to be loved by a woman as remarkable as Mrs. Lizzie Pritchett. But he would spend the rest of his life showing her just how much he loved her back.

EPILOGUE

Graceview Manor
Folkestone, Kent
Spring, 1818

S IN SPOTTED LIZZIE sitting with Bethany and Celia on the picnic blanket, playing with baby Michael and baby Elizabeth, all three women deep in conversation. Patting his waistcoat pocket, he made sure the small gift was still there before stepping behind his wife and giving her a light kiss on her cheek. "Hello, ladies—how is the planning going?"

"Hello, darling," a beaming Lizzie replied, her extraordinary green eyes glittering like emeralds. "Very well—the Celia's fundraiser for the expansion of the orphanage is certain to be a great success."

"I am pleased to hear it. Anything I can do to contribute, let me know."

"You've already done so much mobilizing your former battalion to assist with all the work," Celia said, bouncing her gurgling infant on her lap.

"I suspect we'll get the work done in record time," Bethany added, picking up the rattle her infant son had dropped.

Sin, Romney, Wright, Armstrong, and the workers they'd hired had already laid the foundation and erected the brick façade for the addition—a much-needed expansion, given the number of orphans they had rescued from Blackwood.

"Might I steal my wife away for a few minutes, ladies?" Sin asked.

"Oh, Edward, I don't think I can get up without making a cake of myself," Lizzie said, chuckling. "You'll need to help. Sitting on the ground might not have been the best idea in my condition. I feel as big as a house."

"Nonsense! You grow more beautiful each day," Sin said, gently pulling her to her feet. He couldn't wait to meet his son or daughter. He wanted a big family, with many children. They were off to a good start, having adopted Simon and Bobby, and now expecting their own baby.

How strange life could be. How unexpected the changes. Until he met and fell in love with Lizzie, he'd avoided marriage, let alone becoming a father. But Lizzie had changed all that. His only regret was that circumstances had separated them after their meeting in America. But Sin had vowed not to let any more time slip away from them, which was why he had asked Lizzie to marry him the same night they rescued her from Blackwood's clutches. Or rather, Simon and Bobby rescued her.

"Oomph! That feels immensely better!" Lizzie said, shaking the wrinkles from her skirt.

"I thought some refreshing lemonade and small sandwiches might be a welcome respite," Sin said, escorting her to a table he'd arranged to be placed under the shade of a leafy oak.

"Oh, how lovely. I was just craving those delicious cucumber sandwiches. Oh, and lemon biscuits too," Lizzie said as he helped her into one of two comfortable armchairs. "Then again, I've been craving almost everything lately."

"Anything you desire, my love, I will see that you have it." He dropped a gentle kiss on her lips and sat across from her.

"You've already given me everything I could ever want," she said softly.

"You're everything I want. You and our children," he said,

reaching for her hand.

"Thank you, my darling." She blushed prettily. "Isn't it wonderful that Romney and Bethany have a house party to celebrate little Elizabeth's first birthday? I can hardly believe a year has passed since we were here last. And this time we have so much to celebrate and be thankful for."

"I agree," Sin said. "But I do have some news to share with you. Blackwood's execution is scheduled a week from now in London."

"He's an evil man who did such horrible things," Lizzie said with a shiver.

"His conviction for treason is what's bringing him to the gallows, not the abuse of all those children. But he will be punished just the same. Luckily, we gathered the information we needed, and the munitions he stole were returned."

"Thank you for stepping back from your position with Wellington," she said, squeezing his hand. "I confess, the constant worry would have done me in."

"And I confess that I much prefer this new consultive role. Besides, there's plenty to keep me busy at our country estate and the townhouse in Mayfair. And I plan to devote as much time and resources as I can on working to pass laws that will protect children from men like Blackwood."

"It's definitely something we need," Lizzie said, pouring them each a glass of lemonade.

"I also have something else I wanted to tell you," he said, popping a sandwich into his mouth.

"Oh dear—I hope it's not more news about Blackwood."

"No, my love. This is infinitely better," he said around a mouthful of cucumber sandwich.

"Well, then I am all ears." She grinned.

"Actually, it's a surprise."

"What kind of surprise?" Lizzie asked, arching a delicate brow. "It's not a special occasion I've forgotten, is it?"

"I promise it's not. We'll call it a 'just because' gift. Just because I love you," Sin said before leaning across the table and capturing her lips in a kiss. She tasted sweet and tart from the lemonade she'd sipped. His lips hovered over hers, and a groan escaped him as he beheld the sensual gleam in her eyes.

"If that's my gift, I can't wait for more," she said in a husky voice.

"There will be more, tonight in our suite," he said, waggling his eyebrows.

Lizzie giggled as she placed a cucumber sandwich on her plate.

"Now…for your present." He withdrew a small black velvet box from the interior pocket of his jacket and opened it. Inside was a gleaming opal surrounded by diamonds. The moment the jeweler showed him the finished ring, he could hardly contain his excitement, deciding to present it to Lizzie at the house party.

Lizzie's mouth formed an O. She started to speak and then stopped, brushing away tears from her cheeks. "It's so beautiful. I love it."

"It was my late mother's. I hope you don't mind, but I had it refitted for you and added the diamonds. The ring was burning a hole in my pocket, and I could wait no longer. As your birthday is October, as was hers, I thought it would be the perfect mother-hood gift."

"But my birthday is months away…"

"Nonsense. Remember, this is a 'just because' gift," he said, placing the ring on her finger.

She started to speak but had to swipe away tears before she could say a word. "It's so beautiful. I love it," she said, holding it up. "It's exquisite. Thank you, my darling." She smiled and crooked her finger.

He grinned and leaned in to accept her kiss.

"I wish I had thought about something for you…to celebrate your pending fatherhood," she said.

"My gift will come later." He planned on both of them retiring early from the day's festivities.

The sound of a dog barking and boys giggling drew their attention. Aunt Millie was supervising Simon and Bobby as they taught Josie and her three cats to roll over.

"I cannot believe my aunt is allowing the cats outside, let alone to play on the lawn with a dog."

"Those cats think they are her children. But I detect the boys have made significant inroads," Lizzie said. "The children plan to perform a little show for us with the animals and show the tricks they have taught them. Millie has been such a dear helping with the boys."

"I suspect the boys have been helping Aunt Millie just as much. I've never seen her look so happy," Sin said. "But I am relieved the governess will be starting in two weeks."

"I confess, it was becoming a challenge for me between giving the boys their lessons and preparing for the baby. I can barely see over my belly. Until there is a magic carpet that can ferry me up the stairs to the nursery, we shall have to rely on the governess."

"Every day with you is like a magic carpet ride," Sin said. "Shall we take a stroll about the grounds?"

"I would love to."

He helped her up, and she slipped her arm through his. They strolled down the garden path, enjoying the sun glinting off the pond.

Sin looked up at the sound of men's laughter. Wright, Armstrong, Romney, and Robinson were playing a game of croquet. Although Robinson still had a pronounced limp, he had recently stopped using his cane.

"I'm glad Michael seems to be enjoying himself. I've been so worried about him," Lizzie whispered.

"I wouldn't worry too much about your brother. The man just inherited an earldom. He'll have plenty to keep his mind occupied."

"I hope we can find a nice young lady for him. And Wright."

"I doubt Wright will be ready to marry anytime soon," Sin

said, laughing. "He's not as lucky as I am."

"And you are so very lucky, then?" She smiled up into his eyes.

His breath caught as he gazed at his wife's golden beauty. "I may have been at death's door the day I met you, but it turned out to be the luckiest day of my life," he said, bending down to claim Lizzie's lips once more.

Not the end.

About the Author

Anna St. Claire is a big believer that *nothing* is impossible if you believe in yourself. She sprinkles her stories with laughter, romance, mystery and lots of possibilities, adhering to the belief that goodness and love will win the day.

Anna is both an avid reader author of American and British historical romance. She and her husband live in Charlotte, North Carolina with their two dogs and often, their two beautiful granddaughters, who live nearby. *Daughter, sister, wife, mother, and Mimi*—all life roles that Anna St. Claire relishes and feels blessed to still enjoy. And she loves her pets – dogs and cats alike, and often inserts them into her books as secondary characters. And she loves chocolate and popcorn, a definite nod to her need for sweet followed by salty…*but not together*—a tasty weakness!

Anna relocated from New York to the Carolinas as a child. Her mother, a retired English and History teacher, always encouraged Anna's interest in writing, after discovering short stories she would write in her spare time.

As a child, she loved mysteries and checked out every *Encyclopedia Brown* story that came into the school library. Before too long, her fascination with history and reading led her to her first historical romance—Margaret Mitchell's *Gone With The Wind*, now a treasured, but weathered book from being read multiple times. The day she discovered Kathleen Woodiwiss,' books, *Shanna* and *Ashes In The Wind*, Anna became hooked. She read every historical romance that came her way and dreams of writing her own historical romances took seed.

Today, her focus is primarily the Regency and Civil War eras, although Anna enjoys almost any period in American and British history. She would love to connect with any of her readers on her website – www.annastclaire.com, through email – annastclaireauthor@gmail.com, Instagram – annastclaire_author, BookBub – www.bookbub.com/profile/anna-st-claire, Twitter – @1AnnaSt Claire, Facebook – facebook.com/authorannastclaire or on Amazon – amazon.com/Anna-St-Claire/e/B078WMRHHF.